"Take off your dress and leave it on the floor on the way out."

"My dress?" Juliana inquired. Her voice was hesitant. Alarmed.

Hunter smiled despite his fatigue. "The servants will expect some evidence of a romantic evening. I'll close my eyes, I promise." He obediently closed his eyes. Never had he imagined that the whisper of fabric against skin could be so tantalizing.

"My father warned me about rich boys like you."

"Your father is a smart man," Hunter retorted, "but you're safe with me." A vision of her naked before him turned his body to pulsating awareness. He counted her footsteps across the room, his breath exploded in his chest, and he reminded himself that asking her to remove her clothes was his idea.

"Hunter?"

He hoped she wasn't going to ask him whether she could expect to find him in her bed when she woke up. He couldn't trust himself with the answer to that question.

Dear Harlequin Intrigue Reader,

This month Harlequin Intrigue has an enthralling array of breathtaking romantic suspense to make the most of those last lingering days of summer.

The wait is finally over! The next crop of undercover agents who belong to the newest branch of the top secret Confidential organization are about to embark on an unbelievable adventure. Award-winning reader favorite Gayle Wilson will rivet you with the launch book of this brand-new ten-story continuity series. COLORADO CONFIDENTIAL will begin in Harlequin Intrigue, break out into a special release anthology and finish in Harlequin Historicals. In *Rocky Mountain Maverick*, an undeniably sexy undercover agent infiltrates a powerful senator's ranch and falls under the influence of an intoxicating impostor. Be there from the very beginning!

The adrenaline rush continues in *The Butler's Daughter* by Joyce Sullivan, with the first book in her new miniseries, THE COLLINGWOOD HEIRS. A beautiful guardian has been entrusted with the care of a toddler-sized heir, but now they are running for their lives and she must place their safety in an enigmatic protector's tantalizing hands! Ann Voss Peterson heats things up with *Incriminating Passion* when a targeted "witness" to a murder manages to inflame the heart of a by-the-book assistant D.A.

Finally rounding out the month is *Semiautomatic Marriage* by veteran author Leona Karr. Will the race to track down a killer culminate in a *real* trip down the aisle for an undercover husband and wife?

So pick up all four of these pulse-pounding stories and end the summer with a bang!

Sincerely,

Denise O'Sullivan
Harlequin Intrigue, Senior Editor

THE BUTLER'S DAUGHTER

JOYCE SULLIVAN

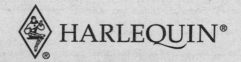

TORONTO • NEW YORK • LONDON
AMSTERDAM • PARIS • SYDNEY • HAMBURG
STOCKHOLM • ATHENS • TOKYO • MILAN • MADRID
PRAGUE • WARSAW • BUDAPEST • AUCKLAND

ISBN 0-373-22722-1

THE BUTLER'S DAUGHTER

Visit us at www.eHarlequin.com

Printed in U.S.A.

ABOUT THE AUTHOR

Joyce credits her lawyer mother with instilling in her a love of reading and writing—a fascination for solving mysteries. She has a bachelor's degree in criminal justice and worked several years as a private investigator before turning her hand to writing romantic suspense. A transplanted American, Joyce makes her home in Aylmer, Quebec, with her handsome French-Canadian husband and two children. A visit to the Thousand Islands, where this story is set, gave her the inspiration to write about a hero and his castle.

Books by Joyce Sullivan

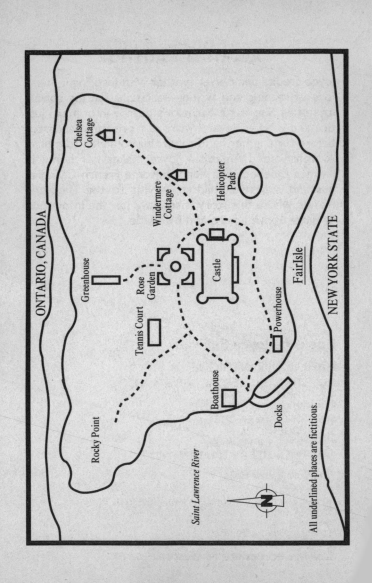

ONTARIO, CANADA

Chelsea Cottage

Windermere Cottage

Helicopter Pads

Greenhouse

Rose Garden

Castle

Tennis Court

Powerhouse

Fairlsle

NEW YORK STATE

Rocky Point

Boathouse

Docks

Saint Lawrence River

N

All underlined places are fictitious.

CAST OF CHARACTERS

Ross and Lexi Collingwood—He was the Baron of Wall Street. After their baby daughter was kidnapped and never returned, they went to extreme measures to hide the birth of their son and new heir from the world.

Goodhew—What did the butler know about the explosion that killed Ross and Lexi Collingwood?

Juliana Goodhew—She was the butler's daughter, who'd agreed to raise the Collingwood heir as her own son.

Hunter Sinclair—This reclusive multimillionaire lived a double life as The Guardian. He'd do anything—even marry a woman he'd never met—to save his godson from a killer.

Annette York—Lexi's sister. The baby was her only family left.

Kendrick Dwyer—The president and chief financial officer of the Collingwood Corporation. Was he too eager to fill Ross's shoes as CEO?

David Younge—The controller. Had he been on his way out of the corporation? Or on his way up?

Sable Holden and Phillip Ballard—Ross Collingwood had ruthlessly bought out their companies in hostile takeovers. Did they want revenge?

Nonnie Wilson—Was the Collingwoods' missing cook somehow involved in the bombing?

Stacey Kerr—Lexi's personal secretary. Who was she sleeping with?

Gord Nevins—Could the household manager of the Collingwood estate be trusted?

To my daughter Elise
for the joy she brings me.

Acknowledgments

My sincere thanks to Denise O'Sullivan,
who recognized *The Butler's Daughter* before I did.
And to the generous people listed below who answered
my tedious questions about their lives and their jobs
or provided valuable input to my plot.

From the Ottawa-Carleton Regional Police services:
Jackie Oakley; Constable Bob Arbour, Bomb Tech;
and Sergeant Dave Lockhart, Intelligence Section.

Also, Mr. Victor Robles, The City Clerk, The City of
New York; Tom McCormick, W. J. Van Dusen Professor of
Management, UBC Commerce; New York State Police
Trooper Lieutenant Jamie Mills; Dr. Steven W. Maclean;
Pilot Pierre Duchaine; Ellen Hall; Judy McAnerin;
T. Lorraine Vassalo; and Rickey R. Mallory.

Chapter One

They weren't going to make it to Severance tonight, Juliana Goodhew realized, resigning herself to that fact as another heart-wrenching wail erupted from her five-month-old charge who was strapped into the infant carrier in the back seat of the SUV. Cort Collingwood's cry fractured into a refrain of sharp, desolate sobs that reverberated off the windows like steel balls.

Poor Cort was making it clear he'd had enough of traveling for one day. They'd missed their morning flight from Cleveland because he'd spent a restless, irritable night, and she'd taken him to the doctor only to discover Cort had an ear infection. The pain reliever she'd given him a few hours ago must have worn off.

"Oh, sweetheart, I'm so sorry," she crooned, trying to soothe him with her voice as she searched the dark New York interstate for an exit and lodging for the night. "I was hoping you'd sleep for most of the trip and before you knew it…you'd be in your parents' arms."

Emotion gathered tight in her throat at the thought of Lexi waiting anxiously for their arrival. Spending one more sleepless night without her baby. Lexi hadn't seen her son since she'd tearfully handed him over to Juliana's safekeeping when he was three days old. "They're so anxious

to see you again, pumpkin. They love you so much. But
the reunion will have to wait until morning, after we've
both had a rest.''

Cort snuffled as if he completely agreed with her, then
let out another wail that sounded like a wounded tomcat.
Juliana couldn't see him, but she could hear him squirming
in the carrier, completely fed up with being confined.

Her fingers gripped the steering wheel as she debated the
risks of pulling over to the side of the road to comfort him
for a few minutes. It was almost midnight and the traffic
along the highway was sparse. She had a gun in the diaper
bag that she knew how to use. But still, she couldn't take
a chance with Cort's safety. Not after what had happened
to the Collingwood's first baby.

Anger and grief abraded her heart like bits of broken
glass ground into an open wound. In the blink of an eye,
Ross and Lexi Collingwood's one-day-old daughter, Riana,
had been abducted from the hospital nursery. The heir to
one of America's wealthiest families had gone missing.
There had been one aborted ransom demand. Then nothing.
Twenty-eight months later there were still no clues in Riana's abduction.

And poor Lexi blamed herself. Juliana had taken Lexi's
request to see Cort as a sign of hope that she was finally
ready to go on with her life after the tragedy. Surely after
holding her delightful son in her arms—and experiencing
just one of his bubbly sunshine smiles—she'd know that
Cort's rightful place was with his parents and not with the
butler's daughter.

''You are going to love your mommy, Cort,'' she bab-
bled reassuringly, still scouring the roadway for a hotel.
''She's so beautiful—she has a smile that begins with a
starry twinkle in her eyes. It infects everyone she meets
with an uncontrollable urge to smile back at her. Just like

yours, pumpkin. And unlike some of the well-to-dos who shall remain nameless because I don't tell tales about what I see behind closed doors, she's kind and sincere all the time, not just when she's in public. She's generous, too.''

Despite her distress over Cort's cries, Juliana's heart swelled with gratitude for Cort's mother. She knew full well it was Lexi's glowing praise of her design and organizational skills that had resulted in her pick of a dozen job offers from wedding consulting firms across the country. A car hurtled past her on the left, blowing its horn, making Juliana realize she was driving well below the posted speed limit.

She sped up. Keeping her left hand on the steering wheel, Juliana stretched her other arm into the back seat and gently stroked Cort's downy head with her fingers. He was hot and sticky, poor darling. She kept talking to him in an effort to soothe him. ''Do you remember me telling you how your parents met at a hospital charity ball for sick children, pumpkin? Your mommy worked as a social worker for the hospital. Your father flirted with her—shamelessly, I might add. She didn't know who he was, but she thought he was too handsome and too arrogant for his own good. He asked her out, but she told him she wouldn't even consider going out with him unless he donated one whole week's salary to the hospital because a man who didn't care about sick children wasn't a man she cared to spend five minutes of conversation with, much less an evening. Oh, I'd have loved to have seen your father's face when she said that! Would you believe your father took your mother's hand, pulled her to the stage of the ballroom and made a pledge for 1.2 million dollars?''

Cort let out a discontented roar.

The corners of Juliana's mouth tilted. ''You think he should have offered more, do you? Spoken just like a Collingwood.'' Juliana steadied her grip on the steering wheel as a gust of wind from a passing eighteen-wheeler buffeted the SUV. ''They don't call your daddy the baron of Wall Street for nothing. He certainly proved he was smart enough to convince your mother to marry him—and I got to help your mommy plan their wedding.''

Juliana's gaze flickered toward the star-studded sky, remembering the music and the twinkling lights and the thousands of flowers for that spectacular December night. She'd never seen two people more in love. Lexi had looked like a princess in an exquisite silk gown with diamonds sparkling in her chestnut hair. Juliana had planned every detail of the wedding and every detail had been perfect. Even her father had said so.

''That's how I discovered I wanted to be a wedding planner. It's sort of like being a fairy godmother to brides. They get to be Cinderella with their own prince.'' Juliana sighed softly and stroked Cort's head, missing the glamour and the romance of her job. She even missed the thousand and one details that had required her constant attention. While she hoped she'd be returning to that life after this weekend, a part of her ached at the thought of being separated from Cort.

After five months together, she knew each of her tiny charge's smiles and cries. She knew the plump rounded curves of his cheeks and limbs and the delicious scents of his skin and his hair. Her heart folded into a tight contented box whenever she held him. Saying goodbye was not going to be easy.

''But for the moment, pumpkin,'' she mused as Cort continued to whimper and grumble like a radio with static, ''I'm *your* fairy godmother—until your mommy comes to her senses and realizes she can't hide your birth from the rest of the world.''

To her relief, Juliana rounded a dark curve and the headlights flashed on an accommodations sign for the next exit. "It won't be much longer now." She gave Cort's head one last caress and put both hands on the steering wheel.

Within fifteen minutes, she'd managed to secure a motel room and juggle the baby, his diaper bag, her purse and her carry-on bag up to the second-floor room. She gave Cort another dose of pain reliever, changed his diaper and snapped him into a miniature baseball sleeper while a portable crib was brought up to the room. Then she put a bottle in the warmer. Cuddling Cort against her, she pulled the cell phone from the diaper bag to call her father.

"Juliana? It's practically midnight." Her father's voice was stiff with disapproval. "Where are you?"

"Sorry, Papa. I thought I could surprise the Collingwoods tonight, but Cort is fussing. His ears are bothering him still. The doctor said it would be a good twenty-four hours before the antibiotics took effect." Juliana rocked from side to side as Cort started to whimper, his fingers clinging to her cotton sweater. "We've just checked into a motel about two hours from Severance. We'll leave first thing in the morning and arrive for breakfast. Cort usually wakes around six."

"Well, then, I suppose it can't be helped."

Juliana closed her eyes, hearing the unspoken accusation that she'd failed him yet again echo in her ears. Typically, her father viewed the baby's ear infection and her failure to arrive by the designated hour as a poor reflection on him. Would she ever stop failing him? Probably not. Why did she even try?

"I need to go, Papa. Cort needs his bot—" Her words were drowned out by an explosive roaring transmitted over the phone line. What on earth? "Papa! Are you there? Answer me! What's happening?"

Juliana strained to hear as she pressed the receiver close to her ear, her heart thundering in her chest, while her other arm clutched the baby. Oh, dear God. The phone line was not dead. She could hear distinct crackling and popping sounds. Flames?

"Papa!" she shouted into the receiver. "Can you hear me?"

To her relief she heard her father's voice, fading in and out, as if coming from the end of a tunnel. "There's been an explosion—a bomb. Take the baby, Juliana. Protect him with your life. Operation Guardian. Promise me as a Goodhew that you'll…" His voice faded, snatching away the rest of his words.

Horror gripped her. "I promise—"

With a loud pop, the line went dead. Juliana stared at the phone and started to shake. Operation Guardian could only mean one thing. Ross and Lexi Collingwood were dead.

SICK WITH FEAR over the safety of her father and the Collingwoods, Juliana called the police and reported the explosion, then punched in the number she'd been asked to memorize in the event of an emergency such as this.

"Yes." The voice that answered was curt and concise. One word, but totally male and in charge. She knew instinctively that he was the enigmatic security consultant Ross Collingwood had hired to head up the search for Riana. The man known only as The Guardian.

Juliana had never met him. But then, few people ever met The Guardian in the flesh or knew his real name. His existence and the services he supplied were a closely guarded secret of the world's upper class.

"Operation Guardian," she replied numbly, the code word falling from her shocked lips like a blunt instrument onto a table. She gripped the phone tightly as tears seared her eyes.

Please God, this wasn't happening. Not to her father. Or Ross and Lexi. They couldn't be dead.

Tremors wracked her body in undulating waves of disbelief and grief. If not for Cort's ear infection, she and the baby would have been caught in the explosion, too!

A softly muttered curse whispered over the line, the hint of raw emotion it conveyed so genuine it snagged her heart like a hook, connecting her to him. "Tell me your name," he commanded.

The clear authority in his tone evoked a comforting image of an indomitable muscle-hewn Marine sergeant. Juliana caught the tiny precious foot of the child who lay on the bed beside her. Cort's golden gossamer eyebrows arched over his sooty blue eyes in surprise as he gnawed on a teething ring of plastic keys. She swallowed hard and glanced nervously over her shoulder toward the door, half expecting someone to kick it open. Whatever fate had been dealt her charge's parents, Cort was not alone. Not while breath still remained in her body.

"My name is Juliana Goodhew," she said as calmly as she could.

"Juliana, I'm The Guardian. Tell me what's happened."

Wanting to tear her hair out with the fear that was expanding in her until she thought her skin would burst, she told him about the secret rendezvous with the Collingwoods at a rented home in the Adirondacks and the horrible explosion she'd heard a few minutes ago when she'd called her father to inform him she and the baby would be delayed until morning.

"My father believed it was a bomb. He told me to call you. I called the police first to get them some help…." Her voice broke.

After all her problems with her father…was this how it was going to end? *I'm sorry, Papa.*

A sharp stab of guilt lanced her side, torturing her with memories of a rainy autumn afternoon and a gleaming banister—a forbidden and irresistible temptation to two young children. The day that had changed their lives forever.

She fanned her fingers over Cort's plump belly, her heart melting at the snugly warmth of his compact body and his gummy irresistible smile. Tears slipped down her cheeks, splashing onto his sleeper. *I won't let the baby out of my sight, Papa. I promise.*

The Guardian's voice penetrated her thoughts. "You did the right thing, Juliana. Your father is wise to be cautious. Until we have more information confirming the cause of the explosion, I'm going to implement measures to keep you and the baby safe. Where are you now?"

"A motel in Utica." She gave him the name and room number.

"Stay inside, away from the windows. Don't go out to your car. I'll catch a chopper and be with you in an hour and a half, two hours tops. Did you call your father or the police from the phone in the motel room?"

"No, I used my cell phone."

"Good. So only the police know of your location."

"Yes."

"And you didn't tell them who the child is with you?"

Did he think she had the IQ of an idiot? "Of course not," she said shortly. "I told them I was the butler's daughter, and I'd been talking to my father when the explosion occurred."

"Are you armed?"

The implication of his question slid over her like the blade of a razor. He thought the danger was real.

"Yes. Mr. Collingwood insisted I be trained properly in how to use a gun."

"Excellent. I'm on my way. Stay alert and be ready to move." The line clicked off.

She dropped the phone onto the bed as if it had burned her.

Be ready to move.

But moving with a baby required thinking ahead. She'd given Cort his second dose of antibiotics when she'd stopped for gas at 10:00 p.m., but he would need a bottle. Wary of casting a shadow across the window, she crawled on her hands and knees to the bathroom to grab the bottle from the warmer she'd set up earlier on the counter. Then she unplugged the device so she could pack it back into the diaper bag.

Returning to the bed, she pulled the semiautomatic pistol from the diaper bag and laid it on the floor beside her within easy reach, then pulled Cort into her arms and leaned her back against the wall so she could keep an eye on the door while she fed him. Cort took the nipple of the bottle into his mouth, sucking greedily. His fingers curled and uncurled blissfully around the bottle as his eyelids slowly drifted downward.

Juliana kissed his sticky-sweet forehead as terror brutally clutched her heart in a white-knuckle grip. "Please, God, let them be okay."

Beyond Cort's sucking noises an ominous silence hung outside the thick drapes covering the window.

EXACTLY ONE HOUR and forty-two minutes later, Juliana heard a light tapping on the door.

Leaving Cort sleeping on a pillow on the floor, she approached the door stealthily with the gun in hand. Surely, it could only be The Guardian, but she wasn't taking any chances.

Through the peephole she saw a man standing in the exterior hallway—his posture rigid and controlled as if his body were formed from black steel, his head turned in profile to scan the corridor and the parking lot below.

He was younger than the image she'd conjured from his voice. But no less intimidating. Instead of the military fatigues she'd imagined, he was dressed all in black. The black leather of his jacket gleamed almost malevolently in the muted glow of the corridor light piercing the chilly autumn night. He tapped again lightly on the door.

Juliana jumped, her heart dropping to her stomach. "Who is it?" she called softly, staying to one side of the door.

"Operation Guardian."

Relief whisked through her. There was no mistaking his voice. "Just a minute." Tucking the gun into the waistband of her jeans at the small of her back, she unhooked the chain and opened the door. His brown hair was cut short and combed back, revealing every bone and hollow in a face that was hard and uncompromising. His eyes were the azure blue of a Mediterranean Sea.

The instant their gazes connected she knew the news wasn't good. His face was grave, each tight line carved in stone.

She fell back two steps, instinctively retreating from the harsh truth in his eyes. "M-my father?"

He entered the motel room, closing and locking the door with fluid efficiency, then put his hands on her shoulders. His firm fingers held her captive, upright, though her knees threatened to sink right to the carpet. "Juliana, I'm afraid your father has been seriously injured."

Her fingers twisted into the cold supple leather of his

jacket, felt the impenetrable hardness of his chest beneath. "He's alive, then?"

"They found him unconscious. He was apparently outside when the explosion occurred."

"Oh, thank God! He was probably waiting for me and Cort to arrive." Juliana stopped suddenly. A cold horrible truth was still suspended between them on a taut thread. "How serious are his injuries?"

"I don't know. He's been rushed to the hospital, and I haven't received an update on his condition. But someone will call." He paused and Juliana felt the slow pound of his heartbeat against her fingers. She couldn't explain it. She was terrified, yet she'd never felt so safe or so grateful for this man's presence. It was as if every beat of his heart shielded her in a secure airtight bubble from the grim truth of what had happened tonight.

"And the others?"

His face might have been carved of stone, but for an instant his eyes gleamed with moisture. Confusing her. Scaring her.

A well of grief savagely ripped open within her. "Oh, no!"

His fingers dug into her shoulders, preventing her from collapsing. "I spoke with the police at the scene. They don't expect to find any survivors in the house."

"Oh, my God." Juliana pressed a fist to her mouth, hot tears stinging her eyes. This was not happening. It was too much. She'd grown up on the Collingwood estate. Had spied on Ross Collingwood and his friends living their golden lives in a world she could never be part of. Ross ran a billion-dollar corporation and amassed companies in takeover bids as if capturing checkers on a checkerboard. And he remembered to take her and her father out to lunch on their birthdays and wrote them silly poems for birthday cards.

A sob exploded in her chest like a fireball. He could *not* be dead. Nor could Lexi. They were madly, totally in love with each other. This was too horrible, too ugly to contemplate.

The Guardian pulled her against his chest, his hands stroking her back. Heat seeped into her cold body in slow widening circles.

"I'm sorry."

Juliana bit back a sob and lifted her head to look up into his rock-hard features, her heart registering the compassion she saw in his eyes. She'd heard stories of The Guardian. Whispered tales that made him sound mysterious and invincible, like a cross between a comic-book superhero and James Bond. But in that fraction of a second before he hid the emotion banked in his eyes she saw a man who truly cared about the people he tried to protect. "Was it a bomb or an accident?"

"It's too soon to tell. The fire department will investigate, but they say the explosion is suspicious. It appears to have originated in an upstairs bedroom. Were Ross and Lexi the only ones in the house? The police would like to know."

Juliana nodded, her mind still trying to grapple with the horror of what he'd just told her and the frantic desire to rush to her father's side, ensure he was okay even though he'd told her to keep Cort safely away. "There were only the three of them, my father and the Collingwoods," she said shakily. "The Collingwoods were being extra careful, following the precautions you gave them. They left the members of their traveling staff at home—even the chef and the chauffeur. No one knew they'd rented the house in the Adirondacks. My father secured the booking under his own name.'' Juliana paused, suddenly aware that she was still standing there with The Guardian's arms around her.

Self-consciously, she pulled out of his embrace and wiped her face with her palms. She needed to be strong. Ross and Lexi and her father were counting on her. She had promises to keep. ''What about the baby?'' she asked, her legs trembling as she walked around the corner of the bed to check on Cort. He was still sleeping peacefully, his little arms suspended in midair as if ready to receive a hug. ''What happens to Cort?''

The Guardian followed her movements, his gaze narrowing on the sleeping infant. He didn't ask why the baby was lying on the floor rather than in the crib. ''He'll be raised by his godfather.''

Juliana stepped defensively between him and the infant, alarm snapping her to attention. His godfather? That was news to her. Had Lexi and Ross had the baby christened shortly after his birth? Perhaps that was information they'd only shared with her father. ''Who would that be?'' she demanded, feeling as if more of her world was about to change.

''Me. I'm Hunter Sinclair.''

The strange, reclusive multimillionaire who'd sent Ross and Lexi a canoe as a wedding present? Juliana instantly recognized his name and remembered the rumors associated with it. Rumours of dementia. Wasn't there a history of mental illness in the family? She didn't give a damn if he was James Bond or the President of the United States. She was *not* surrendering Cort to him. Ross and Lexi had trusted The Guardian to find their daughter and protect them from harm. He'd failed on both counts.

''Over my dead body,'' she said sharply, breaking twenty years of protocol by raising her voice to her better. ''You are *not* taking that baby away from me.''

Hunter stiffened at the unexpected threat. Juliana Good-hew glared at him out of almond-shaped eyes that reminded him of richly polished mahogany. Her lips, bearing a faint trace of pink lipstick, thinned into a determined line.

Ross had trained the nanny well. Slim and youthful in blue jeans and a thick creamy cotton sweater, her silver-blond hair escaping a French braid, Juliana looked ready to carry out her threat. Her hand moved, reaching behind her for the Glock he could see in the mirror on the far wall.

Hunter cocked a brow, his hand snaking out to grab her wrist. He could snap the fragile bones in her arm with one movement. "Please, don't for even one foolish moment, consider reaching for the gun at your back. I would hate to hurt you."

"Release me instantly," she snapped, her face glowing white with anger.

Hunter released her, eyeing her warily. The nanny he'd hired to care for his sister's children would never dare speak to him like this. Nor was she this pretty, he noted, his inner radar for trouble sounding a silent alarm.

"Thank you." Frost clung to Juliana's tone. "I repeat, you are not taking that baby from me. I don't care who you are. Where were you when Riana was abducted? Or for Ross and Lexi? The Goodhews have served the Collingwoods for sixty-three years. The Collingwoods person-ally entrusted him to my care. He's staying with me." She folded her arms across her chest and drew herself up to her full height; the top of her head barely reached his chin.

Grief lashed Hunter's heart along with her accusations. He frowned down at her, hesitating between a grudging admiration for her show of loyalty to her charge and his innate suspicious nature. He knew painfully well that trusted servants betrayed their employers. Money could be a powerful motivator.

He'd been nine years old when he'd seen pictures in the newspapers of his mother's indiscretions with two of his father's friends. The Sinclairs' butler had secretly orchestrated a blackmail scheme, certain that Hunter's father would pay up to prevent the photos from being released to the media. Convinced his wife would never betray him, Hunter's father hadn't met the blackmailer's demands. Their marriage was destroyed when the pictures appeared and his mother committed suicide. His father had told Hunter and his sister that their mother had suffered from a mental illness.

Hunter took in the sharp thrust of Juliana's chin and the defensive stance of her body.

He could count on one hand the other individuals who'd known the Collingwoods had another child. There was the doctor who'd delivered Cort. The lawyer who'd drawn up Ross's and Lexi's wills. Lexi's sister Annette. And Juliana and her father. Yet someone had obviously gotten wind of the child's existence, despite the care the Collingwoods had taken to keep Lexi in seclusion during her pregnancy.

Where had the breach in security occurred?

"Juliana, I have no intention of wrenching that child from your arms. Not now or in the near future," he said, striving to reassure her. "But you are both coming with me. These are extraordinary circumstances. We will have to work together. I'm sure it has occurred to you that Cort was an intended target of the explosion, as well. Whoever planned it is undoubtedly aware that you're caring for the child. That puts you both in danger."

"Why should I trust you? How do I know the almighty Guardian wasn't behind the explosion?"

He stepped toward her menacingly. "I know you are hurting and wanting someone to blame, but Ross was my best friend. I would never hurt him, nor was I after his money.'' A bitter laugh erupted from him. ''I have enough damn problems dealing with my own family fortune.''

She didn't budge an inch. ''If you were so close, how come he never mentioned you? Oh, excuse me, your name was among the eight hundred others on the guest list to his wedding. But as I recall, you didn't bother to attend.''

Hunter towered over her, feeling the tension and the distrust emanating from her body like shrapnel. He just happened to be the nearest target. ''How do you know that?''

''I helped Lexi with the guest list. And I was there when your regrets arrived along with your wedding gift.'' Her voice quavered, her brown eyes taking on a faraway cast as they glistened with fresh tears. ''Ross had the canoe you sent put in the swimming pool so he could recite poetry to Lexi in the moonlight. He did, too.'' She wiped away a tear slipping onto her cheek with a jerky movement. ''He loved her so much.''

Hunter risked squeezing her arm, needing the human contact with Juliana to help ground his own tormented feelings. So much of his life he'd mastered on his own, coldly and calmly discarding any emotions that got in the way of his job. But he'd lost a friend tonight—Ross had been an anchor—and Hunter was treading water to keep himself from sinking under into the pain. ''I know. Ross and I met at Harvard. We were roommates our last year. In fact, he's the one who nicknamed me The Guardian.'' Pain laced his words. ''I take the credit for teaching him how to be a little more ruthless in his judgment. We stayed close, but I was afraid I'd be recognized if I came to the wedding. Ross sent me a video of the ceremony.''

She pulled away from his touch, leaving Hunter reeling alone in memories of his friendship with Ross. Her suspicions were still plainly apparent on her face.

''You've never even been to the estate,'' she said in a

clipped tone. "I was a boy-crazy teenager in high school when Ross was bringing his friends home from Harvard. You weren't among them."

His lips thinned. He knew the friends Juliana was referring to. She must have gotten quite an education from watching Ross with his self-indulgent buddies…if that was all she'd gotten. She'd probably been as pretty in high school as she was now. His impatience with the conversation grew.

"Juliana, you're wasting time with these questions. We must leave quickly. I'm obliged to trust you to keep The Guardian's real identity confidential, and you're going to have to trust me. Understood?" His gaze locked with hers, studying the shadows flickering in her unusual mahogany eyes like minnows darting in the shallows.

Color rose from her pale throat and splashed onto her cheeks, but her voice was as suitably controlled and decorous as he would expect from an employee. "Quite, Mr. Sinclair."

Hunter nodded approvingly as he reached for the bags lying on the end of the bed. "My household doesn't stand on the same ceremony as the Collingwood household. You may address me as Hunter in private. The Guardian is addressed as sir when he's on duty. Clear enough?"

She gave him a subdued smile. "Yes, sir."

"The chopper is waiting. You take the baby. I'll carry your luggage."

"What about my car?" she asked as she slipped an apricot wool blazer over her sweater and transferred the Glock into one of the blazer's front pockets. From the way she handled the weapon, Hunter had no doubt she was proficient in its use. Hooking a caramel leather purse over her shoulder, she knelt down to scoop up the baby.

"I'll send one of my men to pick up your car. You won't need it where we're going."

"We'll need Cort's car seat."

"We'll go without it. Someone could have tampered with your car since you left it in the parking lot."

She glanced over at him, alarm sparking in her eyes as she gently tucked a blanket around the sleeping infant. The baby cried out in his sleep and Juliana spoke softly to him, pressing a kiss onto the crown of his head.

The intimate gesture caused anger to rise inside Hunter—anger and unbearable guilt that Ross and Lexi would never kiss their son—or the daughter who'd been snatched from their lives over two years ago. All the security precautions in the world could minimize the chances, but not always prevent a determined lunatic bent on destruction.

In the hospital, all it had taken was for one night-duty nurse to be overpowered by a stun gun and little Riana Collingwood was gone. Though Hunter had vowed to do everything within his means to find the infant, chase every lead that came in over the 1-800 tips line, the grim odds were that they might never find her. Or learn the true reason for her abduction.

The timing of the explosion tonight in a rented house where the Collingwoods had planned to be reunited with their son was suspicious—especially following their daughter Riana's kidnapping. And it cast Riana's abduction and the aborted ransom demand into a whole new light.

Ross Collingwood had some powerful enemies. Men whose companies he'd ruthlessly overtaken, who had the financial means to discover his secrets and his vulnerabilities. And who might be determined to destroy his entire family and the Collingwood empire. The aborted ransom demand could have been part of the kidnapper's goal to emotionally cripple Ross by leaving him agonizing over his daughter's fate.

Hunter knew far too keenly, far too deeply that all the money in the world couldn't protect a man's heart. Love made a man vulnerable to his enemies.

While Hunter couldn't be sure at this point, he had to assume the security measures set in place to shield Cort's identity had been breached. He needed to take countermeasures to protect the baby from another possible attack. He owed it to his friend.

Carrying the diaper bag and Juliana's carry-on bag he moved to the door, motioning for Juliana to wait while he opened the door and checked the exterior corridor to ensure the coast was clear.

"Where are we going?" Juliana demanded sotto voce as they headed out in the brisk night air, their footsteps muted on the concrete walkway.

"New York City," he said in her ear, cupping her elbow. The scent of her hair reminded him of springtime and apple blossoms. He shook the distracting thought away and focused on checking their surroundings. He didn't know how much time they had before details of the explosion hit the news.

"Is that where you live?"

"No, but I have a residence there where I can set up a command post to deal with the police and the lawyers and whatever else needs to be done. There will be some reaction in the stock market to his death and the future of the company." Hunter grimaced inwardly as he scanned the parking lot. Ross Collingwood had been his friend, but he didn't have time for grief. He was The Guardian. He had to do his job—protect Ross's son.

The vehicles were dark and silent. Not a sign of movement. They descended the stairs. "The chopper's in the parking lot of a mall just down the street."

The street was deserted. The streetlights cast pools of light on the sidewalk.

Juliana adjusted the blanket around Cort. "Where do you call home, then?"

"A private island in the St. Lawrence Seaway. I hope you don't like crowds."

Her arms tightened around the baby. "I can put up with anything to keep Cort safe."

Ahead, the chopper crouched like a giant glass grasshopper in an asphalt field. "I'm relieved you feel that way, because it's going to take some ingenuity to keep Cort's identity secret from the world. I don't think it was a coincidence that the explosion occurred tonight when Ross and Lexi would have been reunited with their child. And I can't help wondering if Riana's kidnapping and the explosion tonight are related—that someone wanted to destroy Ross Collingwood and his empire by killing him and his family. We need a strategy to protect Cort. If the media learns of his existence, there'll be a circus trying to find him."

Juliana halted in her tracks and a suspicious gleam entered her eyes. "I've done a good job protecting Cort on my own. What did *you* have in mind?"

Hunter hesitated, momentarily blindsided by the brilliant simplicity of the plan that formed in his thoughts. Sweat dotted his brow. Could it work? Juliana was pretty enough. It wouldn't be much of a stretch to feign an attraction to her. At all.

"Hide him in plain sight," he said slowly as if his words were weighed down with lead by the decision he was making. "I live on an island. People in the surrounding community would be curious if I suddenly brought home an infant and a nanny. Bringing home a wife and a son wou rouse less suspicion. Marginally less," he added wryly. "But less."

Her mouth dropped open. "A wife and a son? Just what are you suggesting?"

Every muscle in his body tightened with foreboding. He'd told himself a thousand times he'd never subject himself to the state of matrimony. Sinclairs were cursed in that regard, experiencing more bitterness than bliss.

But he wasn't offering Juliana his heart, his bed or his money, he told himself rationally. There'd be a prenup. "I'm suggesting that we get married."

Chapter Two

Juliana stared at Hunter in mute shock. Then she got angry and said the first thing that came to mind, the wrong thing, "You are absolutely insane."

She regretted it instantly as his eyes narrowed on her like rapier blades and his mouth flattened into a deadly line. "Given my family history, I'd say that's a foregone conclusion. What's the matter, Cinderella, you never wanted to marry a prince?"

"That remark was completely inappropriate, Mr. Sinclair, but excusable considering my own poor choice of words," Juliana retorted sharply, feeling heat blister her cheeks. She was half out of her mind with worry about her father's condition and this man expected her to take his marriage of convenience proposal seriously. Still, caution honed from years of domestic service whispered a gentle warning in her ears. Whether she liked it or not, Ross had appointed Hunter Sinclair as Cort's guardian. If memory and gossip served her correctly, the Sinclair family owned luxury hotels. Lots of them. She was at this man's mercy and his whims if she wished to remain in Cort's life and uphold her promise to her father.

She took a deep breath. "I assure you, I intended no disrespect toward you or your family. You simply caught me off guard. Are you sure someone will call about my father?''

''Yes. I've dispatched two operatives to ensure he receives the best medical care and personal protection. Someone will call as soon as there's news.''

''Thank you.''

One of Hunter's dark eyebrows rose. ''You haven't answered my other question. Had you planned on marrying a prince?''

He was baiting her. Intentionally. Maybe even testing her. Juliana had no intention of sharing her private dreams with this intimidating man. Nor did she want to offend him. She held Cort's warm bundled body against her heart, knowing her father would urge her to do whatever duty necessitated.

After all, her father hadn't thought twice about asking her to give up her career and branding her an unwed mother to protect Ross and Lexi's son. She doubted her father would object to her skyrocketing up the social ladder by marrying a multimillionaire.

But as far as Juliana was concerned, it was a leap in the wrong direction.

Her insides trembled at the prospect of playing the mistress of Hunter Sinclair's home—and the mistress of his bed, where, in the shadowed folds of the night, he'd surely look just as intimidating as he did towering over her now.

Lexi had been the daughter of a middle-class family. She'd boldly and elegantly leaped into Ross's elite world with her grace and charm, blissfully ignorant of the rules. Juliana, by contrast, had been schooled in the rules of behavior long before she entered kindergarten. The butler's daughter did not play with the children of the Collingwoods' guests. She did not speak until spoken to. And she did not once ever let herself think that any of Ross's fancy friends would look at her as anything more than a diversion.

She rather doubted Hunter even considered her a diversion. From his perspective he was negotiating a business merger with all the rules to be spelled out on paper in legalese. "My personal desires are none of your business, Mr. Sinclair," she said coolly. "But allow me to allay your fears. I'm not the least bit interested in the number of zeroes in your trust fund. All I care about is this darling little boy's safety. If marrying you will achieve that, then so be it. But I want a prenup with your agreement that I shall be appointed Cort's guardian in your will. And should the marriage end in divorce, I want joint custody."

"That's all? No zeroes from my trust fund?"

She held his mocking gaze for a long moment, convinced that behind his tight mask and the sarcasm was a man who truly cared about protecting Cort. No doubt he was as reluctant as she to enter into this absurd agreement. "Not a one. You may keep them all to yourself. I have employable skills—it's so hard to find good domestic help these days. Do we have a deal?"

Those azure eyes transformed, thawing with sudden warmth. "Deal. The helicopter is waiting. The performance begins now. We can't have anyone suspecting we aren't in love—especially the hired help. You know how they gossip below stairs."

Before she could stop him or think to protest, he brushed a kiss along her cheek, then nuzzled her jaw as if she were a delectable offering. Juliana stood paralyzed inhaling the scent of him, mesmerized by the seductive play of his lips over her skin and the moist heat of his breath. He was so big, so hard, so utterly dangerous her pulse fluttered on tiny wings. What on earth had she gotten herself into?

Shyly, tentatively, she let her lips touch the corner of his mouth. Felt the firmness of those lips and the prickle of stubble on his cheek.

Oh, my. Her stomach did a free fall to her toes as his lips settled, coaxing and demanding, over hers. Juliana clutched Cort to her, aware of his precious slumbering body between them as Hunter skillfully swept his tongue into her mouth and kissed her as she imagined all rich boys kissed. Thoroughly. Powerfully. As if the world and her body were his for the taking.

And they were. Her bones threatened to disintegrate beneath the onslaught of sensation.

It was only when she felt the cold imprint of the night air on her face did she realize Hunter had pulled back and was gazing down at her beneath half-lowered lids. The intensity gleaming in his eyes sent a tremor rippling through her. ''We'll tell everyone I met you in Europe. That you only told me recently I'd fathered your baby,'' he said.

Juliana told herself that if he kept looking at her as he was looking at her now, as if he'd been interrupted during a favorite meal, no one could possibly doubt that he'd fathered Cort. This crazy scheme might work. ''Where in Europe?'' she said breathlessly. ''People will ask.''

''Germany. The Black Forest. They'll believe that. We camped at adjoining campsites. Everyone knows I never stay in hotels, especially my own hotels.''

''I know absolutely nothing about camping.''

''Which is why I came to your rescue, Cinderella, out of fear that you'd light your clothes on fire.''

She ground her teeth behind clamped lips, subduing the urge to insist he stop calling her Cinderella. She forced her lips into a smile. ''How complimentary.''

''I'm glad you approve.'' He gripped her elbow again

and hurried her across the parking lot toward the chopper.
Juliana felt as if she were leaving one world and entering
another.

TO HIS CREDIT, THE MAN she'd just agreed to marry was
solicitous to a fault during the chopper ride to New York
City. For the limousine ride to the penthouse apartment
overlooking Central Park, Hunter thoughtfully closed the
privacy window between them and the driver. Juliana tried
not to let her grief over the Collingwoods' deaths or her
fears over her father's condition show in her face. What
was happening with her father? Why didn't the doctor call?

The apartment was as enigmatic and masculine as Hunter
himself. An oasis of muted earth colors on the walls, comfortable leather furnishings, and artwork that probed to the
soul.

Juliana restrained herself from offering an apologetic
smile to the middle-aged butler and housekeeper who'd obviously been roused from their beds and awaited them in
the foyer, with appropriate smiles of welcome.

"Juliana, darling, this is Marquise and his wife Valentina, who make life much simpler in the Big Apple,"
Hunter said warmly, slipping the stiff band of his arm
around Juliana's shoulder and dropping a kiss on Cort's
downy head. "Marquise, Valentina, this handsome young
man is my son, Cort. And his beautiful mother is going to
be my wife as soon as we can arrange a quiet wedding.
Please make them comfortable. They're both exhausted
from their trip."

Juliana blushed as Marquise, a short man with a precisely
trimmed goatee and velvety black eyes, bowed slightly.
"Very good, sir. And congratulations. A crib has been set
up in the nursery for the little one."

Cort let out a grumpy wail. Gratitude and awkwardness
spilled through Juliana. It felt alien to have someone antic-

ipate her needs before she'd thought of them herself; she was used to the shoe being on the other foot. "Thank you, Marquise. The baby's not feeling well. I'm sure he'll rest better in a comfy bed."

"You follow me, please, madam," Valentina said in heavily accented English. Hunter excused himself to take care of some phone calls. Neither Marquise nor Valentina seemed to think it odd that he would be making phone calls at 4:00 a.m. Juliana prayed that one of those phone calls would bring news about her father's condition. Please, let him be all right.

Unpretentious and quiet, Valentina led the way down a thickly carpeted hallway to the nursery. Even though the lights were turned low, Juliana could see this was a room used by children. Boys, she presumed from the twin set of race car beds and the buckets of blocks, trucks and action figures neatly arranged on the shelves near the window.

She didn't ask Valentina what boys used this room. As Hunter's fiancée, it would be expected that she know this. Did Hunter have children from a previous marriage? Was that why he'd seemed so sarcastic about the subject of matrimony? Had his first wife relieved him of some of his much prized zeroes?

Although she'd successfully hidden Cort's existence from the world for the last five months, Juliana was overwhelmed by the enormity of what the task now entailed. It was one thing to pretend to be a single mother living on her own. Quite another to find herself suddenly married, pretending to be in love with a stranger. A large, intimidating stranger.

While Juliana changed Cort's diaper, Valentina helpfully warmed a bottle for him, then unpacked the diaper bag. Juliana experienced a flicker of alarm, wondering if the housekeeper found it odd that there was only a few days' worth of clothes in the bag.

Hunter had been right, they couldn't have the servants talking, thinking there was anything remotely suspicious about their wedding or Cort's parentage. "I had most of the baby's clothes sent to the island," she extemporized. "And I planned to do some shopping—for the wedding and for him while we're here in New York. He's growing so fast."

Valentina laughed. "Marquise will drive you to find what you need. He knows all Brook's favorite stores. She comes many times with the boys to visit their fathers and to shop."

Fathers? Juliana distractedly absorbed this information, wondering if it was a grammatical error on Valentina's part and still uncertain as to who Brook could be. Cort whimpered and snuffled as Juliana changed his diaper, her fingers fumbling with the snaps of his sleeper. Had the news of the explosion reached the media yet? "There, there, everything's going to be fine," she whispered to Cort, rubbing his back until he quieted. Then she lowered him into the crib and covered him with his favorite blanket.

With any luck, he'd sleep for a few hours.

Valentina waited outside in the hall, her dark-ginger eyes eager to please as she led Juliana to a room across the hall that was distinctly feminine in tones of ivory and powder-blue. A bedroom fit for a princess, with dainty upholstered furniture and a bed draped with yards of powder-blue velvet, ivory satin and gold-tasseled cords. Not a bed fit for the butler's daughter.

Resentment and anger teemed inside her. This pampered luxury was not her life. It rightfully belonged to Lexi and Ross. She wanted to scream.

Valentina was gazing at her in concern. "Hunter say to

prepare this room. His room is adjoining, yes? He gets lots of phone calls in the night. No good for a new mother who needs her sleep.''

Juliana reminded herself to play her role. ''How thoughtful of him, although I doubt anyone's going to get much sleep with Cort in the house,'' she murmured ruefully. With a practiced eye she sought out the details she'd been trained to note: the bed neatly turned down, the fresh flowers, the spotless tabletops that would pass a white glove test. ''The room is very comfortable, Valentina. Thank you.''

The housekeeper bobbed her head and beamed. ''Hunter not bothered by crying babies. He love babies—very good with babies. I unpack your bag for you, yes?''

Juliana felt woozy, as if she couldn't hold herself together a moment longer. ''Please. I'm so exhausted I can't think straight. Our flight was delayed for hours. Leave my robe out. I'll have a shower before I turn in.''

Escaping into the bathroom, she removed her jacket, wondering what to do with the gun in the front pocket. Where could she hide it from Valentina's prying eyes? She tucked it between the folds of a plush towel stacked in a basket on the handsome wood vanity until she could return it to her purse. Violet smudges cut beneath her eyes as she stared at herself in the gilt-framed mirror. The situation was absurd. She didn't look anything like a happy bride-to-be. Just the thought of pretending to be in love with Hunter Sinclair made her shiver.

Shedding her clothes, she turned on the water in the large marble-tiled shower. Here, at last, was privacy beneath the veil of steam and the pulsing drum of the water. Juliana sagged against the cool marble wall and let the sobs come.

''THANKS, KEEP ME POSTED.'' Hunter hung up the phone and massaged his temples, holding his grief at bay through

sheer force of will. From his study window, Central Park
was a dark abyss with a halo of fire rising along the horizon, the sun dawning on a terrible day. The fire department
had recovered two bodies from the house in the Adirondacks. Autopsies would be done later today or tomorrow
to identify the remains. Hunter had contacted the Collingwood lawyers, then alerted the senior vice president of the
Collingwood Corporation. Coverage of the explosion was
already hitting CNN on one of the TVs on the opposite
wall.

Hunter dialed Lexi's sister's number again, wishing he
could deliver this news personally. But Cort's safety was
his top priority.

"Hello?" Annette York's voice had the breathless, disoriented quality of someone roused from a deep sleep.

Hunter introduced himself as The Guardian.

Lexi's sister woke instantly, wariness rippling into her
voice. "Why are you calling?"

"I'm afraid I have some difficult news."

"Is it Riana? Have you found her?"

Hunter's stomach tightened into a lead ball. "No. It's
Ross and Lexi. There's been an explosion. I wanted you to
know before it hit the news. They were both killed. I'm so
sorry."

"Oh, my God! Are you sure? There's no chance you're
mistaken?" The shred of hope clinging to her voice nearly
obliterated his self-control.

"There's no mistake." He gently told her about the
rented house in the Adirondacks and the suspicion that the
explosion was caused by a bomb.

"But I talked to Lexi two days ago. She didn't mention
they were going," Annette protested in numb disbelief.

Hunter selectively chose what information he could share
with her. He saw no point in informing Annette of the

purpose of the trip. Or that Juliana and Cort had narrowly missed being caught in the explosion.

"Perhaps the decision to go away was made last minute," he said tactfully. "Ms. York, I realize this is a terrible shock, but you must listen to me carefully. Ross gave me instructions to protect Cort in the event something like this should occur. Someone killed your sister and her husband—quite possibly the same person who abducted Riana. You and Cort could be next on the list."

Dead silence greeted his explanation.

He forged ahead. "It would be prudent to act with extreme caution. We must be very careful not to let slip any information about Cort. I want you to pack your bags. I've sent a car for you. You'll be brought to a hotel here in New York where I've registered you under another name. I don't want any reporters finding you. You can issue a family statement to the press via Ross's lawyers."

"What about Juliana and the baby? Where are they?"

"They're safe. For your nephew's protection, I'd rather not tell you any more than that until we have a chance to speak privately. I'm sure you understand."

"No, I don't understand. My sister and her husband are dead. I want to know where my nephew is *now*." Her shrill voice scraped his ears like a blade cutting glass. "I'm his aunt—his *only* living relative. You have no right to keep him from me."

"On the contrary, Ms. York. I'm acting on Ross's wishes and at the specific request of the infant's legal guardian, whom Ross and Lexi appointed in their wills. You'll be informed of Cort's whereabouts and a visit will be arranged when his guardian feels it's safe to do so."

"Just who did Ross and Lexi think was fit to raise their son—the butler's daughter? Or someone in that damned company?"

Hunter genuinely felt sorry for her. He knew what it felt like to have your family shattered and suddenly be set adrift in a sea of uncertainty. Her hurt and disappointment that her sister hadn't chosen her to rear Cort were obvious. Anger was only one of the emotions she would be experiencing in the painful days ahead. "I regret that I'm not at liberty to reveal that information."

"I'll go to the media," she threatened.

Hunter felt the beginning pound of a headache. "Ms. York, take a deep breath. You're upset. You're not thinking clearly. Going to the media could endanger your life, as well as Cort's. I'll contact you at the hotel and we'll discuss this privately. Is there anyone you'd like to stay with you? The next few days are going to be very rough."

"No," Annette said very softly. Quietly. "Our parents died just after Riana's abduction. And Lexi was my best friend."

Hunter's chest tightened with the dull ache of his own heavy heart. "I'm very sorry for your loss." Somehow the words seemed inadequate.

He hung up the phone, promising himself that he'd find out who had done this. Make them pay for destroying a family. And he'd do his best to be the kind of father Ross had wanted for his son.

Hunter made a couple more quick phone calls, checking on the increased security measures he'd put in place on the Collingwood estate. Apparently, the press was already gathering at the gates. One of the operatives he'd dispatched to the hospital called with Goodhew's doctor on the line. Hunter convinced the doctor he was Goodhew's son-in-law and listened grimly to the doctor's report on the extent of the elderly man's injuries. At least he was expected to recover.

Feeling much older than his thirty-three years, Hunter made his way down the hall to Juliana's room.

If she was sleeping, he'd let her rest.

His knock went unanswered, but the sound of the shower running in the bathroom told him she wasn't sleeping. He entered the room. The bed hadn't been touched.

The door to the ensuite bathroom was closed, steam escaping the crack at the bottom of the door. Hunter frowned. How long had she been in there? Concerned, he rapped briskly on the door. "Juliana?"

There was no answer. Beneath the rhythmic drum of the water, he thought he heard a sob. Was she crying?

He knocked once more on the door. "I'm coming in."

Mist surrounded him, ghostly fingers of it swirled around him as he stepped into the bathroom. He couldn't make out Juliana's shape through the mist-cloaked glass doors of the shower, but the water was running.

What on earth? Where was she?

"Juliana? Are you here? Are you all right?"

A muted sound like an animal in pain echoed from out of the shower stall. Hunter opened the door to the stall and saw her huddled on the marble floor, a sodden trembling ball of white flesh. Her arms were wrapped tightly around her knees and damp ribbons of hair were plastered to her shoulders and back.

Sympathy pierced his body like a sword from his groin to his heart. Hunter quickly shut the water off and reached for the thick white towels she'd set out.

He snapped one open and stepped into the shower, crouching down to gingerly wrap it around her. Somehow he hadn't associated a marriage of convenience with the inconvenience of having a sodden naked young woman in his life.

"Juliana, we have to get you out of here," he said gently, worried she was in shock.

She lifted her head, looking at him with red-rimmed eyes. Fear, dark and turgid, shadowed her gaze. Hunter fervently wished that he were anywhere else in the world but here. Her eyes were a mirror into his own soul. "My father?"

"I just spoke to his doctor." Fighting a reluctance to touch her in this vulnerable state, he massaged her back through the thickness of the towel, careful to keep his gaze from drifting onto the gleaming damp softness of her limbs or the delicate shape of her feet peeking out beneath the towel. She looked like a frightened swan, ready to take flight. "It's good news. Your father's made it through surgery—he'd been struck by some flying debris. He broke a few ribs and shattered his shoulder blade, but the surgeon has repaired the damage. Apparently your father's suffered some burns on his face and hands, but the doctor expects him to make a full recovery. They're moving him into ICU to keep a careful eye on him. He's heavily sedated."

Her eyes shuttered closed. "Thank God. I should be there with him, but if I went he'd only be angry. He told me to stay with Cort."

Hunter didn't contradict her. A tremor was shuddering through her body. He wasn't letting her or Cort anywhere near that hospital. If the killer was intent on finding Juliana, that would be the first spot the killer would look. "You're exhausted," he said. "And you're shivering. You need to be in bed." He lifted her effortlessly against his chest, his senses reacting simultaneously to the feel of her buttocks molding sweetly to his abs and the scent of apple blossoms clinging to her damp hair.

She didn't protest.

The shock of what had happened was setting in.

Carrying her into the bedroom, he yanked the covers back from the bed and laid her gently on the crisply ironed powder-blue sheets. Stopping long enough to extinguish the bedside lamp and curse his predicament under his breath, he removed his shoes and climbed in bed beside her.

Every self-protective instinct in his body rebelled, his legs and arms moving as if hindered by rusting armor as he wrapped his arms around Juliana, awkwardly spooning his body to hers. Despite the steaming heat of the shower, her limbs were ice cold.

"It's going to be okay," he whispered.

Hunter closed his eyes, not caring that the dampness from her hair seeped into his pillow. He grudgingly allowed the exquisite softness of this woman he'd committed himself to marrying to register on his senses, to distract him from the headache grinding at his temples.

The faint shallow sound of her breathing gradually deepened and became regular.

She'd fallen asleep.

Hunter told himself he could leave her now, strip himself away from the forced intimacy of their joined bodies. Take some pain reliever for his headache. It would be light soon. There were numerous tasks still requiring his attention. But he didn't move. Ross and Lexi were dead, their lives extinguished far too soon. Though Hunter never would have thought it possible, somehow, holding Juliana close to him like this made his own grief more bearable.

A MONTAGE OF PHOTOGRAPHS of Ross and Lexi Collingwood flashed on the TV screen, each looking as if it had been lifted straight out of the pages of a storybook fairytale romance—white teeth, stylish clothes, not a pimple to be seen or a hair out of place. There was no mention of the butler's daughter or the baby.

A curled fist hit the desktop. Damn!

After all that careful planning, the baby had escaped his fate.

Not for long, though. Not for long.

Ross and Lexi's killer smiled smugly and rose to thumb through the clothes hanging precisely one inch apart on the row of expensive wooden hangers. The specially chosen attire purchased for the funeral waited expectantly at the back of the closet like a gift to be unwrapped and savored on Christmas morning. The brand-new black leather shoes lined up beneath it, toes and heels aligned as if at attention. Half of the plan had been achieved. The baron of Wall Street and his oh-so-perfect wife were dead. How hard could it be to find the butler's daughter?

The baby would be with her.

Soon, very soon, all the Collingwoods would be dead.

Chapter Three

Cort's cries tore Juliana from sleep, uprooting her from what felt like a tangle of heavy branches until she realized that the branches flung over her torso were long and muscled—and belonged to a man.

Sunlight peeped through the partially closed drapes allowing her a glimpse of the slumbering man beside her.

He looked just as handsome and dangerous this morning as he had last night. What was Hunter doing in her bed?

A draft of cold air on her bare shoulder brought an even greater worry. How had she ended up *naked* in bed with him?

His eyes fluttered open, pinning her in the sights of his azure gaze. Juliana stared at him, transfixed, as his pupils narrowed to tiny dots and shifted downward to her breasts. Too late, she scrambled to pull the sheet up to cover herself, conscious of the heat that exploded in her stomach and crept over her body to sear her face.

"The baby's crying," she gasped. "Where's my robe?"

Hunter blinked as if orienting himself, then threw back the covers and leaped out of bed. He was fully dressed. Memories slapped her like physical blows to the heart as she remembered the explosion. The Collingwoods were dead. Her father was in the hospital, clinging to life. And

Hunter, the man she'd woken up beside this morning, expected her to hand over her freedom and her dreams and marry him to protect Cort's identity.

"I'll get Cort," Hunter said gruffly, "and bring him in here while you find your robe."

"He doesn't know you—" she protested, searching the floor and the bedclothes for the practical toffee-colored velour robe her father had given her last Christmas.

He cut her off abruptly. "Then it's time we got acquainted. Besides, a new father would be eager to see his son. Marquise and Valentina would expect it."

He was right, Juliana realized, finally spotting her robe on the carpet on the opposite side of the bed. It looked like a mud puddle on the pale-blue wool—as glaringly out of place as she was in this apartment. Had Hunter climbed into her bed last night because he'd thought the servants would expect that, too?

She snatched up her robe, jamming her arms into the sleeves and hurried to the dresser to find fresh underwear and clothes. She doubted Hunter knew the first thing about diapering a baby.

Cort's cries had stopped by the time Juliana had changed into a pair of black slacks and a sleeveless black cowl-neck sweater. Her hair was a mess, so she twisted it into a ponytail. Then she hastily brushed her teeth and splashed cold water on her face. She'd call the hospital and get an update on her father's condition right after she'd checked on Hunter and Cort.

The deep murmur of Hunter's voice coming from the nursery pulled at her in a curious way. She paused in the doorway, feeling both protective of her charge and uncertain of the man holding him near the window.

Cort's blond head leaned trustingly on the biceps of Hunter's arm as the infant cooed and gurgled up at the dark, unshaven face hovering over him. Hunter's eyes were intent on the infant, but he glanced up as if he'd sensed Juliana's arrival. Her heart locked solidly in her throat when she noticed moisture glimmering in the clear blue of his eyes.

"He's beautiful," he said simply. A muscle flexed rigidly in his jaw as if capping the pain inside him.

Juliana took a hesitant step into the room, torn between conflicting duties. The butler's daughter would never intrude on his private sorrow. But as Hunter's bride-to-be she supposed she should say something. Offer some comfort.

She stood there awkwardly, feeling completely out of her element, yet drawn to this dangerous-looking man who could be abrupt and cynical one moment and deeply compassionate the next. Words whispered from her, razor-edged with grief for Cort's parents who would never know their son's delightful nature. "He's a bundle of joy. How did you do with his diaper?"

"No sweat. Just peel and stick. I've changed diapers before."

"You have?" Why did her heart beat so fast when he looked at her like that—as if he could intuit every thought, every secret she'd ever harbored? She crossed her arms over her chest and resisted the urge to reach for Cort. Somehow seeing him so secure in Hunter's arms seemed threatening, a reminder that Hunter had all the power to make decisions for Cort's care.

Hunter shrugged his massive shoulders, Cort's eyes widening at the sudden movement. "My sister, Brook, has two sons resulting from two of her three failed marriages. Both boys' fathers work in New York and she brings them for visitation." Juliana didn't miss the wry curl to his tone.

"That explains the nursery. How old are they?"

"Mackensie is eight and Parrish is three. They're rascals." Hunter frowned, thinking of his nephews' dubious futures and the way Juliana had her arms drawn over her breasts as if she thought he might pounce on her. Of course, she'd been somewhat underdressed when they'd awoken this morning. And the glimpse he'd had of one sleep-warmed, pearly breast and its rosebud tip had been so disconcerting he'd practically pole-vaulted out of the room to attend to Cort.

Even now, in that typical chic black New York getup, her wild tangled hair and the circles under her eyes, there was a freshness in her clear skin. An honesty dwelling in those rich brown eyes and a sweet sensuality to her curves that made the prospect of marrying her doubly alarming.

He'd never once considered taking a wife. His sister's three disastrous marriages had cemented that resolve. And thankfully, had produced the requisite heir and a spare to the Sinclair family coffers.

Hunter had no illusions that he'd be any better than his sister or his father in choosing a soul mate.

How many times had he cautioned his clients about marrying in haste? Rushing into a relationship based on physical desire or—especially among the wealthy—an attraction to an individual's net worth. He'd been worried when Ross had told him Lexi was pregnant and they were getting married.

But Ross had assured him he'd learned his lesson from their Harvard days when women were eager to fall into his bed, and more than one had tried to trap him into marriage. Lexi was different.

And Hunter acknowledged the truth of that. Even though her parents had been pushy and middle-class with aspirations of grandeur for their daughter, Lexi had been Ross's soul mate in every way. Even after Riana's abduction, a tragedy that would have destroyed many relationships, the core of love between them had remained rock solid. The looks they exchanged excluded everyone else around them because Ross and Lexi had a private world unto themselves. Ross would have moved heaven and earth for his wife's happiness, even asking the butler's daughter to raise their precious son.

And Hunter could understand Ross's reasoning. He'd met Juliana's father and knew how highly Ross had regarded Goodhew, who'd looked after Ross like a second father after J. Ross Collingwood had died of a massive heart attack when Ross was barely out of college.

Goodhew knew how J. Ross had run the Collingwood empire, knew which senior executives and which board members could be trusted and which were sharks circling for a meal. While he'd brushed suits and laid out Ross's Oxford button-down shirts and silk ties, he'd dispensed advice. And Ross had taken the Collingwood empire further than his father had ever dreamed.

Cort playfully drummed his heels against Hunter's forearm, vocalizing his little heart out with chirps and coos. Hunter smiled down at his godson, feeling a laugh trying to burst its way to the surface.

The tender look he caught on Juliana's face as he stole a glance at her told him they were at least on the same page when it came to Cort's care. Her fierce loyalty to the baby was obvious.

Hunter had no intention of dishonoring Goodhew's daughter, or ruining a perfectly good business arrangement by letting lust creep into his marriage and muddy the waters. A man in his position had the means to discreetly deal with his physical needs.

Since Juliana's arms were still folded like bars across her body, he decided there was no time like the present to clarify their arrangement. "About my being in your bed this morning," he began, finding it more difficult than he expected to broach the subject with her. "It was only for show.... You shouldn't expect a physical side to our marriage. Or children."

Her arms dropped to her sides. "Oh."

Hunter wished he could interpret the thoughts flickering behind her dark polished eyes. She was relieved. He was sure of it. "I wanted that to be clear before we proceeded with the ceremony," he continued, "in case it altered your decision."

"Hardly."

Hunter looked with renewed interest at his self-sacrificing Cinderella. Judging from the way she lovingly cared for Cort, he'd assumed that she was the type of woman who would want children of her own. She probably did, but she wasn't going to admit it. His admiration for her went up another notch. "Do you feel up to coping with the world? I'll have Valentina prepare breakfast."

"I'd like to call the hospital again. Check on my father."

"Of course. I have the number in my study."

"I'm going to call the Collingwoods' household manager, too. Let him know of my father's condition and that he'll need to supervise the preparations for the funeral. Annette won't know what to do or the protocol involved—" Juliana broke off suddenly. Her palm tapped her forehead. "Annette. I completely forgot about telling Lexi's sister! She'll be devastated. Lexi was her only family. I don't think Annette is seeing anyone whom she could lean on to help her get through this. She was engaged when Lexi was planning her wedding to Ross, but the engagement was called off for some reason."

"I already called her. One of my operatives was dispatched to collect her and put her up in a nearby hotel as a safety precaution."

"A safety precaution? You think she's in danger?"

"If someone knows of Cort's existence, it's logical for them to suspect that Lexi's sister would know where the baby is."

Juliana ran her fingers through her tangled hair. "Yes, of course, you're right. Annette must be terrified."

"She's being well guarded."

Her pointed gaze threw his words of reassurance back in his face. He knew she was thinking he hadn't protected Ross and Lexi. He couldn't blame her, not when he was thinking it himself. Why hadn't he considered that Riana's abduction might have had deeper, darker roots, especially after the abandoned ransom demand? He set his jaw. He couldn't second-guess himself. There was no way to be certain that first ransom demand had been genuine.

He had to focus on the situation as he knew it now. On keeping Cort safe and hidden. On playing this role with Juliana of a man eager to wed the mother of his child.

He held Cort out to Juliana. "Take him. I need to shower and change. I'll meet you at the table for breakfast. I talked to my lawyer last night, he's preparing the prenup. We'll need to apply for the marriage license Monday. There's probably a waiting period. We'll need rings, and you'll need clothes—"

"The waiting period is one day in New York. I know because I helped Lexi plan her wedding, remember? And I worked as a wedding planner before I got drafted as the nanny. How about I handle the details for the wedding, and you concentrate on finding out who did this horrible thing so Cort will be safe?"

Hunter looked at her, surprised, remembering how magical Ross and Lexi's winter wedding had appeared in the video. She'd had her hand in that? He felt a prickle of guilt. A civil ceremony in the Manhattan city clerk's office would be a far cry from whatever dreams she'd spun of her own romantic wedding. Well, they were both making sacrifices.

He'd suddenly had enough of the conversation and the cacophony of thoughts and emotions driving him in cross directions. "Consider yourself hired," he replied with a dismissive wave of his hand, grateful for her offer and already turning his mind to the tasks demanding his concentration as he headed back to his room.

"Hunter?" Juliana called after him. "One more thing."

He paused in the doorway and looked back at her; Cort was tucked in her arms, hungrily gnawing on a tiny fist shoved in his mouth. "Yes?"

Her pink lips parted in a faint smile that seemed apologetic, contrite, and made him wonder how she would taste if he kissed her. Really kissed her. Sweet, like a perfectly ripe peach? Or tangy like dry white wine?

His blood pounded in waves to his brain.

Color dusted her cheekbones. "I'll need a credit card," she said. "I suspect Hunter Sinclair's wife has a higher credit limit than the butler's daughter. It would probably be safer if I weren't flashing my own credit card around, too. Credit cards can be traced, can't they?"

He let his gaze twine with hers, felt his body's stiffening response to her simple beauty and the intelligence embedded in her eyes. What the hell was the matter with him?

Shock. Loss. And the fact that Juliana was more intriguing than his ego was willing to admit. "Yes, they can be traced. And, in this case, your paranoia is good. Brook has a personal shopper for each of her major haunts. Marquise will make the necessary arrangements with each store for your purchases to be put on my account if you feel up to venturing out today. I'll see that you receive your own cards as soon as possible."

"Thank you. Since visiting my father isn't an option for

the time being, I might as well do something useful or I'll go absolutely crazy. I'll bring my cell phone with me so I can keep in touch with the hospital. Cort will need clothes and a new car seat. Do you have a crib for him on this island of yours?''

''Yes, there's a nursery. You'll both need warm, comfortable clothes for the island. And plan to pick up something for the funeral while you're at it. The butler's daughter will be attending it…under close surveillance.''

''I am?''

''Yes, and you're going to keep your eyes and your ears open, especially to what's being said in the servant's quarters.''

Her eyes narrowed on him, glassy as marbles. ''The servant's quarters? Are you suggesting that someone on the Collingwood staff was involved in this?''

He shrugged and glanced down the hallway to ensure their conversation was not being overheard by the servants. ''It's a possibility we can't afford to overlook. Think about it. How did someone find out the details of the reunion in Severance? You said your father made the arrangements himself. So someone either overheard him make the booking by phone or searched his quarters and found the information. Reason suggests someone in the house may have been involved.''

Cort let out a discontented squawk, reminding them he was hungry. Juliana rocked him against her hip, her body swaying with gentle motion. ''Maybe the house was bugged,'' she argued. ''An estate that size requires constant upkeep. Maintenance people coming and going fairly frequently, deliveries being made. My father would know if—'' She broke off, biting her lip. Tears swam in her eyes. ''I really should call the hospital. See if he's regained consciousness. Maybe he saw or heard something that will help.''

The determination that seemed to glow from her skin with translucent fire melted one more barrier in Hunter's resistance. She'd had a lot to deal with in the last ten hours and he wasn't making it easier. If she gave him the same loyalty she devoted to Cort, he'd at least have a wife who was more loyal to him than his mother had ever been to his father. ''Give me this little man,'' he said more gently. ''He's about ready to swallow his hand. I'll have Valentina prepare him a bottle while you call the hospital. You can use the telephone in your bedroom. Marquise will bring you the number.''

The scent of her hair and the delicate softness of her hands impacted his senses as she transferred the baby back into his arms.

''You're in good hands, pumpkin.'' The soft wool of her sweater grazed Hunter's side as she rose on tiptoes to kiss Cort's cheek, reminding Hunter of visits his mother had made to the nursery when he was a boy. He remembered his mother's fragrance—as exotic and elusive as the flowers she'd tended in her private greenhouse—and her light kisses that felt like a feather against his cheek.

He remembered the sting of her betrayal.

His throat tightened. ''Juliana, if you do manage to get through to your father, be careful what you say. His life and our lives may depend on it.''

''Please, let him be okay.'' Juliana's stomach bunched in a tight lump as her call was transferred to the ICU. A nurse told her that her father was heavily sedated and hadn't regained consciousness from the surgery. But he was breathing on his own.

Helplessness and fear welled in Juliana, torn by divided loyalties to her father and Cort.

"Could you hold the phone up to his ear, please?"

"Hold on." There was a brief pause. Then a distant, "Go ahead, ma'am."

Juliana heard the steady *beep-beep* of a heart monitor and her throat swelled with gratitude. He was alive. "Papa, please get better. I wish I could be with you. I love you."

She hung up the phone, her body trembling. She hadn't told her father she loved him in over two years—not since the day he'd hugged her when she'd returned home to the estate to help after Riana's abduction.

The direct line to the administrative household manager's office as well as the main line to the Collingwood estate were constantly busy. Lexi's private line was picked up by her voice mail. The sound of her vibrant voice moved Juliana to more tears. She kept speed-dialing the manager's office as she applied her makeup and pulled a hairbrush through her hair.

Finally the line rang through, but it was Stacey Kerr, Lexi's personal secretary who answered, rather than Gord Nevins, who examined and supervised all expenditures on the estate.

Stacey's genteel Southern composure broke as soon as she recognized Juliana's voice. "I can't believe they're gone!" she said, bursting into tears. "Those two beautiful people—and after what they went through with their poor baby's abduction. Then Lexi losing her mother and her father. Tell me, how is your father doing? Gord told us that he'd been seriously injured, but we didn't know which hospital to call to check on him."

"He's doing as well as can be expected," Juliana said, reaching for a tissue and struggling to keep her voice steady as she updated Stacey on her father's condition.

"We'll be praying for him. It's terrible what they're saying on the news. The police are here asking questions of the staff. Is it true it was a bomb?"

"I'm not sure," Juliana hedged, remembering Hunter's warning that someone on the staff might be a mole. "I've been so worried about my father that I haven't spoken to them directly."

"Well, you stay with your father. He needs you. We're managing here, though it is difficult. Cook is missing—she took the week off when the Collingwoods told her she wouldn't be needed on their getaway and we haven't been able to reach her. She hasn't called in either. The sous-chef is helping Gord plan the menu for the reception after the funeral."

Juliana frowned. Should she mention the cook's disappearance to Hunter? It was probably nothing. Maybe Cook hadn't turned on a TV or seen the morning paper yet. "Do you know when the funeral is scheduled?"

"Wednesday or Thursday, we're told. Gord received a fax with instructions for the funeral from Mr. Collingwood's lawyer. We haven't seen hide nor hair of Lexi's sister. Apparently, as a security precaution, she's under guard. Poor thing. We've had too many funerals in this family in the last few years. With the Collingwoods gone, I imagine the staff will soon be looking for employment elsewhere."

Including her father, Juliana thought despondently. The household staff was a gregarious family with a hierarchy all its own. They had their conflicts and their slights, but they also pulled together when the need arose. She couldn't imagine one of them voluntarily being involved in a murder plot. "I'll keep you posted on my father. He'll appreciate your good wishes."

Juliana brooded over the phone call as she transferred

the gun from its hiding place in the bathroom to her purse, then hurried downstairs to give Cort his morning dose of antibiotics.

The kitchen smelled deliciously of sausages and French-roast coffee. Valentina reluctantly surrendered Cort to Juliana, reassuring Juliana that he'd drunk a full bottle. Valentina returned her attention to slicing fresh fruit into crystal bowls, but Juliana felt the housekeeper's attentive eye on her as she squeezed a syringeful of bubble-gum-flavored medicine into Cort's mouth. Cort fussed, his lips scrunched into a cupid's bow of distaste.

She gave him an indulgent smile as she stored his medicine in the refrigerator. "The coffee smells divine. Where is breakfast usually served, Valentina?"

"In the breakfast room, madam. Straight through that door." She gestured with her paring knife. "Marquise found a high chair for the little one."

Juliana carried Cort into the breakfast room, which looked out onto a terrace garden. The walls were a burnished gold that reminded her of the summer days she'd spent in Provence visiting her mother's family when she was a girl. Her mother, Juliette, had been the social secretary to the wife of the American ambassador to France. Her father had met her mother below stairs when Ross's parents were guests of the American embassy in Paris.

Juliana was settling Cort in the soft high chair clipped onto the table when Hunter joined them, his hair still damp from the shower. He was wearing black slacks and a charcoal sweater. The scents of soap and money still clung tantalizingly to his skin as he nuzzled her neck in greeting, his fingers dropping lightly onto her shoulders.

She froze for a fraction of a second, goose bumps tingling her skin despite the fact she knew this was all for the servants' benefit. She slid her hand up to his smooth-shaven cheek. How could a man's face feel so incredibly appealing? She tilted her head back, awareness rising in her as she bravely dipped her gaze into the azure ocean of his eyes. "Can I expect that every morning?"

"That, and then some," he retorted with a teasing grin.

They broke apart as Marquise entered, carrying the coffeepot.

Juliana gratefully accepted the steaming cup of fragrant coffee and tried to get her mind to settle on the notion that this would be her everyday life. Having breakfast with her husband and son, though she noticed Hunter's appetite was as meager as her own. Fortunately, Cort's babbling eliminated the need for meaningful conversation. After picking at his meal for a few minutes, Hunter excused himself and leaned over to whisper in her ear, "Duty calls. Annette is expecting me, and I have a private meeting with the senior management of Ross's company. Will you be all right here with Cort? The building is secure."

"Of course." She was armed. Without thinking, she smoothed the deep lines bracketing his mouth with her fingers. Her heartbeat stumbled as his eyes met hers. His eyes glowed with pure amusement. Knowing that he was amused by her feeble attempts at playing his loving wife made her fingers tremble. "I have a wedding to plan, remember? And shopping arrangements to make. We'll be fine."

His firm lips formed a sardonic smile beneath her fingertips. "Ah, yes, the shopping. Don't let it be said that the Sinclair family hasn't made a meaningful contribution to the economy."

Her voice lowered as she placed a lover's kiss on his cheek. "Be careful. We need you."

He drew back. The amusement was gone from his eyes, replaced by an intensity that awakened a slow warmth curling through her belly. "You can reach me on my cell phone.'' He grabbed one of Cort's hands and blew a raspberry into his tiny palm. Cort chortled.

As Hunter left the room, Juliana's smile faded, chased away by misgivings. If someone knew she'd been caring for Cort, did that person also know The Guardian's identity?

Chapter Four

"Is the team in place?" Hunter demanded into his cell phone as the limousine whisked him through the fleet of cabs zigzagging the city's streets. Saturday morning shoppers were out in full force. Though it was nearing noon, the overcast sky visible between the high corridors of the buildings made it seem even later.

"Yes, sir. We'll be invisible," Del Lanham, the commander of The Guardian's elite security force, assured him. "She won't even know we're there."

"Good. I don't want to alarm her any more than necessary. If anyone so much as looks at her the wrong way, I want details, right down to the names of their second cousins. Understood?"

"Yes, sir. They're in good hands."

"I'm counting on it." Hunter disconnected the call, still debating whether or not he should have told Juliana about the team he'd assigned to secure the apartment building and watch over her and the baby. Del was assigning their best team to this detail, handpicked ex-military and police officers, even a former Secret Service agent. Until Hunter knew who'd murdered Ross and Lexi, he wasn't taking any chances. He couldn't ignore the fact that only a handful of people knew of Cort's birth.

Hunter arrived at his family's flagship hotel via a rear entrance reserved for celebrities. He met briefly with the head of Clairmont's security to ensure that the special measures he'd requested to protect Lexi's sister were being carried out to the letter. Then he was escorted up to Annette's suite.

A security officer was stationed outside her suite. A butler opened the door and showed him inside.

Annette York was almost lost in the ornate grandness of the suite. Hunter found her burrowed in the corner of the plush sofa, a silver tea tray resting on the coffee table in front of her. Attractive in an elfin sort of way, her short frosted hair framed features that were thin and expressive, and swollen from crying. Beside the tea tray, her leather satchel lay open, piles of typewritten pages and her agenda visible. Hunter remembered she worked as a copy editor for a women's magazine. She eyed him warily, her brows arching when he dismissed the butler.

"Are you The Guardian?" she demanded.

"Yes, I am," he acknowledged. "We spoke several hours ago by phone. Again, my deepest condolences for your loss."

Annette sandwiched her hands into the brocade cushions surrounding her. Hunter had the impression she was fortifying herself for an emotional onslaught. "Is it really necessary for me to be kept here like this? I have obligations. Mr. Nevins has questions about the funeral arrangements. I should be at the estate."

Hunter had no intention of telling her that no one would be allowed at the estate other than the staff until the police had finished sweeping it for hidden listening devices. "You should be here, where you are safe and can be protected. Mr. Nevins is extremely competent. This will be a difficult period, Ms. York, I ask for your forbearance."

"You don't intend to keep me from attending the funeral?"

"No."

"Good." Annette drooped, some of the tension leaving her petite body. "I would still like to see my nephew, reassure myself that he's okay."

Hunter refused to be moved. "He's safe and well cared for."

Her lips set in obvious irritation at his response. Her green eyes snapped with fire. "And you still refuse to tell me who Ross and Lexi appointed to take care of him?"

"I'm afraid so."

"Then why are you here?"

"Because I know you and Lexi were close and that you were a frequent guest at the estate, particularly when your sister and her husband were entertaining. I was hoping I could pick your brain about some of the senior executives in Ross's company and members of the board of directors."

Annette made a face. "Egotistical jackasses, most of them. Don't know why Lexi thought I might ever hook up with one of them. But then, marrying a billionaire was her idea of happiness, not mine." Her tone grew edgy. "Do the police really think someone from within the company is involved?"

"It's a possibility that must be considered seriously," Hunter explained patiently. "Your impressions could be important. Ross was the president, CEO and the chairman of the board of directors. What do you know about Kendrick Dwyer? As the senior vice president and chief financial officer, he'll be stepping into Ross's shoes, taking over as CEO and reassuring the shareholders that the company will remain stable."

A frown inched across Annette's brow. "He's been with the company for ages—at least twenty-five years. Ross's father trusted him, and so did Ross. If Kendrick had any ill feelings toward the family, you'd think it would have surfaced earlier when Ross took over as CEO after his father's death.''

''What about the company's three vice presidents— they'd have the most to gain after Kendrick Dwyer.''

''Well, Simon Findlay's the ultimate brownnoser and heads up human resources and corporate relations. He did whatever Ross told him, but his most charming quality is his ability to hire people with IQs vastly beyond his own so that he can take the credit for their brilliant work.'' She rolled her eyes. ''Other than that, I'm sure he's a decent human being. His mother probably loves him. And I'm sure his new fiancée loves his salary. He, no doubt, loves her implants.''

Hunter hid a smile. Annette shared her sister's expressiveness, but with a caustic edge that Lexi hadn't possessed. ''What about Paulo Tardioli and David Younge?''

''Not that either of them ever considered me worthy of anything more than a polite hello, but Tardioli's the general counsel. He's a player. Competitive. Gutsy. A don't-get-in-my-way attitude. He doesn't acknowledge you unless there's something in it for him.''

''And Younge?''

''Younge's the controller. He's quiet and intense. He's got a family, five kids. His wife, Sarah, is into causes. She's an interesting dinner companion, at least, even if she only eats organically grown vegetables. Lexi told me David has ulcers, though she never mentioned if they were caused by the pressures of his position or raising five kids. One of them got suspended recently—for threatening a teacher or going on a hunger strike. I can't remember which.''

Hunter digested the information, adding it to what he already knew about the senior executives in Ross's com-

pany. ''What about the board of directors? Anyone leap out
who might have a grudge against Ross?''

Annette hesitated. ''Well, I don't know them all personally, but I do know that Lexi used to take special pains to
seat Sable Holden and Phillip Ballard as far away from
Ross as possible. They secured their board positions as part
of the hostile takeovers of their companies. Phillip Ballard
is a maverick, doesn't like the corporate game playing. Sable is a total bitch. Amusing, but a bitch. Lexi thought
Sable was hot for Ross, but she wasn't seriously worried
about it. I mean, how could she be? Lexi was so per—''
She paused and swallowed hard, pain haunting her green
eyes. Her hands fluttered in front of her as she struggled
for control. ''Well, Lexi was Lexi,'' she finished softly,
curling into a defensive ball against the cushions. ''Now,
if you don't mind, I'd really like to be alone.'' Her eyes
shuttered closed, dismissing him.

Hunter excused himself and left her to her grief.

THE HEAD OFFICE of the Collingwood Corporation in lower
Manhattan reflected the solemnity of the day. A portrait of
Ross had been placed on an easel in the reception area and
draped with black bunting. An employee carefully arranged
a bank of floral deliveries around the foot of the easel.

The artist had captured Ross's bold personality down to
the golden aura that seemed to shimmer around him to the
candor lodged in his blue eyes. The candor that won him
friends and enemies.

Who did this to you, my friend?

''Are you here for the press conference?'' the reception-
ist at the desk asked him, drawing him away from the paint-
ing. ''It's scheduled for three o'clock.''

''No, Mr. Dwyer is expecting me. I'm William Holmes.''

''Yes, of course. Please follow me.''

She ushered him down a wide hallway displaying pieces from Ross's extensive art collection. When he saw the empty leather chair before the plate glass window that looked over New York's financial district, the extent of Ross's loss hit Hunter like an oar to the gut.

At his entrance, the four men occupying the office halted their conversation in midsentence. Hunter surveyed the men. A slightly stooped, silver-haired man with a drink in his hand came forward and introduced himself as Kendrick Dwyer.

Simon Findlay, slick as an otter in a shiny pewter-gray suit, his light-brown hair and sideburns touched with pomade, rose and offered a limp handshake. The brownnoser Annette had described. "Good of you to come. We're all at a loss, but unanimous in the belief that Ross would want us to carry on his legacy."

"Cut the bull, Simon," said a well-heeled man in a black suit, shirt and tie who had the body of a prize fighter and a Roman nose that had never taken the battering end of a fist. "Ross would want justice and the bastard who did this strapped into the electric chair." His black eyes pegged Hunter. "Paulo Tardioli. General counsel."

"Down boy," said the remaining gentleman, a heron-thin male in his late forties with a pinched expression about his lips. Hunter had the impression the liquid in his glass was spring water. "David Younge, controller. Do the state police have any viable leads?"

"None that they're currently sharing. The investigation is only beginning. It may be some time before a suspect or suspects emerge."

"What about you?" Tardioli quipped, his black eyes reminding Hunter of a vulture planning to pick a bone clean. "Who do *you* think did it?"

Hunter eyed him steadily until he could feel Tardioli

back down. "I'm more interested in your opinions. The four of you had intimate knowledge of Ross's business dealings. It shouldn't be difficult for you to give me a list of people who bore an animosity toward him."

"And you intend to include us on the list, I presume?" Tardioli asked, taking a sip from his drink.

"Naturally. And you can bet your life that the police are working the same angle. You four stand the most to gain from Ross's death, so be prepared for some hard questions. I want a complete accounting of your time on Thursday and Friday. Where you were, who you spoke to, who saw you."

Kendrick Dwyer's face reddened. "You've got nerve to come in here and throw accusations around—"

"Sir," Hunter coldly interrupted him. "Whoever killed the Collingwoods had the arrogance to think they could get away with this—and perhaps implicate one or all of you in their murders. I'm putting you on notice. You're either with me in this investigation or I'll consider your lack of co-operation an indication of your possible involvement. Is that understood?"

Paulo Tardioli broke the stunned silence created by Hunter's threat. "Gentlemen, I suggest we cooperate fully with The Guardian's request. We'll have enough difficulties in the days ahead convincing the shareholders that the company is stable. It's only to our benefit to find out whether there's a Judas amongst us."

Hunter nodded. "Excellent advice, Counselor. Someone will be by at four o'clock to pick up your schedules. Do feel free to list anyone you feel may warrant further investigation and your reasons for concern." He laid four business cards on the coffee table. "Here's a number where I can be reached 24/7. Good day, gentlemen."

He'd have paid a million dollars to be a fly on the wall in Ross's office after he left the room.

"GOOD GOD!"

Darren Black's finger froze on the remote control as he flipped through the channels, hoping he could catch the last quarter of the football game. Ross and Lexi Collingwood had been killed in an explosion?

When the hell had that happened?

He'd spent the morning and most of the afternoon in meetings with his Ph.D. students, disproving their wild mathematical ideas on algebraic topology. Not one of them was showing signs of potential. Yet.

Darren upped the volume on the TV set, his heart twisting with bleak hope. Would this change anything between him and Annette?

He still wore the engagement ring she'd given back to him suspended from a chain around his neck. Some day she was going to see how wrong she'd been to break off their engagement. See how much he could offer her. He wasn't a billionaire, but he was well on his way to becoming a hotshot in his field with his plum new teaching position at Cornell.

Maybe that day had finally come.

Darren turned off the set when the news brief ended and tossed the remote onto the coffee table littered with empty soft drink cans, the collection of wooden puzzles Annette had given him and the mechanical pencils and discarded doodling of math research.

He needed to see Annette.

The least he could do was offer his condolences to the woman he loved with all his heart.

JULIANA TACKLED the shopping with the cell phone glued to her ear, requesting hourly updates on her father's condition and driving Valentina crazy, phoning the apartment every twenty minutes to check on Cort. Leaving him in Valentina's care for a few hours made her far more anxious than she cared to admit. But time was of the essence and she couldn't very well drag Cort through the Madison Avenue shops, especially after the last two rough nights he'd spent.

Thanks to the efficiency of the personal shoppers whom Marquise had lined up, she was able to make a sizable dent in her list of necessities in record time. Once the limousine's trunk was filled with clothes, diapers, toys, formula, a car seat and a stroller for Cort, she'd focused on clothes for herself and preparations for the wedding.

Although it was only going to be a quick civil ceremony, Juliana was determined to make it special enough to satisfy any prying minds. She was a wedding planner. She could pull this off! It was all in the details. Not the least of which was Hunter.

Amid the other emotions teeming in her heart was the keen disappointment that she would never have children of her own. Leastwise, not with Hunter. He'd made it so plain that her face burned just thinking about it. She'd have to content herself with being Cort's stand-in mother. And who knew, maybe Riana would one day be found, safe and sound, giving Cort a sibling? Though, if Hunter was right and Riana's abduction was linked with her parents' murders, it was unlikely the infant was alive.

Juliana experienced a chill as the limo pulled up outside Tiffany & Co. She'd picked out a Valentino dress for the ceremony, but she and Hunter still needed rings. Then she could focus on making their wedding night an event to remember—even though she knew it would be an experience she'd just as soon forget.

A WEDDING NIGHT was all about fantasy, Juliana thought ruefully as Hunter joined her at dinner later that evening, his fingers brushing the loose tendrils of hair adorning her neck after she'd pulled her hair into a chignon.

Her heart skipped like a stone over her ribs and plopped into the pit of her belly. She hadn't seen him in hours and she was conscious of everything about him: the fatigue biting hollows into his lean cheeks, the texture of his gray wool blazer, his smoothly shaven jaw, the spicy scent of his aftershave and the faint dampness of his hair as if he'd recently showered.

His eyes glinted in warning as he slanted his mouth over hers in a welcoming kiss. Her fingers pressed against the lapel of his jacket in a futile effort to hold him and his invasive kiss at bay, but the warm coaxing pressure of his lips trampled her resistance, luring her into a dizzying vortex of contrasting sensations: hard muscle against soft flesh. Racing heartbeats and slow dizzying pulses. Dark bottomless kisses and blinding points of light that left her breathless and light-headed when he finally pulled away.

She blinked, trying to get her bearings. Planning a wedding night to reflect Hunter's strong, compelling personality would take more daring than she'd first imagined.

The dark pinpoints of his pupils were narrowed on her, cool and assessing as if estimating the cost of the sleek cobalt dress and the diamond stud earrings she was wearing. "Miss me?" he said with dry amusement.

Juliana felt a furious blush erupt over her skin. The confidence she'd felt when she'd dressed for dinner crumbled tremulously beneath his gaze. The dress and the shoes and the earrings she had thought so perfect earlier, now made her feel as desirable and as invisible as a chambermaid.

She lowered her gaze and gestured toward the table she'd made certain was perfectly set with flowers and candlelight.

"I would think that's obvious. I asked Valentina to hold dinner until your arrival. But you look tired. Would you prefer a tray in your room?" She smiled at him uncertainly. "It would be more private. And Cort's out like a light— for the night, I hope."

One of Hunter's eyebrows darted up. Juliana tried not to jump out of her skin when he slid a hand around her waist to the small of her back. "Are you propositioning me?"

She wet her dry lips, her heartbeat rattling in her chest like a door improperly latched. "Consider it a suggestion." And she could ask the questions about the bombing that she'd hungered to ask all afternoon, rather than playing out this farce of being head over heels in love with Hunter.

Hunter's nerves were pulled taut as cables as he took in the color infusing his bride-to-be's flawless skin. Nothing had prepared him for the sight of Juliana standing near the table in the dining room, the candlelight glowing off her translucent skin and winking like stars off the midnight-blue fabric that clung to her delicate curves. At the end of this horrible day, his breath had stuck in his lungs hot and heavy as smoke from a smoldering fire at the vulnerability and the quiet determination shining in her eyes.

He'd kissed her, wanting to blot it all out, prove to himself that this wasn't real, that the last twenty-four hours had been a nightmare and the fantasy would end when he kissed Juliana. Cinderella's coach would turn back into a pumpkin.

Only it didn't end. It became more real. Her skin tempted him, gliding beneath his fingers like the satiny embrace of the St. Lawrence on a misty morning. Her mouth pleasured him, a cove of delights shyly given up for his exploration. And her eyes compelled him to resist this madness.

He wasn't sure which would be worse, playing out this farce in front of the servants or being alone with his reluctant Cinderella in his bedroom. But he needed food. And they needed to talk.

"Marquise," he said over his shoulder, inhaling the scent of her skin. She smelled different than she had that morning. More sophisticated than apple blossoms. He presumed she'd bought a new perfume to go with the new clothes and the diamond earrings. The clothes and the earrings met with his approval. The perfume did not. "Set up a table in my room. Juliana and I will be dining alone tonight."

His fingers remained possessively on her lower back as he guided her toward his room. He'd had a meeting with Tom McGuire, Ross's lawyer, before he'd come back to the apartment, and he was still mulling over the list of monetary gifts Ross had bequeathed in his will, particularly the size of the gift to Juliana's father. True, Goodhew had been a faithful family retainer for many years. But two million dollars was a considerable sum of money by any standards.

His mouth settled into a grim line. God help Juliana and her father if either one of them was even remotely involved in Ross's and Lexi's murders.

"WELL, WHAT DID YOU find out?"

Hunter warred between suspicion and amusement at Juliana's unaccustomed directness.

He dabbed at his mouth with the linen napkin. "According to the state police, the bomb was some kind of high explosive. It had been concealed in a small chest in the master bedroom. The bomb was set off by a pager. They're attempting to piece together the pager so they can trace it."

"Do the police have any idea how the explosives were put there?"

"Not that they're revealing. They're interviewing the

owners of the property and anyone who visited the house within the last few days, hoping to come up with a lead. How is your father? Has he come around from the surgery? He may be able to answer some questions.''

Anxiety flickered in Juliana's brown eyes. ''I've been checking with the hospital every hour for updates. He's still groggy from the surgery. The ICU nurse said he's in a lot of pain and they've heavily medicated him. I'm hoping tomorrow he might be stronger. The nurse told me the police had come to the hospital this afternoon to ask questions, but they were turned away. Your security guards are still there.''

Hunter cut himself another piece of roast beef, almost too tired to wield the knife and fork. ''Did you call the estate?''

''Yes. Things were in an uproar. It took several calls to get through. I spoke to Lexi's secretary, Stacey. She said the police were there asking questions.''

''Did she happen to mention they were sweeping for bugs?''

Juliana winced. ''No. That topic didn't come up. Did they find any?''

''Apparently not. If the house had been bugged, someone's removed the evidence.''

''You mean someone on the staff, don't you?''

Her defensiveness was charming. Hunter deigned not to point out to her that no listening devices would have been necessary if she or her father was involved in the murders. Or that both she and her father had escaped the bomb.

He'd feel a lot better once the police checked with the doctor who'd diagnosed Cort's ear infection. Hunter had gotten the doctor's name from the bottle of antibiotics in the refrigerator. Juliana wasn't taking one step out of this apartment with Cort until he knew she was everything Ross had purported her to be. "Your father was seriously injured in the explosion, I would think you'd want the person responsible held accountable."

"I do. But my father used to tell me that if you treat servants fairly, they'll reward you with loyalty. Ross might have been the cutthroat of Wall Street, but he was a generous employer. My father weeded out employees whose work ethics weren't in sync with domestic service."

"Everyone has a price."

"It may be true for some people, but not everyone. Do you have a price, Hunter? Is that what the work you do as The Guardian is all about—the right price for the job?"

"Prices aren't always about money. The payoff can be about pride, revenge, retribution, thrills."

"What's your payoff?"

"All of the above?"

"Liar."

Hunter eased back against the leather club chair, mildly irritated that she looked so pleased with herself. What was it about women that made them so certain they could guess what a man was thinking? That she knew why he dedicated so much of his life to being The Guardian? "Tell me, did you agree to care for Cort purely out of loyalty?"

Juliana remained as composed as a marble bust in the candlelight. "That was the main reason. I truly didn't think Lexi could bear to be parted from her baby for long. And Ross offered enough incentive that I knew I'd have the capital to open my own wedding planning firm when the job ended." Her expression grew somber. "And here I am ending my wedding planning career by planning my own wedding. Ironic, isn't it?"

"It's not too late to change your mind."

Her warm mahogany eyes settled unwavering on him.

"No, Cort needs a mother. And some promises are meant to be honored for a lifetime."

It was probably his deep fatigue, but Hunter felt something stir within him like a stone rolled aside to reveal cold, bare earth to the sunlight. Was she implying she would also honor her marriage vows to him for a lifetime?

"If it makes you feel any better, Ross's offices are being swept tonight for listening devices. I met with the senior management of the Collingwood Corporation today after I paid my respects to Annette."

"How is Annette?"

"Distraught. And frustrated that she can't see Cort."

"Can't say as I blame her," Juliana said softly. "This must be such a terrible shock to her, especially after losing both her parents so recently. Her mother died of a heart attack just after the one year anniversary of Riana's abduction. The doctors said it was probably stress related. Annette's father died about six weeks later in a car accident. He went through a stop sign and hit a garbage truck."

Hunter nodded, remembering how Ross had been so worried about Lexi that he'd come to FairIsle. Hunter had taken one look at Ross and poured him a drink. Ross had told Hunter that Lexi was growing increasingly fragile. She wasn't eating. He'd insisted on taking her to a doctor and they'd discovered she was pregnant again. Instead of being happy, she was terrified something would happen to this baby, too. Goodhew had suggested an outrageous scheme to hide her pregnancy from the world and protect the baby's existence and Ross had wanted Hunter's opinion. Who could have guessed it would lead to the present situation?

"Annette gave me an earful on the senior management of the Collingwood Corporation," Hunter said neutrally. "I was hoping you could supplement her comments."

"My father would really be the one to ask. He had Ross's confidence. But I'll do my best."

Hunter poured himself another glass of red wine and sketched out the information Annette had told him. Juliana confirmed that Ross had trusted Kendrick Dwyer, the CFO of the corporation, implicitly. She'd never heard her father suggest anything otherwise.

"My father called Paulo Tardioli a shark. He predicted that Tardioli would eventually find a way to oust Ross's favor with Simon Findlay. But Simon knew Ross didn't want a human resources manager who questioned his decisions. David Younge and his wife, Sarah, were very supportive of Ross and Lexi after Rianna's kidnapping. Especially Sarah. She dropped by or called every day and helped organize the poster campaign." Juliana paused, her slender fingers toying with the stem of her wineglass. Hunter noticed that the third finger of her left hand was bare. He'd check with Marquise to ensure that she'd picked out a suitable engagement ring.

He found his mind drifting, imagining that hand resting on his own, bound to his by duty and loyalty. Would she feel isolated and trapped on FairIsle? Exhaustion tugged at his spirit and he felt his eyelids droop, but he wanted to finish the conversation. He struggled to keep his mind alert, away from distracting thoughts of Juliana.

Each of the officers had provided him with alibis of their whereabouts on Thursday and Friday as he'd requested. But it would take time for his operatives to verify the accounts. They'd each also given him a short and interesting list of suspects. After what Annette had told him about Sable Holden and Phillip Ballard, whose positions on the board of directors were a condition of the takeovers of their respective companies, it was not surprising they garnered top spots on two of the four lists.

Ballard's name didn't ring a bell with Juliana, but she straightened thoughtfully when she heard Sable's name. "Oh yes, I remember her from the wedding. She was the snippy woman who rudely eyed Lexi's pregnant tummy when she passed through the receiving line and asked if Ross was the father of her baby. Lexi called her the 'thorn in Ross's side.' Ross hadn't wanted Sable included in the guest list for the wedding, but Lexi thought it would be insulting if she was the only member of the board of directors who wasn't invited."

Hunter spoke his thoughts out loud. "I wonder how insulted Sable was by the takeover deal. If she felt Ross had screwed her over, she might have resorted to kidnapping and murder. I'll look into it. And I'll check out the deal with Ballard's company, too." He stifled a yawn.

Juliana placed her napkin on the table and rose. "It's been a long day. You need some rest. You're falling asleep in your chair." She tucked a stray wisp of blond hair behind her ear and leaned across the table to blow out the candles.

Hunter had a beautiful image of her face radiant with golden light before the candles were snuffed out. The room darkened around them, shadows settling. Juliana's laughter touched his ears. "I probably should have turned on the lights before I did that."

He reached out to stop her, making contact with her arm. "No, don't. It's fine." His voice tightened. "But take off your dress and leave it on the floor on the way out."

"My dress?" Her voice was hesitant. Alarmed.

Hunter smiled despite his fatigue. He squeezed her arm gently. "The servants will expect some evidence of a romantic evening."

"Oh."

"I'll close my eyes, I promise." He released her arm and obediently closed his eyes. "Go ahead."

Never had he imagined that the whisper of fabric against skin could be so tantalizing. A certain part of his anatomy took special note of the sigh of midnight-blue fabric settling onto the carpet. "Your panties and bra, too."

She hissed in her breath, but her voice was calm. "My father warned me about rich boys like you."

"Your father is a very smart man," Hunter retorted, "but you're safe with me, Cinderella."

"Don't call me that." The shifting of her feet and a light thud indicated her compliance with his request.

A vision of her naked before him in the high heels she'd been wearing turned his body to pulsing awareness.

"I'm leaving my shoes, too. Don't trip over them."

Hunter grit his teeth, hearing two plops as if she'd tossed them in different directions.

"Good night."

He counted her footsteps across the room; his breath exploded in his chest when she seemed to stop before reaching the door connecting their rooms. He reminded himself that asking her to remove her clothes was his lamebrained idea.

"Hunter?"

"Yes?" God, he hoped she wasn't going to do something ridiculous like ask him whether she could expect to find him in her bed when she woke up. Hunter couldn't trust himself with the answer to that question.

"Ross and Lexi's cook appears to be missing. The staff can't locate her. You might want to check into it."

The door closed firmly behind her. Hunter sat alone in the dark. Cinderella had just given him a nugget of her trust.

Chapter Five

Exhaustion finally catching up with her, Juliana slept past noon on Sunday. She peered blurry-eyed at the alarm clock, then leaped out of bed, anxiety rising like mercury within her when she realized she hadn't even heard the baby. She yanked on a bathrobe and shoved her feet into slippers and hurried out into the hall. Cort's crib in the nursery was empty, but her anxiety eased when she heard his characteristic happy chortles behind the closed door to Hunter's room.

She knocked on the door and at Hunter's gruff command to enter, she found Cort in the middle of the bed, propped squarely on Hunter's broad naked chest, patting at the newspaper his godfather was trying to read.

Hunter lowered the newspaper and Juliana forgot to breathe. She'd dated in university, had seen a few male bodies, but she'd never have described any of them as dangerous. Or beautiful. But Hunter, with sleep-tousled hair, that devilish whisk of morning stubble and all those tanned knotted muscles contrasting sharply with Cort's smooth baby-perfect skin sent a shock wave of desire to the core of her being. The sheet barely covering his waist left her little doubt that he was naked under there.

"Good afternoon." He flexed an eyebrow at her. "Sleep

well? I'm teaching Cort to read the financial pages. Think his father would approve?'' He indicated Ross's picture dominating the front page of the financial section and his suddenly misty gaze melted Juliana's heart into a puddle.

''Very much.'' Juliana fought back a sob. Okay, so marrying this carelessly wealthy, mysterious man was the craziest, most reckless thing she'd ever done. But seeing him lying there with the baby on his chest and obvious uncharacteristic emotion dampening his eyes made her want to be crazy and reckless and forget that they would never be equals in this relationship. Needs she'd been denying since Hunter had proposed their arranged marriage surfaced in her heart: the need to be loved and protected; the need to have a home and children of her own.

Juliana quickly closed the door to those imprudent thoughts. ''You didn't have to get up with him, I would have—''

''A phone call woke me anyway.'' His voice lost its dispassionate edge. ''The autopsy results are back. Ross and Lexi were positively identified.'' He paused, his jaw tightening. ''They died instantly and didn't suffer. I hope that will be some comfort to your father, and you.''

Juliana's legs couldn't hold her up anymore. At least Ross and Lexi hadn't suffered. She sat down on the edge of the bed, aware of the precise number of inches between her thigh and Hunter's large feet. Cort, his smile lighting up at the sight of her, crawled over the ridges of Hunter's body toward her.

Juliana laughed, almost crying as Hunter gently kept the baby from straying accidentally into any sensitive areas. ''Come here, pumpkin.'' She stretched out her arms to Cort, love and adoration for this baby twining bittersweetly with her grief. Cort tumbled off Hunter's knee, landing in a nest of sheets and blankets.

"Oopsie," Juliana exclaimed, scooping him up. She peppered his sweet rounded cheek and the button-tip of his nose with kisses, glancing past her precious charge to Hunter. She had to keep Cort safe. "We'll get the marriage license first thing tomorrow?"

"Yes. I'll protect you both with my life, Juliana."

She fitted her arms more snugly around Cort. "Please, God, don't let it come to that."

JULIANA FELT HER FEARS darken along with the ominous clouds building on the horizon as the afternoon wore on. She'd called the hospital, hoping to talk to her father only to be told that he was still holding his own, but unable to communicate. Juliana asked the nurse to keep her posted.

Her call to Gord Nevins at the estate to discuss the funeral arrangements was just as disquieting. Nonnie Wilson, the cook, was still unaccounted for. Gord had phoned the cook's emergency next-of-kin number and spoken to the cook's sister. But as yet, the sister hadn't called back to say that she'd located Nonnie.

Juliana passed the information on to Hunter, who was sequestered in his study, making calls and going through several boxes of files he'd requested from the Collingwood Corporation. Hunter had told her that the sweep of the Collingwood Corporation offices hadn't turned up any listening devices.

Juliana wasn't sure whether this was comforting news or not. She wanted the killer to be caught, but she hated the idea that someone in Ross's company may have been involved.

When her cell phone rang just before five, as she was enlisting Marquise's help in carrying out her romantic secret plans for her and Hunter's wedding night, Juliana put Cort down in his playpen and rushed to answer, praying it was good news from the hospital. Maybe her father had regained consciousness.

To her surprise, it was Hilde Epstein, the elderly woman who occupied the condo alongside Juliana's in Cleveland. They often met for tea and watched chick flick videos together. Hilde had been teaching Juliana an old form of lace making called tatting. "Juliana, I'm sorry to bother you, but you did tell me you'd be out of town this weekend, didn't you?"

Juliana was instantly cautious. "Yes, I'm visiting friends," she said, walking down the hall toward Hunter's study. "Is something the matter?"

"I'm afraid someone's broken into your home and they were quite messy about it. They forced your door open and went through every drawer and cupboard in sight. They must have been after smaller valuables because they didn't touch the TV or your sound system. I've called the police."

Juliana's heart thumped. Someone had broken into her home and disabled the security alarm.

She barged into Hunter's study without knocking. He was on the phone. He looked up frowning, but quickly ended his call and rose to offer assistance when she silently gestured at her cell phone.

Her eyes pleaded with him as he laid a calming hand on her shoulder. She spoke into the receiver, hoping he would catch on by her words. "I'm glad you called me, Hilde. But you shouldn't have gone into my condo. The burglar could have still been in there."

Hunter grabbed a pad on his desk and wrote: "Don't tell where you are."

Juliana nodded.

"What should I do when the police arrive?" Hilde asked.

Juliana gripped Hunter's arm and repeated Hilde's question.

"Officer's name. Report number," he wrote out.

"Just get the officer's name and report number and I'll call him when I get back. I'm not sure when I'll be home. I may stay here for another week." Juliana felt sick lying to her neighbor like this. Thank God there was nothing in the condo to indicate her relationship to the Collingwoods. She didn't have so much as a phone number written down. She shredded her phone bills as soon as she paid them.

"What about the door, dear?" Hilde asked.

"Don't worry about it. I can call a locksmith from here."

Juliana quickly ended the call before Hilde could ask any more questions.

The fear stamped on Juliana's face as she disconnected the call completely undermined Hunter's pragmatic resolve to keep his bride-to-be at a distance when they were in private. She looked paler than a porcelain saucer and about ready to shatter.

"They know where I was living with Cort," she whispered, her eyes wide. She took a step toward him, then paused uncertainly, clasping her hands as if attempting to trap her emotions between her palms. "What if they find out we're with you?"

Hunter's defenses toppled with a silent crash that shook the foundation of his life. The break-in at her condo indicated the killer was intent on finding her and Cort. Finishing the job.

Though his mind warned him against behaving rashly, trusting too deeply, too soon, he anchored her against his chest and promised himself that they wouldn't live in fear for the rest of their lives—assuming their marriage lasted longer than he anticipated. Then he called Investigator Bradshaw, the Bureau of Criminal Investigation investigator with the New York State Police, who was the lead detective in the homicide investigation. Maybe the killer had been careless and left some fingerprints in Juliana's condo.

"AND?" ROSS AND LEXI'S killer waited expectantly for the update on the butler's daughter and the baby.

"She's gone. Her car's gone. No sign of her passport or personal documents so she must have them with her. I went through her papers. I have a checking account and credit card numbers." He paused slightly, significantly, "And she has a cell phone. She likely has it with her. I have the number."

The killer jotted down the number on a thick creamy sheet of stationery from the desk drawer, reveling in this stroke of good fortune. It was amazing what money could buy.

LATE SUNDAY NIGHT Darren returned home to Ithaca to the empty clapboard four-bedroom house that he'd bought for Annette within walking distance of the campus. It wasn't a mansion, but he thought she'd love the clean simple lines of the house, the dark oak floors and the yard spacious enough for children. He slammed the front door behind him, frustrated by a nine-hour round-trip drive that hadn't achieved his objective.

The doorman at Annette's apartment had told him she'd left early Saturday morning in a limo with a driver and bodyguard. He was certain she had to be at the Collingwood Estate. Where else would she be?

He'd fought his way through the horde of journalists demanding admission at the gates and gave his name to the security guard, who'd called up to the house, then told him that he was very sorry, but Ms. York wasn't receiving any visitors.

She didn't want to see *him*. His ego still throbbed from the bruising.

Like the hundreds of other people keeping vigil outside the gates, Darren had camped out overnight, hoping his love might leave the estate by car the next day and catch sight of him.

God he missed her. Missed how perfectly they'd fit together like a very elegant proof of a known mathematical result—clever and aesthetically pleasing. With her parents and her sister gone and no longer putting ideas in her head, it would be easier to convince Annette that they still belonged together. That he was all she'd ever needed in a husband.

Darren grabbed a beer out of the refrigerator and twisted off the cap. His Adam's apple bobbed as he downed half the bottle in one gulp. Whether she liked it or not, Annette was going to see him. The funeral was scheduled for Wednesday.

He'd cancel his classes so he could attend.

MONDAY MORNING Juliana felt buoyed by a call from the ICU nurse; her father had spent a good night. After breakfast she went with Hunter to apply for a marriage license in the Manhattan city clerk's office with hopes that her father was rallying and she'd be able to talk to him later today—tomorrow at the latest.

Juliana balked at once again leaving Cort in Valentina's care, but Hunter was adamant that Cort was safer in the secured building. Reluctantly, she had to admit he was right.

They didn't need blood tests to get married, but there was a twenty-four-hour waiting period. They'd have to return the next day for the ceremony.

After they'd obtained the license, they stopped at

Hunter's lawyer's office. Hunter signed a new will reflecting his anticipated marriage and appointing Juliana as Cort's guardian in the event of his death. Then the lawyer handed them copies of the prenuptial agreement.

Though Hunter's lawyer had urged her to seek her own representation to review the prenuptial agreement before signing, Juliana had dismissed his suggestion. "That won't be necessary. My fiancé is a man of his word and that's more binding than a piece of paper for me."

Juliana couldn't interpret the appraising look Hunter shot her. She had no idea whether her comment had pleased or annoyed him, but watching his dark head bowed and the sharp concentration in his eyes as he read the legal document before signing it, brought a rush of conflicting emotions to her chest.

When she was little, her mother used to tell her, "Handsome is as handsome does." Through the hot jab of tears pricking her eyes, Juliana doubted there was any man on earth more handsome than Hunter at this moment. As much as she hated to admit it, she was seriously in danger of feeling something for her husband-to-be that she had no business feeling. He treated her like a servant, expecting his orders to be obeyed without question. The agreement he was reading so seriously was a contract to him. Everything clear-cut and explained. No entanglements.

He'd keep his end of the deal and expect her to keep hers.

But that didn't stop her from wondering what background events had shaped Hunter's perspective on the world. What motivated a man with his wealth to go to such extremes to help others while protecting himself from involvement? Juliana suspected it was quite possible that beneath Hunter's cynicism about marriage in general, he valued love.

Once the papers at the lawyer's had been dispensed with they headed back to the apartment. But their plans changed en route when Hunter received a call on his cell phone from the BCI investigator who was assigned to Ross and Lexi's murder case. Hunter gave the address of the New York State Police's NYC troop installation to Marquise, then closed the limo's privacy window.

"Investigator Bradshaw needs to ask you some questions," he explained quietly.

Juliana felt a quiver of anxiety that only increased when Hunter's strong fingers wrapped around her hand as if bracing her for bad news.

His gaze met hers, intractable as a stone wall. "He knows about Cort."

"He what?" Anger flared in her heart like a struck match. She yanked her hand from his. "You told him?"

His hands curled into fists on his knees. "We can't hide that kind of information from the police—not without facing charges for hindering a criminal investigation. And it's critical to the case. Investigator Bradshaw understands the sensitivity of the information. I have several retired BCI investigators on my payroll and they tell me I can trust Bradshaw."

Juliana's stomach rolled. Hunter could trust a trooper on a word-of-mouth recommendation, but not the woman he was going to marry. She would dearly love to know if he distrusted her specifically or just relationships. "Does he know about our arrangement, too?"

"He knows that Ross and Lexi appointed me the guardian of their living children, and I have assured him that I am instigating measures to protect Cort's identity. And yours. Just answer the questions, you may know more than you realize."

She leaned against the leather seat back not the least bit

appeased. She had a sick feeling that Hunter was very interested in her answers to the investigator's questions, as well.

INVESTIGATOR BRADSHAW was a compact man in his late forties with a long sharp nose and somber gray eyes. He greeted Juliana with a handshake that seemed both sincere and compassionate and asked after her father as he escorted them to a back room of the police installation reserved for interviews.

"We'd like to interview your father as soon as possible, Ms. Goodhew." The investigator indicated that Juliana and Hunter take a chair at the table in the center of the room. "We may be able to piece together how someone else found out the location of the rendezvous in Severance. Did he reveal any details to you in your phone conversations?"

Juliana shook her head. "I'm sorry. All I know is that my father handled the arrangements himself and booked the house under his own name."

"Would those arrangements include ordering flowers to be delivered to the house?"

Juliana glanced at Hunter uncertainly. He shrugged his shoulders, indicating the significance of the question was unknown to him. She wet her lips. "It's possible. That would be the kind of thing he might do to ensure the Collingwoods were comfortable in their surroundings. Lexi loved freshly cut flowers. But my father didn't mention anything about ordering flowers. Why do you ask?"

"Because we've interviewed the property owners who claim that a floral delivery was made to the house Thursday morning—three large arrangements designated for the living room, dining room and master bedroom. The delivery person insisted on placing the arrangements himself and making finishing touches per Mr. Goodhew's request. The owners didn't object."

Investigator Bradshaw's inquisitive gaze shifted from Juliana to Hunter and back. "A large basket arrangement was carried into the master bedroom and placed on a table near where we believe the explosion originated."

Juliana grew absolutely still as the horror of the investigator's insinuation sank into her fogged mind. The room seemed to be closing in on her. She glanced at Hunter, unconsciously seeking his support as her fingers dug into her palms. This was insane. Her father would never hurt Ross and Lexi. He'd die for them. And a part of Juliana feared that her father's slow recovery might be a subliminal reluctance to face life without Ross. Beneath the table she felt Hunter's leg surreptitiously nudge hers as if reassuring her that he was close by and she wasn't alone. She took a calming breath, drawing strength from this unexpected show of support and felt the walls starting to recede. She had to stay calm. Be as cooperative as possible. "You think my father was involved, Investigator?"

Bradshaw locked his fingers on the table. "It's early in the investigation, Ms. Goodhew. We're following every lead. That includes checking with every florist within a one-hundred-mile radius to ascertain who ordered the flowers. We can't ignore the fact that your father was not in the house when the bomb went off."

Juliana's face grew warm with indignation. "He was outside waiting for me and the baby!" She told the investigator about Cort's ear infection and her father's command that they arrive by midnight to surprise Ross and Lexi. "I did my best, but the drive was too much for Cort. We stopped in a motel near Utica."

The BCI investigator pressed on relentlessly. "The break-in at your condo yesterday suggests that someone is aware you're caring for the Collingwoods' son. Are you certain that no one on the estate other than your father, Ms. York and the Collingwoods was aware of the child's true parentage?''

"There's no way I can be absolutely certain, but we were all very careful. Whenever I visited the estate, I wore those pregnancy pads that actors use and pretended to be nauseous and tired so everyone would be convinced I was expecting.''

Investigator Bradshaw nodded. "How were your living expenses provided to you?''

"Ross gave me a check for two hundred thousand dollars and I set up an account at a bank in Cleveland,'' she replied.

"So, the money didn't come out of the household accounts that Mr. Nevins manages?''

Juliana shook her head, adamant. "No. I'm sure Mr. Nevins would have been curious about such an arrangement. The check was from one of Ross's business accounts.''

At that, Hunter deigned to interrupt. He knew the BCI investigator had to ask his questions, but Juliana could use a moment to compose herself against the steady barrage. He could see fine blue veins beneath the pallor of her face. Had she eaten this morning? Why hadn't he noticed?

"If the check came from one of Ross's business accounts it's possible that it came to the attention of Kendrick Dwyer, the chief financial officer, or David Younge, the controller,'' he interjected. "More likely Younge as he would be responsible for the day-to-day spending.''

"Looks like I'll have a few more questions for Mr. Dwyer and Mr. Younge,'' Investigator Bradshaw said dryly.

Hunter rubbed his jaw, considering motives and opportunity. He'd already given the investigator copies of the alibis he'd gathered from the Collingwood Corporation's senior management.

"Either of them could have had their eye on the CEO position. And they both have the resources to hire assistance. Did the homeowners provide a description of the delivery person? Perhaps Ms. Goodhew will recognize the description."

"Yes. We got a Caucasian, male, approximately five-foot-ten-inches tall, medium build, maybe midforties wearing blue coveralls and a blue ball cap. No distinguishing characteristics. Ring any bells?"

"I'm afraid not," Juliana said, her brow crumpling with worry.

"From what you've told us, Investigator," Hunter continued undaunted, "the bomb was either carried into the house concealed in the arrangement or the delivery man left a door or window unlocked so that someone could enter the house at a later time and plant the bomb."

Investigator Bradshaw loosened the blue-striped tie knotted at his throat. "That's correct."

Hunter drummed his fingers on the scarred wooden table. "Was the home monitored by a security system?"

"Yes, but the homeowner said it was only used in the winter months when the house was unoccupied. Break-ins are rare in Severance. Most people leave their doors unlocked in the daytime."

"Has the Trace Evidence Section been able to determine what kind of explosives were used?"

"Unfortunately, no. There was nothing left. All we know is that it was a high explosive. We're still working on piecing the pager together. We might know more in a few days. And, of course, the Cleveland police are dusting Ms. Goodhew's apartment for fingerprints. The floral delivery man could be the same person who broke into her apartment. We'll want to take Ms. Goodhew's prints before she leaves today so they can be eliminated from any found at the scene.''

''What about Nonnie Wilson, the missing cook?'' Hunter asked, noting that Juliana's head snapped up and her rich mahogany eyes sparked to attention at his mention of the Collingwoods' chef.

Discomfited, he tore his gaze from Juliana's pale face and the sharp jut of her chin and focused on Bradshaw. Had he jeopardized the trust she'd placed in him by passing along the information she'd given him about the cook's disappearance to the police? To Hunter's consternation, earning more of Juliana's trust and keeping it ranked high on his priority list. Right up there with being a loving and attentive father to Cort.

''Nonnie Wilson's still unaccounted for,'' Bradshaw said wearily. ''A neighbor saw her put several suitcases in her car Friday morning and drive off. We've got an APB out for her car, and we're checking the airports and bus stations.'' The investigator checked his watch. ''I've taken up enough of Ms. Goodhew's time for today. If you'll both follow me, someone from the Forensic Identification Section is waiting to take Ms. Goodhew's fingerprints.''

Relief flowed through Juliana as she rose from the table. She was bone tired and heartsick with worry about her father's potential reaction to Investigator Bradshaw's insinuations. And she missed Cort. She wasn't used to spending so much time away from him.

As Hunter and Investigator Bradshaw made arrangements to talk later in the day about the security for the funeral a chill eased down her spine. The sooner she and Hunter were married and safely on his island, the more secure she'd feel.

Chapter Six

Hunter holed up in his study when they got back to the apartment as much to get away from the reality of his impending wedding as to keep pursuing the investigation in his own way. He had piles of Collingwood Corporation documents to review, as well as updates from his operatives and a constant influx of tips coming in on Riana Collingwood's 1-800 hotline demanding his attention.

Since the night of the explosion, calls to the 1-800 tips line for Riana Collingwood had catapulted into the thousands and each one had to be taken seriously. Even though an FBI case agent was reviewing the incoming calls for potential new leads in Riana's abduction, Hunter had instructed the staff manning the hotline that he wanted to see a report on every call. He might spot something the agent missed.

Normally, he would review this information in the offices he leased for his covert Guardian operations, but he felt more comfortable being near Juliana and Cort.

Hunter eyed the daunting piles of folders accumulating on his desk and selected Ross's takeover files on Phillip Ballard's and Sable Holden's companies as being the most urgent to review. But the words swam on the page as an image of Juliana—radiant in an ivory wedding gown that brought out the luminescence of her pearly skin—appeared like a specter in his thoughts.

He hadn't kissed her since Saturday night and the memory of that kiss throbbed hot in his veins. It struck him as being exceedingly ironic that while he was adverse to the institution of marriage, he was not adverse to Juliana's charms.

Juliana, the butler's daughter.

Ross would laugh his head off at the irony, then threaten to kill him if he hurt her.

Hunter appreciated women. Appreciated their beauty and the softness of their skin and the special way women had of making their mark on the world, whether in a business meeting or in wiping the tears from a child's face. He understood the intricacies of seducing a woman. Knew the rules of the game and the outcome.

But he'd never been confronted with a woman who confused him like Juliana did. Although he'd laid out the rules of their marriage, he felt as if he were moving from one precarious foothold to another across a vertical rock face. One misstep and he'd fall into Juliana's polished mahogany eyes. Or bury himself deep into her ivory satin skin.

He *wanted* to touch her. Kiss her. And yet, he didn't.

He didn't want to open his heart to his own vulnerability and let in emotions that would affect his judgment. He'd seen what allowing emotions to overrule good sense had done to his father. His father had fallen in love with a pretty office clerk from New Jersey, who worked in the file room, and had decided to marry her despite his family's concerns that he was marrying beneath him.

Hunter didn't know all the details of his mother's unfaithfulness, but he knew his father had gone through a terrible period when he'd wondered how many of his friends had slept with his wife.

Hunter had no intention of making his life more complicated than it had to be by falling in love with his wife. At least Investigator Bradshaw had pulled him aside while Juliana was having her fingerprints taken and told him that Cort's ear infection was genuine. He'd spoken to the doctor who'd examined Cort. With a frustrated sigh, Hunter concentrated on the takeover files. To his consternation, he realized that Sable Holden's nationwide chain, Office Outfitters, had fallen to Ross's mercy two months prior to Ross and Lexi's wedding. The takeover of Phillip Ballard's communications equipment company had occurred six months ago—one month prior to Cort's birth. Both situations warranted further investigation.

Just before 5:00 p.m., Investigator Bradshaw called to tell him that the police had checked out Goodhew's computer and discovered the butler had found the rental property in Severance via the Internet.

"Did Goodhew have a password to access his computer?"

"Yes, but his password was his daughter's name."

"That's a no-brainer."

"Exactly. Anyone on the staff or a cocky visitor could have accessed his office and looked at the sites he'd bookmarked. It only took our expert about five minutes to find the site."

"Did you happen to find any sites for florists?"

"No such luck."

Hunter riffled his fingers through his hair. "Well, at least we have an idea of how the killer may have learned of the Collingwoods' destination." He briefed the investigator on the dates he'd dug up on the Ballard and Holden company takeovers, then they went over the security arrangements for the funeral. Security would be tight with undercover state troopers stationed in the crowd and surveillance cameras strategically planted by the New York State Police Photography Section in hopes of capturing a gloating killer on film.

Lexi's sister Annette would have undercover troopers protecting her. And Hunter had two operatives lined up who'd stick to Juliana like barnacles for the duration of the ceremony.

Hunter planned to attend the funeral, as well. He just wouldn't be visible. He wasn't letting Juliana out of his sight.

As he hung up the phone his attention was drawn to the bank of TVs in his study, which kept him apprised of public opinion. A picture of Ross and Lexi smiling into each other's eyes at a charity function flashed on CNN. Hunter raised the volume on the set, so he could listen to the news update.

The media was having a field day with the tragedy, speculation running high that Ross had made one too many enemies. And conjecture as to what would happen to the Collingwood fortune. Would it be held in trust for the lost heir? Would Lexi's sister Annette eventually end up with all that money if the heir wasn't found? Fortunately, there wasn't a whisper yet of the cook's timely disappearance.

Hunter frowned as a clip from Kendrick Dwyer's press conference on Saturday was replayed yet again as the news anchor reported on the hit the stock prices of the companies owned by the Collingwood Corporation had taken when the market opened this morning. Dwyer's performance had been exemplary. In the clip, he looked paternal and strong, a seasoned senior vice president capable of leading the corporation into continued success as its new CEO.

From Hunter's jaundiced perspective, Dwyer was in his element. Was he stepping up to the plate and showing his loyalty to a company he'd given most of his working life to? Or was he basking in the glory of a dream finally come true?

Hunter massaged the back of his neck, then thumbed through the files on his desk until he found a copy of Dwyer's employee file. Dwyer was in his sixties. Close to retirement age. Hunter paused as he came across a record indicating the number of sick days Dwyer had taken in the last few years. Had Ross been aware that his chief financial officer was obviously experiencing some health problems? Had he suggested Dwyer think about retirement?

Hunter checked the time. If he hurried, he could have a private talk with Ross's secretary and still be back for a late dinner with Juliana.

"PUT MY FATHER on the line," Juliana asked Hunter's operative, gripping her cell phone tightly in her fingers, wishing it could transport her into her father's hospital room.

Tears sprung to her eyes as her father's weak voice touched her ears. "Juli-ana?"

"Yes, Papa. It's me. I'm so glad you're okay. The doctors say you're going to be fine."

"Good girl, Juliana," her father said woozily. "Always so good with her little brother."

Juliana's heart stopped, confusion setting in. Was the medication affecting her father or was this his way of giving her a message about Cort? They never talked about Michael or the terrible day Michael died. She was supposed to have been watching her little brother. She knew her father blamed her for Michael's death and the end of his dream of Goodhews continuing on in the family tradition of serving the Collingwoods. "I'm so sorry about Ross and Lexi. I want so much to be there with you—"

"No!" Her father interrupted her vehemently. "No!"

Juliana cringed, frightened by her father's reaction. "It's

all right, Papa,'' she said, trying to soothe him, ''I understand what you want me to do. You can count on me—''

''I'm sorry,'' the operative's voice cut in, tempered with
compassion. ''The nurse says your father needs to rest
now.''

Juliana swallowed her disappointment. ''Tell my father
I'll call him again tomorrow when he's stronger.''

''Yes, ma'am.''

Juliana hugged the phone to her heart feeling six years
old again, and her father was entrusting her with Michael's
safety. She'd failed him then. No matter what happened,
she wasn't going to disappoint him this time.

HUNTER DIDN'T WANT to feel it, in fact derided himself for
the sense of anticipation that lightened his step as he
stepped off the elevator and rang the bell for his apartment.

He'd taken a cab to the Collingwood Corporation's offices as Marquise had been occupied by a mysterious errand
for Juliana that had something to do with the wedding.
Though what, precisely, the butler wasn't saying. Judging
from the amusement in Marquise's eyes as he took Hunter's
coat and wished him good evening, Juliana was doing a
credible job of convincing the servants that the wedding
was going to be a happy and joyous event.

Which reminded him that he had certain obligations for
the wedding that couldn't be ignored. Not if he wanted to
convince anyone he was madly in love with the bride.

''Was a certain package delivered?'' he asked.

''Yes, sir.'' Marquise slipped his hand into his jacket
pocket and produced a small velvet box. ''Juliana has arranged for dinner to be set up in your *room*.''

Hunter found himself smiling, then frowning at the prospect of being alone with Juliana again in his room. Deliver

us not into temptation, he thought wryly, tucking the box into his trousers' pocket.

"Where's my son?" His throat tightened awkwardly around the unfamiliar words.

"Just finishing his bath."

While Hunter would admit grudgingly, under oath, that he had spent a few minutes in the cab on the way home picturing how Juliana would dress for dinner tonight, his vision hadn't included this charming view of her backside as she lifted Cort from the special ring that helped him sit up in the bath. Tonight she was wearing a loose sleeveless black pantsuit that set off the blond fire of her hair and the ivory temptation of her skin. The back zipper of her top wasn't closed properly, teasing him with a glimpse of forbidden flesh. "There, let's get you dried off, pumpkin."

"Aha," Hunter said, propping his shoulder against the doorway of the bathroom and folding his arms across his chest to prevent himself from giving in to an overwhelming urge to touch that zipper. "I knew every Cinderella had a pumpkin."

Juliana shot him a harried look, which made her all the more charming in his eyes. "Next you'll be asking me about glass slippers."

"There's a thought. Amazing what torture women will put their feet through for a party."

"Uurg!" Cort clasped his toes with his hands and smiled up at them, trying to join in the conversation. "Naa-naa-nah."

"Yes, I agree. Daddy is very silly, Cort," Juliana said smugly as she patted Cort dry.

Daddy. With all that was going on, Hunter hadn't quite prepared himself for the impact of that word. Cort would grow up calling him daddy, calling Juliana mommy. He'd be depending on them both. Hunter hoped he'd be worthy of the task and he wouldn't cause more harm than good.

"Need some help?" he offered, stepping forward. He had every intention of drying the baby, but his fingers had another agenda. With a determined will of their own they sought the tab of her zipper and inched it into place. Juliana froze and Hunter breathed in the forbidden scent of apple blossoms.

Suddenly the memory of her standing naked in the dark before him burned into his thoughts and short-circuited his senses. He could hear the sensuous whisper of fabric gliding over her skin and puddling to the floor. But most importantly he could feel the gift of her trust burrow unerringly into his heart when she'd confided in him about the cook's disappearance.

"Your zipper," he explained, uncertain whether to feel amused or affronted by her reaction to his touch. Inch by inch, he could feel the tension ease from her shoulders.

"Thank you." Her eyes met his in the vanity mirror. "I spoke to my father today."

Torn between a carnal desire to stroke the tendrils of hair that had escaped onto the back of her elegant neck and his determination to resist her, Hunter compromised and ran his thumb along the fine edge of her jaw. His voice dipped to a strangled husky pitch as she moistened her lips. "I'm so glad. Did he mention anything about the explosion?"

She shook her head, lowering her voice to a murmur. "It was a brief conversation. He wasn't that coherent, but he knew who I was. Maybe tomorrow he'll be more lucid and can talk to the police."

Cort squirmed free of the towel and rolled over onto his tummy. "Oh!" Juliana exclaimed and made a quick grab for him.

Hunter ensnared one of Cort's ankles with his thumb and

forefinger. "Hold it there, big guy." Painfully aware of the uncomfortable tightness of his trousers, he bent to kiss the sole of Cort's tiny foot. "Were you a good boy for Mommy today?"

Cort laughed, drawing his knees up to his tummy.

Hunter got a certain enjoyment from watching Juliana's face turn pink as she towel-dried Cort's trunk and waving arms. He had no doubt she'd be a loving mother to his godson.

"He's always a good boy, aren't you, pumpkin? The antibiotics seem to be working. He's back to his happy-go-lucky self." Her eyes lifted to Hunter's, dark with shadows, as if she doubted life would ever be happy-go-lucky again. Cort's parents had been murdered and the killer was still out there.

He silently handed her a diaper and Cort's sleeper, watching as she expertly dressed the baby. "There," she said, snapping the last fastener, "all ready for a bottle, a story and bed."

He reached for Cort. "I'll read him his story tonight."

Hesitation reared in her eyes. "Don't you have something more important to do?"

Hunter held out his hands like a scale. "Let's see, read a story to my new son, have dinner with my bride-to-be, or save the world. Tough choice. But I'm taking all three and in that order. Princes can do things like that."

Juliana bit her lower lip and settled Cort in his arms. Hunter let his gaze drop to that bit of tender pink flesh caught between her teeth and felt the gnaw of an answering hunger that didn't wish to be denied. It was a shame neither Marquise nor Valentina were passing in the hall. It would have been all the excuse he needed to kiss her again.

HE WAS DELIBERATELY baiting her, Juliana thought, wringing her hands beneath the linen-covered table as she waited for Hunter to join her in his bedroom for their private dinner. He'd insisted on putting Cort to bed himself. She hadn't heard a peep of protest out of Cort at this variation in his nighttime routine. But she worried that Hunter's decision to take care of the baby had been a subtle demonstration that she was not irreplaceable, rather than an effort to play the role of a devoted father in front of the servants.

She bit her lip and studied the wooden sleigh bed and the matching tables and armoires that dominated Hunter's room. The dark-green walls gave the room the feeling of an isolated glade. Visitors were seldom, and not welcome.

Deep down she suspected that all his talk of Cinderella and princes was his way of reinforcing that he thought of her as a servant masquerading as a princess, masquerading as his wife.

Which was all the more reason to strictly adhere to the rules of their marriage arrangement and not let herself fall prey to his azure eyes and his cynical smiles and those very thorough kisses. She was not going to be separated from Cort by doing anything so foolish as becoming too attracted to Hunter Sinclair.

She still couldn't quite bring herself to believe that tomorrow this sexy, bewildering, larger-than-life man would be her husband. Her heart squeezed in awe and wonder as Hunter entered the room, followed by Marquise pushing a serving cart.

Pride lit Hunter's features. "So far, so good. No roars. Cort's on his tummy with his bum up in the air."

"That's his favorite sleeping position," she shared, feeling almost as if she were giving precious secrets to the enemy.

Hunter dismissed Marquise with a wave of his hand as the butler removed the wine chilling in the ice bucket and presented it for inspection. "That will do for the night. Leave the cart. We can manage."

A smile twitching his lips, Marquise withdrew with a discreet bow.

Juliana laced her fingers together on the edge of the table as the door clicked softly closed. She felt a new tension arc from Hunter's broad shoulders like an electric charge.

"How subtle," she remarked dryly. "The poor man is probably envisioning an orgy with food."

Hunter laughed as he expertly uncorked the wine. "How inventive. We'll save it for later in the evening."

"We will not." Juliana rose to hide the sudden spurt of her pulse and peeked under the silver domes covering the food. She placed the garden salads and the basket of rolls on the table. "I'm worried about Investigator Bradshaw interviewing my father," she continued, returning to her seat. "Do you think the investigator seriously considers my father a suspect?"

Hunter fingered the stem of his wineglass and Juliana was moved by the lines of fatigue etched in his face and the stern inner fire of determination lighting his gaze. He pursed his lips, his gaze laser-sharp enough to peel the skin off her nose.

"What would you say if I told you that Ross left your father two million dollars in his will?"

Two million dollars? Juliana managed to keep her salad fork from slipping through her fingers and clattering to the table. With great care she placed the fork on her plate, aware that Hunter was watching and evaluating her reaction.

Despite the fact that he'd kept his word in naming her Cort's guardian in his will, she could see now that the trust in this arranged marriage was solely one-way. She should have realized it earlier this afternoon when Marquise had told her that he was very sorry, but on Hunter's orders he couldn't allow her to take Cort for a walk in Central Park. She'd thought Hunter was just being protective.

Now she realized, he didn't trust her alone with Cort. And she suspected that the operatives posted at her father's side had more to do with making sure that she and her father weren't conspiring together, than protecting her father from the Collingwoods' killer.

Hunter's gaze continued to mock her. If she weren't so angry she might have dared to ask him what had happened in his life to make him so distrustful. As it was, she couldn't bring herself to ask him whether he'd advised Investigator Bradshaw of Ross's generosity. No doubt Investigator Bradshaw already knew and was champing at the bit to interrogate her father. The very idea that her father could have killed Ross and Lexi was insulting. Her father would be outraged—and hurt—by the insinuation.

She wiped her mouth with her napkin, fully aware that Hunter was still awaiting her reply. "I don't feel I need to explain or justify Ross's decisions or his relationship to my father. If you'll excuse me, I'll leave you to enjoy your dinner. I've lost my appetite for the company—and the conversation."

To Hunter's mute astonishment, she rose from the table with dignified grace and marched to the door that connected their suites in a cloud of swirling black silk. The door gave a disturbing, final-sounding click as it closed behind her.

Hunter took another swallow of wine and watched the door, almost certain she'd return momentarily and apologize. She needed to understand no one was above suspicion. Not her father. Not even herself.

He was debating whether he should attempt to apologize—he could have phrased the information about her father's inheritance a tad more tactfully—when the door adjoining their suites suddenly opened. Good, she'd come to her senses. They could resume their dinner and he could solicit her opinion about the timing of the takeovers of Sable Holden and Phillip Ballard's companies. Then he could present her with the engagement ring he had tucked into his pocket. Marquise would notice in the morning if she wasn't wearing it.

A feminine hand snaked around the door, a cascade of black silk trailing from it. She sent it sailing toward him. Hunter realized to his shock it was her dress. Then two scraps of black lace arced through the air. Her panties landed smack-dab in the basket of rolls and her bra snagged his shoulder.

He hooked a finger through a strap.

It was still warm from her body, and the scent of talcum powder and apple blossoms clung to it.

He grimaced, trying not to imagine how Juliana's breasts would fill the flimsy peekaboo lace cups. He failed miserably.

He crushed the bra in his palm, his heart hammering. He couldn't take his eyes off the half-open door. What did she think she was doing?

What would *he* do if she stepped into the room now, without the dress, without the filmy underwear?

Without warning, two missiles sailed around the door aimed straight for his head. He ducked, then eyed the weapons. Her shoes.

He shook his head, a reluctant smile tugging at his lips. He was beginning to see that his Cinderella was not the demure, acquiescent creature he'd first assumed.

Chapter Seven

Juliana barely slept, her thoughts consumed by concerns that her father would be seriously implicated in Ross and Lexi's murders and that she'd made a fatal error by walking out on Hunter last night. Today was supposed to be their wedding day, not that it felt like a joyous occasion when Ross and Lexi were going to be buried tomorrow. Would Hunter tell her to pack her bags? Her father would never forgive her if she didn't stay with Cort.

But her fears were alleviated when she saw the velvet box from Tiffanys and a dove-gray envelope resting on the pillow beside her. Hunter had entered her room last night, and she hadn't been aware of it.

The thought that he may have watched her sleep made her tremble. With unsteady hands she opened the envelope first. On his personal stationery Hunter had written, "For Cinderella on our wedding day. Yours always, Hunter."

Yours always. It sounded like a promise.

And it sounded permanent.

Juliana felt a glow like the first colorful wink of a Christmas tree bulb illuminate inside her. He intended to go through with the wedding, after all. And she could only hope that given time they might come to trust one another completely.

She opened the box and gulped.

Oh, dear.

A huge teardrop-shaped diamond glimmered up at her. Juliana was no expert, but judging from her past experience with brides, she was guessing it was in the six- to eight-carat range.

He shouldn't have. He really shouldn't have. The more modest diamond-studded wedding band she'd picked out for herself would have sufficed. But the fact that he'd concerned himself with this detail at all when he was so busy with the investigation gave her reason to believe that Hunter would prove to be a thoughtful husband. And a thoughtful father.

The engagement ring fit her finger perfectly.

But she still felt like a fraud.

HAD SHE CHANGED her mind about marrying him?

Hunter shifted Cort to his other arm and glanced impatiently at his watch as the baby used his three-hundred-dollar silk tie for a burping rag. He paced the length of his living room, gently thumping Cort's back. Where was Juliana? Should he knock on her door?

He'd had enough of this nonsense about it being bad luck to see the bride before the wedding. Marquise and Valentina had barred his earlier attempt to see Juliana. She'd taken a breakfast tray in her room.

Was she still angry about last night? Or was this her way of creating a little prewedding atmosphere for the servants? Valentina had dressed Cort for the occasion in a tuxedo-style sleeper with black velvet tails, which gave Hunter hope that the wedding would take place as planned.

But he couldn't blame Juliana if she'd changed her mind about going through with the ceremony. Especially after the way she'd walked out on him last night.

He wasn't about to offer any apologies for asking questions about Ross's bequest to her father. Two people were already dead and his godson's life was at stake.

Maybe it had been cowardice to leave the engagement ring on her pillow. Not that there had been anything easy about seeing how beautiful and vulnerable she'd appeared, her Cinderella hair fanned over her shoulders and her body tightly coiled on the edge of the bed as if wishing she could escape the circumstances she'd been caught up in.

And maybe a part of him hadn't wanted Juliana to read anything more into the ring's significance than was intended. He couldn't find fault with the wedding band she'd picked out. It was lovely. But a man in his position could well afford an engagement ring to please his bride.

He paused in midstride as Cort elicited a tiny ungentlemanly burp that thankfully didn't leave any more residue on his tie. Is that what he'd been doing when he'd instructed Marquise to select a suitable engagement ring for Juliana? Had he been trying to please her—thinking that an expensive diamond ring would make their marriage somehow more palatable to her?

He stifled a groan.

Judging from the way she'd reacted to his questions about her father's integrity, she probably thought he was attempting to buy her loyalty with the ring.

Hunter eased his tie from Cort's grasp before the infant strangled him. This was precisely the reason he had no business getting married. Ever. It involved too much uncertainty and risk. Saying "I do" the day before a funeral had to be a bad omen.

But he was doing this for Ross. For Ross's son.

His anxiety multiplied as he heard a door open down the hall and Marquise's and Valentina's murmured exclamations. She was ready. Finally!

Hunter prided himself on his ability to remain emotionally detached and objective in the most trying of circumstances. But there was nothing detached or unemotional about his reaction to Juliana when she appeared in the doorway to the living room.

She looked gorgeous.

Be-still-my-heart gorgeous.

Hunter sucked in his breath as the dazzling impact of Juliana in that short ivory satin dress hit him in the solar plexus, as well as other parts. Her dress was simplicity itself—as if the designer knew that the woman inside was the ornament, not the garment. In her left hand she held a bouquet of blue violets and white roses that kept him from learning whether she'd accepted the ring he'd left on her pillow last night.

He gazed hungrily at the swell of her breasts pushing gently against the bodice, the lithe curves of her legs that were a fantasy unto themselves and the tumble of blond curls escaping from an artless do and felt his body tremble with trepidation.

Juliana had transformed herself into a flesh-and-blood Cinderella, minus the tiara. She was the most delectable woman he'd ever seen.

Never in his life had he felt less like a prince.

Suddenly the prenuptial agreement and his insistence that this marriage be in name only seemed like an incredible joke.

On him.

He could almost hear Ross's laughter.

Color infused her cheeks like late-blooming summer roses as she shyly met his gaze. "Well, what do you think?"

"I can't think," he said honestly, determining that it

would be absolutely appropriate to cross the room and kiss her again. For the servants' benefit, of course.

Marquise and Valentina, both looking jubilant, stood hand in hand in the doorway. Ironically, Hunter found himself wondering whether there would be moments in his marriage to Juliana when they could share the good and the bad with the press of a hand. The idea held a much stronger appeal than he'd ever have believed possible. Right, next he'd be believing in a large furry bunny that left baskets of eggs on doorsteps.

"You look wonderful, Cinderella."

He took several steps toward her, intending to prove to himself that feeling those pink lips soft and pliant beneath his was something he could master, not be mastered by, but Valentina intercepted him and shook a reproachful finger under his nose.

"No kisses until after the wedding, Hunter. Is bad luck before, yes? Marquise, come, take a picture of the happy couple. And the baby."

Hunter's disappointment was far too genuine. The frustration he felt stiffly real. He scowled, unable to take his eyes off Juliana, whose cheeks were blooming scarlet now.

"Are you sure, Valentina? It seems like incredibly bad luck on my part not to be able to kiss her now."

Valentina scolded him in Spanish and Hunter consoled himself with slipping his arm around Juliana's waist for a photograph.

Juliana wiped a dab of drool from Cort's face with her thumb, then self-consciously lifted her gaze to meet his. "You both look very handsome. Cort's joining us for the wedding, I hope?"

Hunter couldn't refuse the soft plea in her eyes. Maybe she needed Cort present as a reminder of the promises they would make to one another today. It occurred to him that perhaps he did, too. He'd alert the security team to the change in plans. He gave her waist a gentle squeeze, all of his nerves alerted to the spark of friction generated by his touch. "Of course. It wouldn't be right without him. He's unequivocally our best man."

Juliana's smile brought a glow to her face and cast a crack of sunlight into the dark cavern of cynicism harbored deep beneath Hunter's ribs. "Thank you. And thank you for the ring." She held out her left hand, where the ring sparkled like a star upon her finger as Marquise snapped another picture. "It was very thoughtful of you. I'll treasure it always."

She would? She sounded so sincere Hunter doubted she'd said it for the servants' benefit. And he doubted a woman who didn't fawn over zeroes would fawn over carats.

Hunter studied her bent head. There she went confusing him again. Surely she knew he *hadn't* taken the time to pick the ring out himself.

Too late, he wished he had.

JULIANA HELD HER TEARS at bay as she and Hunter stood in the chapel of the city clerk's office where a deputy clerk for the city of New York officiated over the ceremony. Sunlight streamed through the stained-glass window as if valiantly trying to add a note of jubilance to the occasion. Hunter had been so silent and unapproachable during the limo ride, his arm draped across the back of the seat, his strong fingers resting protectively on Cort's head. His profile etched with an air of sadness Juliana shared.

Thoughts of Lexi and Ross weren't far from her heart as she and Hunter solemnly exchanged vows and exchanged rings. Cort, perched on the crook of Hunter's arm, chirped and cooed through the ceremony like a songbird, making them laugh through their sorrow. Hunter's lawyer served as their witness.

Juliana's one regret was that she hadn't been able to talk to her father this morning. She'd called the hospital twice and the nurse had told her that her father had spent a restless night, but seemed to be sleeping more soundly this morning.

Juliana took his restlessness as an indication that her father was regaining his faculties. Was remembering, perhaps was even experiencing nightmares about the explosion. She'd never felt so far away from him.

But the firm touch of Hunter's strong fingers on hers, the strength of his voice and Cort's wide-eyed innocence gave her courage. She wasn't alone in protecting Cort. She had no doubt that Hunter would do everything in his means to keep them safe. She only found herself foolishly wishing for the unthinkable when Hunter gazed down at her with his piercing azure eyes and promised to love her.

In the quiet beauty of the chapel, with Hunter standing handsome and resolute beside her in a sinfully tailored black Armani suit, Cort secure within the circle of his arms, the truth stole into Juliana's heart. She'd fallen in love with this man. Completely.

She wanted to share his life with him fully, as a real wife would.

She nearly jerked her hand from his at the realization, then let it remain clasped between his. He was flawed and stalwart. She loved his fierce determination. Loved his selfless dedication to helping others.

Of course, he could never know.

No one could.

"I now pronounce you man and wife. You may kiss the bride," the deputy city clerk finished with a dramatic flourish.

Rising up out of the grief and horror of the last few days, Juliana's heart fluttered on hope-filled wings as Hunter cupped her head with one hand. Any sense of pretense in her shattered as his lips claimed her mouth, branding her with the taste and the scent and the feel of him.

She melted into the warmth of his kiss, abashed by the fierce passion with which she welcomed and returned the seeking, velvety thrusts of his tongue. No one would ever kiss her as he did. The thought of sharing his home and sharing the child he held in his arms made her ache for what could not be.

WHAT THE HELL HAD happened to his apartment? Moreover, what the hell had happened to his life? Hunter wondered, shell-shocked, as Marquise opened the door to what he knew *must* be his apartment that had somehow been transformed during their absence into an enchanted forest.

He wordlessly transferred Cort into Marquise's waiting arms. First he'd had to deal with Juliana in that dress, then that insatiable white-hot kiss in the chapel, which had nearly had him shrugging out of his clothes and taking her right there before his lawyer and the deputy city clerk, and now *this*.

The hallway to their right, which led to the master bedroom, had been darkened and lined with potted trees ablaze with twinkling lights. A footpath of burlap strewn with white long-stemmed roses wound between the trees bordered by banks of purple and blue violets. The aromatic scents of evergreens, roses and violets tinged his every breath. Hunter felt his blood slow and start to drum at his temples.

Through the forest of trees, the glow of candlelight could be seen flickering from his room like a lantern in a window guiding a lost voyager home.

He stood rooted to the marble floor, his mind and his heart waging war over the wisdom of walking down that path with Juliana. With each passing day he was learning that she had many facets to her character beyond courage, an acquiescent smile and beauty. Despite the clarity of their written agreement, she was quietly and thoroughly turning his life upside down and inside out.

He was trapped in a purgatory of his own device.

His body stilled as Juliana's fingers curled around his hand, delicate and feminine. He could feel her fingers trembling. Was she afraid of his response? Afraid she'd gone too over the top in trying to make their marriage seem genuine?

Hunter swallowed hard. Not for a moment could he hurt her. She'd done her job so well a part of him wished it truly was all just for him.

"Since I couldn't tear you away from work for a honeymoon just now, I decided to surprise you with one here," she explained in a bright tone to mask the uncertainty he saw creeping into her beautiful eyes. "Marquise, is everything prepared?"

"Yes, madam. Valentina will see to this young man's whims. Your honeymoon awaits."

Juliana tugged on his hand as if to pull him down the path. Hunter finally snapped out of his state. "Not so fast. I believe that tradition demands you be carried over the threshold." With one quick, effortless movement he lifted her into his arms.

She squealed, then laughed as he pulled her soft, enticing body snugly to his chest. Hunter steeled himself against the erotic sweetness of her curves and the silken feel of her legs hooked over his arm. A wry smile creased his lips as Juliana wrapped one arm around his neck.

Purgatory, plain and simple.

He'd deposit her in his bedroom and sneak into his study. The servants would never know.

He started down the path. "This is quite an amazing feat you've wrought. The violets are a nice touch."

"I thought you'd like them. Very woodsy. In the language of flowers, they stand for faithfulness."

He pondered the potential significance of that revelation. "What do the white roses stand for?"

"Girlhood and an innocent heart."

He paused midstep. "And I'm trampling them? How intimidating."

"You, intimidated? I don't believe it." Juliana laughed again.

Hunter, despite the tension and the confusion cording through his muscles, found himself enjoying the sound of her laughter. In fact, enjoying the intimate feel of her in his arms and the faerie-glow of the lights in the trees that reminded him of the dance of lightning bugs on a warm summer's evening. For the first time, he wondered if Juliana would be happy on FairIsle. Would she hate the isolation of his island home or grow to love the beauty of it as he did? He hugged her to him more tightly and continued down the hallway. "Believe it, Cinderella. I don't want to trample you."

Her elegant jaw jutted up and her eyes darkened dangerously as she tilted her head back to look squarely up at him.

"I'm neither innocent, nor a girl. I'm a grown woman," she said, sounding piqued. "I know full well what I'm getting into. You can put me down now. Valentina and Marquise are in the kitchen with Cort. No one is looking."

Hunter shook his head. "Not until I carry you over the threshold." In fact, he was battling a not unwelcome desire to brush his lips along her hairline and whisper in her sexy little ear that he was completely aware she was a grown woman.

A beautiful, enticing woman.

Just what did she have waiting for him in his bedroom?

Juliana settled back in his arms and Hunter couldn't tell whether she was pleased or annoyed. But he could feel a new tension stiffening her body.

The sound of trickling water and the raucous caw of a crow reached his ears before he crossed the threshold, but it in no way prepared him for the sight which met his eyes. Juliana had turned his bedroom into something out of a dream. Trees ringed the walls creating a clearing, in the middle of which was a white silk tent covering his bed. Burning candles had been artistically placed among a pile of logs to resemble a campfire. And the water fountain positioned beside the tent, he presumed, was a babbling brook. A picnic of delicacies—including champagne on ice—was laid out on a table draped with a red-checkered cloth. And when he listened carefully, he could hear the sounds of a forest—the soft sighing of wind in the trees and the twittering of birds.

A smug smile played at Juliana's lips. ''This is my idea of camping.''

Hunter was speechless. She'd recreated their fictitious first meeting in the Black Forest! But all he could picture was her lying naked in his bed with all that white silk billowing around her, waiting for him. He set her down more abruptly than he'd intended, reminding himself brusquely that he had work to do. Stacks of information to read. A killer to find.

Ross would haunt him until the end of his days if he touched Juliana. Hurt her in any way. Her father would probably kill him.

He drew a deep ragged breath and flexed his fingers to

release some of the tension strung taut in his body. He needed a drink. Something strong enough to knock some sense into him.

He gestured at the room, searching for words and finding himself at a total loss. She'd done a spectacular job of making their wedding day convincing and romantic. Anyone would think they were madly in love.

He darted an anxious glance at Juliana, who stood hands clasped in front of her and was obediently awaiting some sign from him. But there was a hint of amusement lurking in her rich mahogany eyes. In his years as The Guardian he'd dealt with stalkers, kidnappers, extortionists and cold-blooded killers, and none of them had brought the high level of fear to his heart that his new wife suddenly had with this honeymoon surprise.

He'd never been in love. Love was a two-sided coin that brought bliss and pain and Hunter would just as soon not have either.

But he was acutely aware that his marriage to Juliana necessitated making some changes to his schedule and his habits. This was only the first of many awkward moments he and Juliana would encounter as man and wife and the way he handled the enforced intimacy of their wedding day would set the standard for dealing with other such moments.

"You…I can see I'm going to have to educate you about camping. But it will do." He extended his hand to her and felt his pulse leap like a fireball into his palm, anticipating her touch. "Would you do me the honor of sharing this picnic feast? I have work to do, but it can wait until after we've eaten."

She placed her fingers lightly on his palm and a shudder of need coursed up Hunter's arm like a salmon battling its way upstream.

"It would be my pleasure." A frown crinkled her brow. "Is there something I can do to help you with the investigation? Notes I can take or papers I can file?" She flushed delicately. "Marquise and Valentina will expect us to be occupied for hours. You haven't mentioned whether you've heard anything more from Investigator Bradshaw since our meeting with him yesterday."

Hunter held out a chair for her, his mind more fixated on the hem of her dress creeping up her silken thigh than her question. She bent down, placing her ivory satin purse on the floor and granting him a glimpse of round, firm breasts.

Sweat moistened his brow. Hunter worked his tie loose with a tug of his finger, then removed his jacket before he sat down. But he didn't feel any more comfortable.

Gritting his teeth, he grabbed the damn bottle of champagne. "Bradshaw's added Sable Holden and Phillip Ballard to his suspect list," he struggled to say in a reasonable tone. As he worked the cork out of the bottle, he told her that the takeover of Sable Holden's chain of office supply stores had taken place six months prior to Ross and Lexi's wedding and that Ballard's communications equipment company succumbed to Ross three months before Cort's birth.

Juliana leaned forward across the table, holding out her champagne flute. "So what you're saying is that theoretically Sable could have orchestrated both Riana's abduction and the bombing. But not Ballard."

Hunter filled her glass, watching the champagne bubbles jettison up to the surface much like the emotions he was trying to contain. "No, Ballard couldn't have done both. He wasn't in the picture when Riana was abducted. But he may have hoped that the circumstances of Riana's abduction would muddy the police investigation into the bombing and throw the police off track. He's a brilliant man. Went to MIT. His company's success is primarily due to his leadership, which is why Ross probably wanted him and the company.''

He filled his own glass. ''But Sable Holden and Phillip Ballard aren't the only suspects. I've been digging into the backgrounds of the senior executives in Ross's corporation. I didn't find much on Paulo Tardioli, the general counsel. But Kendrick Dwyer's had health problems the last two years. I spoke to Ross's personal secretary yesterday afternoon. She told me Ross had expressed concern about Dwyer's health and was thinking about making some changes, but she didn't know what types of changes. But she did say that Ross had had a number of tense private meetings with David Younge lately.''

''Well, David's the controller. Maybe Ross was thinking he would be the logical choice to step up and replace Kendrick Dwyer as the senior vice president and chief financial officer,'' Juliana suggested.

''And maybe not. Maybe Ross was preparing Younge for the possibility that he was going to offer the job to someone else—like Paulo Tardioli or Simon Findlay. Tardioli's a lawyer. He has guts like Ross did.''

Hunter raised his glass to Juliana and felt his heart knot as her eyes became dark guarded pools. Those eyes were a trap that would ensnare him if he wasn't careful. ''To Ross and Lexi. May their love for one another guide us in raising their son.''

A tear rolled silently down Juliana's smooth cheek. He reached across the table and gripped her hand, which bore his ring, as his own emotions threatened to swamp him with guilt and grief.

Juliana smiled at him through her tears and raised her glass. ''To Ross and Lexi.''

And Hunter came undone. For four days he'd been stoically dealing with horror and anger, determined to help the police find Ross and Lexi's killer. Determined to protect their son at all costs. Trying so damn hard not to think about how much he would miss Ross.

He'd loved him like a brother. They'd kidded each other, swapped tales of their business and personal conquests, and he'd used every tactic he could think of to help Ross hold it together after Riana's abduction. A sob hit him so deep in the chest it felt as if he'd cracked a rib. Champagne spilled over the rim of his glass as he set it on the table with a thump.

Tomorrow he would bury his best friend.

Juliana saw Hunter's face contort with pain and heard the harsh agonized sob break from him as his fingers tightened almost unbearably over her hand. Without thinking or realizing how it happened she was kneeling beside him, holding him. Her face was pressed into the hard fortress of his chest as another sob shook his powerful body. A hot flow of tears broke in Juliana's throat. "Oh, Hunter."

Her fingers threaded through his short hair as she sought to offer him comfort, stroking his head and shoulders. Murmuring words of reassurance.

And then she felt it. A kiss, warm and firm, pressed on the crown of her head.

Then another one on her temple.

A frisson of alarm worked from her heart to her soul as Hunter's fingers sought her throat, his thumbs tipping her chin back, forcing her to look up at him.

She searched his face for some sign of apology or explanation, but saw only the stark pain in his eyes and the wet traces of his tears on the tight planes of his face. Hunter Sinclair was an extraordinary man. But who comforted The Guardian when he needed it?

She couldn't stand the thought of him bearing his pain alone.

Her mouth went dry as dust as Hunter's azure gaze locked on her lips. A trail of blistering heat unfurled down to her stomach. Slowly, deliberately, as if he were debating the decision every fraction of an inch, his mouth descended toward hers. His nose touched hers and stilled; Juliana felt the moisture of his tears lubricating his skin.

Her heart crumbled, compassion for his emotional struggle rising in her, overwhelming and unstoppable.

His warm breath bathed her cheek. Her nipples peaked to aching points against the bodice of her dress. The muscles of his shoulders were iron-hard beneath the fabric of his fine cotton shirt. Every cell in her body craved his kiss as she stared helplessly into his eyes, but she couldn't bring herself to break the protocols that had been drummed into her since childhood.

Although she now shared Hunter's name, she was still essentially Cort's nanny. They both knew that.

She couldn't overstep her place, but she couldn't turn away, either. Not when he was looking at her as if he were on the road to hell and she was his only salvation. If it was comfort he wanted…

His eyes shuttered closed and his mouth touched hers in the most poignant kiss ever imaginable. Damp with the salt of his tears and raw and powerful as a breaking wave.

Juliana heard a *beep-beep, beep-beep* that was surely her heartbeat rapping sharply against her chest—until she realized it was her cell phone.

Hunter reared back abruptly as if released from a spell.

Juliana whirled around to find her purse, disappointment and embarrassment staining her cheeks. ''That might be my father.''

What on earth had she been thinking to allow Hunter to kiss her?

She'd been thinking that he was as emotionally upset as she was. That she loved him and he'd needed someone to turn to as much as she did.

"Hello?"

The voice of her father's doctor cut through the chaotic thoughts tumbling in her brain. "I'm afraid I have some bad news. Your father's suffered a stroke. He's slipped into a coma."

Juliana dropped the phone as the searing pain of rejection drove a wedge into her heart. She'd already known how devoted her father was to the Collingwoods, especially Ross, who he'd treated as a son.

Without Ross, her father had lost his will to live.

She took one faltering step toward Hunter and fainted.

Chapter Eight

For years Hunter had suspected that the Sinclair family was cursed when it came to marriage, and now he was convinced of it. His bride had collapsed on their wedding day. Ross would have appreciated the irony of it, were it not Juliana who'd collapsed.

Hunter rubbed his tired eyes, the scents of the evergreens and roses filling his lungs as he kept a watchful eye on Juliana. She lay sleeping in his bed, still in her wedding dress, resembling for all the world a slumbering princess waiting for true love's kiss to awaken her.

Unfortunately he didn't think awakening her with a kiss was going to solve any of their problems.

She'd been sleeping for fourteen hours straight. She was exhausted. He'd noticed she hadn't eaten much in the last few days, but then, neither had he. The call from the hospital about her father's stroke had been the last straw. Hunter had spoken to the doctor and learned there was little the doctors could do but wait and see. Goodhew had slipped into a coma. The CT scan had confirmed an early stroke, but the regular clot-buster medication, which would normally be administered to thin his blood, couldn't be used because of his recent surgery. He could likely bleed to death from such a blood thinner. The doctors had reinserted the endotracheal tube because he wasn't breathing well on his own.

After agonizing over what the doctor had said, Hunter had phoned up Del Lanham, the commander of his elite security force. They'd assessed the risks and hammered out the security arrangements for a visit to the hospital later today.

Del thought he was crazy and advised against it. They had their hands full making sure Juliana would be safe at the funeral and the reception. Why expose her to another risk? But Hunter was adamant. Juliana needed to see her father as soon as possible.

Hunter set aside the reports of the phone calls coming in to the 1-800 hotline that he'd been skimming and leaned back in the leather chair for another catnap. It was 4:00 a.m. He'd napped earlier from 10:00 p.m. until 2:00 a.m., when he'd gotten up to give Cort a bottle and change his diaper. He could rest for a couple more hours before he woke Juliana so they could prepare for the funeral. He needed to brief her on the security arrangements. He wanted her to be strong today. Have her wits about her. The killer could make another move.

JULIANA FELT A NIGGLE of panic like the tapping of a finger on a windowpane when she saw the crowds and the TV cameras outside St. Patrick's Cathedral. A gray sky draped the city as if sharing in the dismal mood of the day. The two operatives seated on either side of her in the hired car should have made her feel safer—Hunter had handpicked them for this detail—but they were no substitute for her husband's reassuring presence. She wanted Hunter beside her, watching over her as he'd watched over her last night while she'd slept.

She'd never forget how she'd woken this morning, feeling disoriented by the white canopy above her head and a soreness in her lower back. She'd desperately needed to pee. At first she'd thought she might still be dreaming or she'd been injured and was in a hospital. But as she'd attempted to push herself up, she'd noticed Hunter dozing in a chair he'd drawn up beside the bed. His jaw slack and covered with stubble. His dark lashes rested against hollows that suggested he'd been up most of the night. Suddenly, the phone call from the doctor had slipped painfully into her mind.

She'd sagged back down into the bed like a twig that had just been broken, remembering her father's stroke. Though she told herself she was a mature adult and that her father loved her, she couldn't push away the irrational thought that her father was withdrawing from her again— choosing Ross, who'd been like a son to him, over her. Juliana couldn't explain it, but knowing that Hunter had stayed with her, had watched over her during the night made the heartbreaking fear that her father might not recover more bearable.

She wouldn't be alone.

She sighed and glanced down at her bare fingers as the car pulled up at the curb outside the cathedral. She'd removed her wedding band and engagement ring and given them to Hunter for safekeeping before leaving for the funeral. Odd how yesterday she'd felt like a fraud when she'd put the engagement ring on her finger. Now she felt vulnerable without it.

With her bodyguards—whom she'd be introducing as her father's cousin Francis and his wife, Gina—flanking her, Juliana was escorted into the cathedral to the private section reserved for family and close friends of the family. Organ music from Mozart's *Requiem* soared poignantly up into the arched ceiling of the cathedral.

Juliana's heart wrenched when she saw the twin coffins placed side by side, surrounded by a heart-shaped garden of white roses, lilies and freesia. Sprays of roses rested on the polished cherry wood of the coffins. Dainty pink roses for Lexi. Bloodred roses for Ross. Juliana's throat clotted. She felt certain her father would have approved.

Lexi's sister, Annette York, looking wan and brave in a black suit with a dignified short black veil attached to her hat, was braced between Gord Nevins, the Collingwoods' robust household manager and Stacey Kerr, Lexi's personal secretary. Leggy, with shoulder-length tawny hair, Stacey looked striking in a black-and-white suit and pearls. Juliana assumed the two men in the modest black suits beside Gord and Stacey were the plainclothes state troopers assigned to protect Annette.

As soon as Annette noticed Juliana's arrival she broke free of her guard and hurried forward, her arms outstretched. Juliana hugged the petite woman hard, tears unleashing. She could sense desperation in the clinging strength of her grip. Poor Annette! This must be so difficult for her!

"I'm so sorry," she whispered in Annette's ear. "I wish I could have been with you these last few days."

Annette squeezed Juliana's shoulders almost painfully. "I *need* to talk to you."

"Not here, not now," Juliana warned, afraid Annette might mention Cort in public. "Later at the house—in private."

Annette's grip eased. "All right. At the house." She stepped back and Juliana felt a twitch of alarm. The glazed look in the petite woman's green eyes reminded her of a spooked horse. "Will you sit with me during the ceremony? Lexi was so fond of you. She considered you a friend." Her voice cracked. "And I want us to be friends, or I don't think I'm going to be able to get through this. At least my parents aren't alive. This would have killed them.''

Juliana silently agreed as she slipped an arm around Annette's waist. Like everyone who entered Lexi's sphere, Lexi's parents had doted on their eldest daughter. ''I'm here for you,'' she promised fervently.

While she'd never felt the immediate warmth and closeness to Annette that she'd felt for Lexi—Annette had always been prickish and prone to mood swings—she realized the situation warranted that she establish closer permanent ties with her. She *was* Cort's aunt.

Annette asked after her father and Juliana felt her body cramp when she told Annette about her father's stroke.

''I'm so sorry,'' Annette murmured.

They were interrupted by the en masse arrival of the senior officers of the Collingwood Corporation and the board of directors. Juliana steeled her spine at the mob of black suits and the power the individuals wearing them represented, her heart palpitating at the possibility that Lexi and Ross's killer might be among them. Would any of them pay her undue interest?

Grateful for the bodyguards hovering close by, she remained steadfastly at Annette's side, observing the expressions and the behavior of the officers and the board members as they stepped forward, one by one, to offer their condolences.

Kendrick Dwyer was first. After telling Annette she could depend on him for anything, he told Juliana that he hoped her father would make a speedy recovery and the company would, of course, pick up the costs of his care.

Simon Findlay made apologies to Annette for his fiancée's inability to accompany him this morning and gave Juliana a polite nod before turning away.

Annette whispered to Juliana out of the side of her mouth that the cathedral wasn't spacious enough to hold Findlay's fiancée's breasts. Juliana contained her shock at the inappropriate remark, but then realized Annette was only letting off steam. Lexi's sister was an intelligent woman, and she'd no doubt already figured out there was a good chance that someone in this church had killed her brother-in-law and her sister. Juliana shared Annette's anger.

Paulo Tardioli offered Annette his condolences, then gave Juliana a glance that expressed such frank sexual interest that she felt tarnished. David Younge and his wife Sarah, who'd been totally supportive of Ross and Lexi after Riana's abduction, hugged Juliana and asked if her father was still in the hospital. They'd sent a basket containing books on tape and a selection of his favorite teas to the house.

"Please let us know if there's anything we can do to help," Sarah offered, tears glimmering in her eyes.

Juliana thanked them for their kindness. She'd always liked Sarah.

Wearing dark, narrow sunglasses and a ponytail, Phillip Ballard stood out—a veritable maverick in the sea of corporate suits. His suit had neither a lapel, nor a tie. A black leather lace secured his ponytail. He and his very pregnant wife didn't give Juliana a second glance, but she didn't sense any animosity from the couple, either.

But Sable Holden… Well, the instant Sable held out her hand to Annette and said she hoped Ross and Lexi would rest in peace, Juliana experienced an unbridled urge to wipe the smug twitch off the woman's lips. In her thirties, Sable had the lacquered finish of a woman who worked too hard to look good. Her body was too sculpted, her clothes were too pretentious—as if she were a widow in mourning. Her hair was coated with too much hair spray and her makeup was overdone. The brunette would have been much more appealing with a fresh-scrubbed face and more conservative clothes.

Annette smirked at Sable. "I'm sure they'll be as madly in love with each other in heaven as they were on earth. I guess you'll have to lust after someone else's husband now."

Sable gave Annette a subzero smile. "You never were half the lady your sister was. But I'm sure you know that." Rattling her jewels, Sable stormed off, her high heels clicking sharply.

Annette trembled with suppressed rage. "What a bitch."

"I can have her removed from the church if you like," Juliana offered. "That's what the gentlemen behind us are for."

"What? And give Sable a story for the tabloids? Not on your life!"

Several more people arrived. Friends and co-workers of Lexi's from the hospital where she'd worked before she married Ross. Friends of Lexi's parents. And a lanky young man with a raggedly trimmed brown beard and owlish hazel eyes in an ill-fitting gray tweed jacket with leather patches on the elbows.

"Darren, what are you doing here?" Annette stammered, color infusing her face as the young man crushed her to him.

"I came to pay my respects. See if you needed anything—a shoulder to cry on? I've missed you."

Annette's features hardened. "Darren, I told you, it's over."

"But I—" Darren broke off and looked at Juliana as if he'd just noticed she was there. "We need to talk."

The conversation was beginning to sound too personal for Juliana's ears. She wondered if Darren might be a former boyfriend or possibly Annette's ex-fiancé. Juliana excused herself and told Annette she'd return in a moment.

Off in a shadowed corner near the confessional she spotted Kendrick Dwyer having a private conversation with Stacey Kerr. Stacey looked upset, her eyes dark in her pale face. What were they talking about?

Visions of Hunter's conspiracy theory filling her mind, Juliana skirted around the pews toward them, hoping to catch a nibble of their conversation. Her bodyguards followed at a discreet distance.

Gord Nevins, however, intercepted her plans. Juliana stepped right into the stocky household manager's bone-jarring embrace. The strain of the last few days showed in the deep white lines scoring his mouth and the puffiness around his eyes. Juliana introduced her bodyguards as her father's cousin and his wife. "I brought them for support." Then, drawing Gord aside, Juliana gently broke the news of her father's stroke. Gord and her father had worked together in harmony for years and respected one another. "He's in a coma, and I'm afraid they don't know if and when he'll come out of it."

Gord's pale eyes glistened. "I'll keep him in my prayers. Your father is strong-willed. Can I see him? Sit with him? It might do him good to have a visit from an old friend. I'll tell him how the staff and the house have gone to hell without him. That ought to rouse him."

She shook her head, tears bathing her cheeks. Her heart felt like a heavy stone in her breast. She hated this. Hated suspecting people whom she'd trusted for years. "I wish you could, but the police are taking extra security precautions. No visitors."

"You're coming back to the house after the interment, then?"

"Yes, for a little while."

Gord patted her arm and kissed her on the cheek. "Good. This is a time for us to be together. I'm being signaled by the funeral director. The service is about to start. We'll talk more at the house."

She glanced toward the corner where she'd seen Stacey and Kendrick Dwyer, but they were gone. Needing a tissue to wipe her face, she flipped open the small black leather purse she'd borrowed from Hunter's sister's closet for today. It was just big enough to hold her cell phone, some tissues and a lipstick. Juliana dried her tears. People were taking their seats and Annette was motioning for her to join her in the front pew.

Juliana gathered her courage for the strength to make it through the ceremony and the interment and wished once more that Hunter were here with her.

MEETING JULIANA HAD changed him, corroded the detachment that he wore like armor when he was working on a job. Feeling as if his heart were suspended in midair, Hunter monitored her every movement on the bank of television screens connected to covert video cameras planted inside and outside the cathedral. He took note of everyone who spoke to her or even looked at her. And made sure her bodyguards were doing their job.

Juliana was too precious to Cort to lose. And somehow, in the long dark hours of their wedding night as Hunter had waited for her to wake, she'd become infinitely precious to him.

Though he knew she was frightened about being the target of a killer and worried sick about her father, you'd never know it by looking at her. She had her chin up and was lending Annette moral support.

He was so damn proud of her! Grace under pressure.

Even when she cried, she wiped her eyes with a quiet dignity and carried on. No histrionics.

Disguised in a groundskeeper's uniform, dark glasses and a thick mustache, Hunter attended the interment, which had been limited to Annette and the household staff. As the short ceremony ended, the wind tore savagely through the trees and the swollen clouds above split their gray underbellies. Rain pounded into the ground as the staff scuttled into limousines that would take them back to the Collingwood estate for the reception. Hunter and Investigator Bradshaw followed behind in an unmarked car.

Upon arriving at the estate and making his way to the command center the troopers had set up, Hunter's tension jackknifed. More covert cameras had been planted in the house to record the reception, but there were many holes in the coverage.

If something happened to Juliana, he'd never forgive himself.

MELANCHOLY SETTLED heavily on Juliana's shoulders as she entered the packed drawing room after leaving her coat with a maid. The Collingwood Estate had been built for glorious parties, and today it was a house in mourning— the atmosphere oppressive with the heavy scents of flowers and wet wool and the sounds of muted conversation. She hadn't the heart to ask Hunter what would happen to this magnificent house. Maybe all that would become known once the will was officially read.

Annette was nowhere in sight. Nor were her bodyguards. Yet Juliana knew Annette had arrived at the house before her.

Juliana slipped through the mourners overflowing into the vast center hall that had soaring Palladian windows on each end, and tried the dining room where a buffet had been set up.

She stopped Stacey Kerr, Lexi's personal secretary. "Have you seen Annette?"

"She said something about needing to lie down, poor thing," Stacey replied. "I didn't have a chance to ask you at the church, but how's your baby? Did you bring pictures?"

Juliana felt a prickle of apprehension at her nape. "He's getting so big! But I didn't think to bring any photos. I will next time, I promise. Excuse me, I want to check on Annette. She shouldn't be alone."

She hurried up the gold inlaid staircase to the second floor, replaying Stacey's interest in Cort in her mind. Was the secretary's question as innocuous as it had seemed? Stacey and Kendrick Dwyer had had their heads together at the funeral. But they could have been discussing the eulogy that Kendrick had given. He'd also read a loving tribute Annette had written.

At the top of the stairs Juliana encountered Sable Holden. She stopped the woman. "May I ask what you are doing upstairs?"

"Who the hell are you?" Sable responded with a curl of her crimson lips.

"Part of the staff. I repeat, what are you doing up here? There's a sign at the bottom of the stairs clearly stating this area is off-limits to guests."

Color slashed Sable's cheeks. "I was looking for a bathroom." She forcibly tried to brush past Juliana, ramming her with her shoulder.

Knocked off balance, Juliana teetered on her high heels and clutched at the banister to keep from falling down the stairs.

Her bodyguards were on Sable in an instant.

An anger-induced tremor worked its way up Juliana's spine. Had they just nabbed Ross and Lexi's killer? "Please escort this woman to security. Have them check her purse to make sure she hasn't removed anything from the house. I'm sure the police will have a few questions for her, as well."

"You can't do this," Sable blustered.

"I can. And I will. Now, please go quietly before you create an unpleasant scene. And, I suggest, in future, you refrain from trespassing."

"Do you know who I am? I'm on the board of directors of the Collingwood Corporation."

"I don't care if you're Santa Claus."

Leaving Sable in the capable hands of her bodyguards, Juliana hurried down the hall, concern for Annette uppermost on her mind. Had Sable followed Annette upstairs? Had she turned back when she'd noticed Annette was well guarded by the troopers?

She tried the guest rooms on the second floor left wing first. But surely if Annette were here Juliana would see bodyguards out in the hallway. Juliana crossed over to the right wing where the family's rooms were. The door to the nursery stood slightly ajar. Juliana grasped the knob and pushed the door open.

The bright room Lexi had lovingly prepared with a Noah's ark theme was empty.

She moved farther down the hall to the room Lexi's parents had shared when they'd moved into the mansion after Riana's abduction. That door, too, was ajar. Juliana saw an imprint on the bed as if someone had lain down for a while. Who, Sable?

She tried Lexi's suite next. Relief expanded in her chest when she pushed the door open and was immediately halted by two troopers. She told them about her encounter with

Sable Holden on the stairs. One of the troopers radioed Investigator Bradshaw while Juliana continued to the bedroom to check on Annette.

She knocked softly on the door and entered the room.

Annette sat on Lexi's bed with some of Lexi's clothes spread out around her.

"She's really gone, isn't she?"

Juliana slipped her purse off her shoulder and joined Annette on the bed. Compassion welled in her as she gently stroked Annette's back. Tension bunched in the petite woman's body like stones tightly packed in a jar. "I'm afraid so."

"It didn't seem real until I came in here. They're all gone." Suddenly, Annette gripped Juliana's knee. "But not Cort, right?"

Juliana cast an anxious glance toward the door and lowered her voice. "Annette, I assure you he's safe and sound."

A frustrated cry broke from Annette's throat and twisted her features. "I need to see him. He's the only family I have left. Tell me where he is. Or better yet, take me to him."

"I wish I could, but I can't."

"Don't tell me you can't. I'm ordering you to tell me where my nephew is."

Juliana looked at her sharply. "I don't take orders from you."

"It's him, isn't it? That damn Guardian! He can't do this! He won't even tell me who has custody of the baby!" Annette jumped off the bed and swung her arm at a collection of crystal figurines—birthday gifts from Lexi's parents—displayed on a mirrored table. Several pieces crashed to the floor.

Juliana leaped up to prevent Annette from wreaking

more damage as the bedroom door flew open. Both troopers filled the doorway, weapons drawn.

"It's all right," Juliana told them. "She's just upset. Annette, you must calm down. Losing control will achieve nothing."

The troopers withdrew, closing the door.

"I just realized—you probably have custody of Cort! The Guardian is working for you." Annette dragged a shaking hand across her brow, her green eyes blazing with anguish. "Oh, my God, I can't believe my own sister chose the butler's daughter to raise her baby over her own flesh and blood. And to think that I postponed my wedding so that Lexi could marry Ross first because she was pregnant!"

"You are so wrong. I don't have custody of Cort, either. I wish I did."

Annette advanced toward her. "But you know who does."

Juliana's back stiffened. "I'm not going to jeopardize Cort's safety—or yours—by discussing this any further. There are enough people dead. I haven't even been allowed to visit my father at the hospital! I'm sure a safe meeting will be arranged for you and the baby as soon as possible. Now, come downstairs. I'll get you something to eat and a nice cup of tea."

It took some doing, but she finally coaxed Annette downstairs. Lexi's sister had been in isolation since the bombing. It would do her good to be surrounded by people and feel their support.

She settled Annette on a sofa in the drawing room with Stacey Kerr and brought her a plate of food from the buffet and a cup of tea. Then Juliana dispatched a maid to clean up the broken crystal in Lexi's room while she circulated through the house to talk with each member of the staff.

To offer comfort and be comforted. The staff was solidly divided in opinions about the cook's disappearance. Half firmly believed she was doing something odd like meditating on her past lives. The other half was convinced she was working her magic in someone else's kitchen.

No one seemed unduly interested in her movements. Juliana found herself praying that Sable Holden was confessing.

At least Annette had pulled herself together and was moving from one group to another thanking people for coming.

Juliana took a moment to dodge into the ladies' room. When she came out into the lounge to wash her hands, Sarah Younge was seated on one of the upholstered stools in front of the mirror replenishing her lipstick with a sienna color that matched her dark-auburn hair.

"I'm glad to have caught you alone, Juliana. I thought you might know if the search will still continue for Riana."

Juliana lathered her hands with scented soap. Had Sarah followed her in here on purpose? Gina, her female bodyguard, had ostensibly engaged the powder room maid in conversation.

"I'm sure the search will continue. I don't think any of us, especially now, have given up hope that she'll be found."

Sarah's lips wobbled into a smile and her gray eyes grew misty. "Well, I'd like to continue to help. If you need a spokesperson, I'd consider it a privilege. Ross and Lexi were so good to us—especially recently. Ross called David into his office last week and told him to take some time off. We've—our son David Jr.'s been having some problems at school. Getting into serious trouble. Ross told David that there was nothing more important in life than your children and—" Sarah broke off with a choked cry, pressing her hand to her mouth. "David finally decided to take Ross's advice."

Juliana used a fresh towel to dry her hands and dab at the new spring of tears welling in her eyes. Sarah's explanation accounted for the tension in David Younge's life and the private meetings with Ross. She'd have to tell Hunter. "I'll pass your offer along, Sarah. Thank you."

"It's the least I can do."

Juliana took a moment to compose herself after Sarah left. Her reflection in the mirror told of the day's emotional drain. Her eyes were red and swollen, her lipstick had worn off and her hair needed combing. She reached for her purse to repair the damage, only to discover it wasn't on her shoulder or the vanity counter. Had she left it in the stall in the bathroom?

She hurried to check.

There was no sign of it.

Fortunately she didn't have any identification or anything of value in the purse—except her cell phone. What if the hospital had called with an update about her father's condition?

She tried to think when she'd had it last and couldn't remember. Had she forgotten it in the limo after the interment?

Left it upstairs in Lexi's room? Or accidentally set it down someplace when she'd brought Annette some refreshments?

Juliana alerted one of her bodyguards who radioed a message to The Guardian in the security command center. Maybe it was nothing, but still…

A quiet search was begun by the staff. The guests were discreetly informed that Annette was overtired and perhaps they should take their leave.

Juliana stood sentry in the foyer keeping a sharp eye out for the missing purse as the guests departed. Try as she might, she couldn't dispel the disquieting fear that someone had deliberately taken her purse.

Chapter Nine

When Stacey Kerr found the purse underneath the buffet table forty-five minutes later, Juliana snapped it open to check the contents, then clutched it to her chest in relief. Her cell phone was there. Everything seemed to be in order.

She must have accidentally dropped it when she'd filled a plate for Annette and it had been kicked under the buffet table.

The day had been rife with too much tension. She was relieved when one of her bodyguards informed her that her car was waiting outside. Her stomach muscles clenched tightly in the fervent hope that Hunter would be in the car waiting for her.

She needed the reassurance that only being with him, feeling the safety of his arms around her, could give.

She wanted him to take her home to his apartment where she could hug Cort and check on her father's condition.

She said her goodbyes to the staff—and to Annette who'd be staying on at the estate for several days helping the staff deal with the Collingwoods' personal effects. Then they collected their coats.

To her keen disappointment, Investigator Bradshaw occupied the front passenger seat of the luxury car. Not Hunter. He extended his hand to her as she slid into the back seat, wedged between her bodyguards. She noticed he was wearing latex gloves.

"I'd like to examine your purse, if I may."

"Of course."

The investigator raised his brows at her bodyguards. "Did she touch anything inside the purse once it was recovered?"

"No, sir."

"No, I did not," Juliana said, offended that her word was not considered good enough. "Nothing's missing. It was a false alarm. I'm sure I mislaid it. I didn't have any ID in it."

"Hmm…we'll check it for latent fingerprints just to be sure. The killer could have searched it looking for a clue to your whereabouts." The car lurched forward down the long drive. "Anyone else in the house touch it?"

"Only Stacey Kerr," she admitted reluctantly. "She found it under the buffet table in the dining room."

She watched Bradshaw's face furrow in concentration as he carefully removed and examined her tube of lipstick, her comb and, finally, her cell phone.

"What was the last number you dialed on your cell phone?"

"The hospi—"

"Damn it. Stop the car," Investigator Bradshaw barked in a low urgent tone, cutting her off.

"What is it?" Juliana gripped the back of the front seat, trying to scoot forward to see.

"There are scratch marks on the phone. Someone's tampered with it."

The investigator shoved open his door and jumped out of the car, moving at a brisk walk toward the center of the wide sweeping lawn.

"Get her out of here," he ordered over his shoulder. "And seal off the area. I want a bomb squad here ASAP."

IT WAS THE LONGEST WAIT in Hunter's life.

His insides quivered as he counted out the minutes until Juliana's car would arrive at the rendezvous point for the transfer. His clenched fist pounded on his thigh. Where the hell was she?

Bradshaw's tense voice on the phone informing him that Juliana's cell phone had been tampered with looped through his brain, replaying itself over and over.

What if a bomb had been planted in her cell phone? She could have been killed. Cort, too.

His mouth firmed into a taut line, his heart pounding like a driven nail into his chest at the thought of never seeing her barge into his study without knocking or holding Cort against her breast with the glow of fierce determination in her eyes. Never hearing her laugh or smelling the apple blossoms in her hair.

Never being able to expect the unexpected from her again.

He'd promised to protect her and he'd come perilously close to losing her. Thank God he and Investigator Bradshaw were cautious by nature.

She'd done her part for the investigation at the funeral today—even nabbing Sable Holden wandering the house where she didn't belong. Now, after a brief stop at the hospital, he was going to whisk Juliana and Cort home to FairIsle. Marquise was already en route with Cort. The helicopter would pick them up in twenty minutes.

He could keep them safe at FairIsle.

When the car carrying Juliana finally entered the parking garage, it was all Hunter could do to remain in the limo. Endless seconds passed as the one car door opened and a bodyguard, followed by Juliana, emerged. The door beside him opened.

Bringing the faint scent of apple blossoms with her, Juliana bolted straight into his arms.

THE KILLER WAS FRUSTRATED. The tracking device hadn't fit in the damn phone as it should. It was too large. Or the damn phone was too small, and there hadn't been enough time.

Pushing the redial button had only resulted in reaching the hospital where the butler was recovering from his injuries. Information the killer already had.

But the engraved monogram on the designer purse from an exclusive Madison Avenue shop was quite distinctive.

The killer slipped into the household manager's office and looked up the phone number for the shop.

"Good afternoon," the killer said in an uppity voice. "I'm calling from the Collingwood estate. Yes, those Collingwoods. As I'm sure you're aware, the funeral took place earlier today. Unfortunately, one of the guests left behind a purse at the reception. It's one of your designs. No, there was no ID inside, but there is a monogram—BES. Does that ring any bells?" The killer described the black leather handbag.

"What was the name again? Thank you. You've no idea how happy you've just made me. I'm sure the owner will be very grateful."

With a smug smile, the killer hung up the phone.

Who the hell was Brook Everett Sinclair? And what was Juliana doing with her purse?

SHE STILL DIDN'T WANT anything to do with him.

Darren stood outside the gates to the Collingwood estate barred from his love by iron bars and security guards. The steady stream of departing Mercedes-Benzes, BMWs and Jaguars told him the reception was over.

He told himself she was distraught. She'd lost both her parents and now her sister and brother-in-law. She wasn't thinking straight.

He'd give her more time. Maybe send her a card telling her he was thinking about her. Then after the media circus had died down he could call her up at the office, ask her out to dinner.

They could linger over coffee and talk into the late hours of the night about art and pop culture and whether or not universal health care would ever happen in the U.S. Just like in the old days.

It had been almost three years since she'd called off their engagement. He'd patiently waited all this time for her to realize that what they'd had was once-in-a-lifetime. What was a few more months?

"WE'RE GOING WHERE?"

"To the hospital to see your father," Hunter explained patiently.

Juliana scooted away from him to the far side of the limo's wide back seat and crossed her arms. "No. I'm not going. We'll go directly to FairIsle."

He narrowed his gaze on the determined set of her chin, trying to figure out what was going on in his wife's mind. He'd thought she'd leap at the chance to visit her father.

"The window of opportunity is here. We should take it. No one would expect you to be able to get from Long Island to the hospital in the Adirondacks so quickly. It lowers the element of risk to an acceptable level. Cort won't come to the hospital with us. I have a team of men who'll stay with him."

"No."

He ran a hand through his hair in frustration. He wanted so much to touch her, feel her melt against him again and reassure her that they would survive this together. "I know the incident with your purse was frightening, but don't let it deter you from seeing your father."

"This has nothing to do with that."

"Then what, Juliana? Please explain it to me. I spoke with the doctor. Your father could die, and I think you'll regret not seeing him." He slid his arm along the rim of the seat back and brushed her shoulder with his thumb. "After all you've been asked to do, I can't ask you to make this sacrifice, too."

She looked at him, her eyes tormented pools in her pale face. "Don't you think I *want* to see him? He's my father. I love him! But it would only make him angry."

Hunter frowned, confused by her logic. "Why would he be angry?"

She clamped her lips shut.

He rubbed his thumb against her shoulder in tiny circles, and felt the slightest weakening in the bow-tight arc of her back. "Tell me, please. Trust me."

"Trust you? Ha!" She jabbed a finger toward the privacy screen. "I've done nothing but give you my absolute trust and you trust the limo driver—who's probably some cop— more than you trust me!"

A muscle ticked in his jaw. There was some truth to her accusation, but he wasn't about to admit it.

"Tell me a deep dark secret, Hunter," she prodded him. "And maybe, I'll tell you mine."

Hunter stared at her, coldly furious, as if she'd drop-kicked him into another dimension without his permission. Words bottled in his throat. But he wasn't sure what upset him more—her impertinence or the reckless temptation to answer her question with frank unvarnished honesty to see what it would garner him.

Recklessness won out.

He was a damn fool, but he wanted, oh, God, he wanted to trust Juliana more than he'd ever wanted anything in his life!

He held her gaze. "How about this, then? My mother had an unfortunate habit of sleeping with my father's friends. She was neither wise, nor discreet. My father learned about my mother's indiscretions from a blackmailer who sought to profit from her lapses in judgment. My father refused to meet the blackmailer's demands because he was convinced my mother would never betray him. He'd fallen in love with a woman his family didn't approve of, a file clerk at the Clairmont Hotel. The blackmailer released photos of her indiscretions to the press. My father filed for divorce. When my mother realized he was determined to prevent her from having any contact with my sister and me, she committed suicide."

His tone hardened. "I'm not sure which was harder on my father, discovering that my mother had betrayed him and had probably only married him for his money—or being made such a fool of in public."

Hunter stopped short of telling her that the family butler had orchestrated the blackmail scheme, believing that he was helping his master by opening his eyes to the truth of his marriage.

Flecks of gold and burnt umber shifted in Juliana's eyes like molten metals. Her back remained taut as a wind-filled sail.

"How old were you?" she asked.

"Nine. FairIsle had been our summer home, but after my mother's suicide, my father retreated to the island and we lived there year-round."

Only nine. He'd never trust her completely, Juliana thought, seeing the shuttered set of his face and the white marks on his knuckles where his free hand unconsciously clenched and unclenched on his thigh. There was too much hurt buried there.

She knew without having to ask that he'd never been married before. He'd never planned to risk his heart the way his father had. And even when his cold calculating mind had urged him into marriage to protect a helpless baby, he'd protected his heart by making it clear from the outset that the marriage would be in name only. He'd be a father to Cort, but he wouldn't make himself vulnerable by fathering children of his own. It also explained why he'd so readily agreed to share joint custody of Cort should their marriage end in divorce. He wouldn't put a child through a messy custody hearing.

Suddenly it made perfect sense to her how and why he'd become The Guardian. Somehow he'd hoped to save others from the ugliness of his own childhood.

Juliana closed her eyes, feeling hot tears scald her eyelids. If anyone needed love, deserved love, it was Hunter.

"I can't see my father because I promised him I'd take care of Cort," she began in a thready voice. "If I went to see him, he'd think I was disobeying him—neglecting my duty to Cort—and he'd never forgive me."

Hunter's fingers closed over her shoulder, dipping into the hollow above her collarbone. "Your father would never forgive you? Never is a long time."

She opened her eyes and looked into the azure blue sea of Hunter's concerned gaze. "You have no idea. Never, so far, has lasted nineteen years and two months."

"What are you talking about?"

"When I was six my father asked me to watch my little brother Michael. Michael was three. We'd seen Ross sliding down the banister of the grand staircase when no one was looking and we wanted to do it, too. We'd been told many times, not to, but we were children. Michael was a little monkey. He climbed up on the railing and before I could stop him he was sliding down like a rocket. About halfway down he lost his balance and fell onto the stairs—and started rolling down. The fall killed him.''

A great emptiness opened inside her, stretching down to the bottom of her soul. ''My father has hugged me only once since that day—and that was the day that I returned to the estate to be with Lexi after Riana was kidnapped.''

Rage shredded Hunter's heart that she should be made to feel guilty for her brother's death. ''Michael's death wasn't your fault. You were a child yourself—much too young to have the responsibility of a three-year-old. You should have been supervised by an adult.''

He leaned down and kissed her temple, wishing there were some way he could heal the hurt of her father's rejection. But knowing from his own life that hurts such as those left permanent scars. ''I'm sorry about your brother. But I'm still taking you to see your father.'' At the flash of protest in her eyes, he laid a finger on her lips.

''I'll tell him you had no choice but to follow The Guardian's orders. And after, we're going home with Cort. Which reminds me…''

He reached into his coat pocket for her wedding rings, which she'd given him for safekeeping when they'd left for the funeral this morning. Even if she felt he was once again breaching her trust by insisting on this visit with her father, he was listening to his gut on this one. He'd never had a chance to say goodbye to his mother. He wouldn't deny Juliana this chance with her father.

He took her left hand and slid the rings over the third

finger, more solemnly aware than yesterday of the commitment he'd undertaken when he'd claimed this woman as his wife.

THE EXTENT OF HER father's injuries hit Juliana hard. It was all she could do to keep the sharp cry of anguish from her lips. She gripped Hunter's hand in silent communication to steady herself as she approached the bed.

Her father, who'd always possessed an authoritative bearing, lay motionless in the bed, garish bruises mottling his face, a turban of bandages circling his head. There were red areas on his arms and neck resembling a sunburn. And the tubes! Some sort of tube protruded from his chest. Another tube helped him breathe and a feeding tube had been inserted in his nostril.

Only when she reached the side of the bed could she detect the damage from the stroke on her father's poor battered body. The features on the right side of his face drooped.

Releasing her grip on Hunter, Juliana slipped her hand gently under her father's, careful not to cause him further discomfort by touching any of the burns.

"Papa, I'm here," she said softly, seeking an undamaged spot on his face to kiss him. Tears welled in her chest as if caught in a dam. "I'm here with you."

She felt a gentle supportive squeeze on her shoulders. "I'll be right outside," Hunter told her. His eyes gleamed with warmth and moisture as he brushed a kiss on her cheek. "You need your privacy."

Juliana looked at her husband and nodded, her throat too choked to express the love and the appreciation she felt for his being here with her. Hunter had been right. As apprehensive as she was about her father's reaction to her visit, she could see now that her father had needed her here as much as she'd needed to see him. She had so much to say.

The ICU nurse had told her that even though her father was in a coma, he could still hear what was being said to him.

She prayed that was true. Summoning her courage, she said the words she should have said to her father years ago, "Papa, I'm very angry with you...."

"THERE WAS NO BOMB."

Investigator Bradshaw's brisk voice scraped over the phone line. "But we got some prints off the purse. We'll run them through the system and see if we pick up anything."

"Good. Better safe than sorry." Holding his cell phone to his ear, Hunter paced the front walkway outside the hospital. Relief bounded through him that the scare earlier over Juliana's missing purse had been just that—a scare.

"How's the butler?" Bradshaw asked. "Any chance we're going to get any information out of him in the near future?"

Hunter pinched the bridge of his nose. Smoke from a cigarette butt dropped on the pavement nearby curled up into the chilly September night. "He's still in a coma. The doctors aren't sure how extensive the damage is from the stroke. It's definitely wait-and-see. What's the story with Sable Holden? Did you get anything out of her?"

"She insists the ladies' room downstairs was crowded and she decided to try upstairs. There was nothing in her purse to indicate she'd been helping herself to a few souvenirs."

"Annette was upstairs at the time—that could have been Sable's motivation for being there. Sable might have changed her mind when she saw the bodyguards."

"I've got ten witnesses who'll swear Sable was seated at a dining table at a family party at midnight on Friday—" Investigator Bradshaw broke off abruptly. "Hold on a sec."

Hunter waited impatiently, intending to point out to the BCI investigator that Sable could have put her hands under the table and called the pager that detonated the bomb with a cell phone.

Bradshaw came back on the line, excitement rising in his voice. "We've just been given the lead we've been waiting for on the pager. The call to the pager that set off the bomb was made from a pay phone in lower Manhattan."

From the financial district, no doubt, Hunter thought.

"The pager was bought a month ago by a man named Robert Lance in Soho. Only one call ever made to the number. He doesn't have a record. Does the name ring any bells?"

"No. But he could be the person who delivered the flowers. Maybe he made the call, too."

"We're on our way to pick him up. I'll keep you posted." Bradshaw disconnected the call.

Hunter looked up into the night sky that was blurred by the lights of the hospital compound and hoped this lead would break the case wide-open.

SEEING JULIANA'S HEAD bowed over her father's comatose body when he returned to the ICU made Hunter feel helpless and frustrated and willing to do just about anything to ease some of the pain she was going through.

"It's time to go."

Juliana lifted her head and he saw the silvery traces of tears on her cheeks. Her eyes were red. Her defenses were down, bringing all his protective instincts roaring to the surface. He slipped an arm around her waist and helped her stand. He'd tell her about the new lead as soon as they were someplace private. Now, she needed some food. She looked about ready to keel over.

Once outside the hospital the cold air seemed to revive

her a bit, bringing color to her cheeks. Hunter told her that the scare with her cell phone had been a false alarm. She seemed to be barely listening as he explained that the police had lifted some fingerprints from her purse and hoped to come up with something positive. But hope lit up her eyes when he told her the troopers had traced the pager to a Robert Lance.

"The name Robert Lance doesn't sound familiar to me, either. I'm sure he wasn't on the wedding guest list."

"He could be a hired goon. Maybe an explosives expert. We'll know soon enough. The state police will be bringing him in for questioning."

She gripped the lapels of Hunter's wool suit jacket as if a gust of wind might carry her off. "Thank God! Maybe there will be an end to this nightmare. You've no idea how difficult it was at the funeral today—watching people, wondering if they were up to no good."

Hunter listened intently as she told him about Kendrick Dwyer's huddled conversation with Lexi's secretary at the church. "For all I know they were discussing details of the service, but Stacey asked me questions about Cort later— how he was doing, if I had pictures. Even Sarah Younge cornered me in the ladies' room and asked if the search would continue for Riana. She said she wanted to volunteer as a spokesperson for the search."

"What'd you tell her?"

"That of course it would continue. And she said something that might explain the nature of the private meetings between Ross and her husband. Apparently Sarah and David have been having some trouble with their oldest son. Ross was strongly encouraging David to take a month off to be with his family." Juliana's voice caught. "Sarah said Ross had convinced David that family was the most important thing a man had."

Hunter silently agreed. "I'll check it out. You did well today. I know it couldn't have been easy when you had your own grief to deal with."

A crooked smile touched her lips. "Well, I didn't tell you everything. Gord Nevins, the household manager, asked if he could visit my father. They've been friends for twenty years. I was hoping that under the circumstances you'd consider allowing Gord to visit. I refuse to consider him a threat to my father's well-being."

Hunter cupped her jaw, stroking the fine perfection of her skin. She was at her most beautiful when she was displaying her unwavering loyalty to the people she cared about. And Hunter couldn't refuse her, not when she was so terribly torn between her duty to Cort and her love for her father. Odd, he didn't trust easily, but he was beginning to trust his wife's instincts.

"Consider it done," he said.

"Thank you," she breathed. It was all Hunter could do to resist the temptation to kiss her. "I'll feel better knowing he's being visited by someone he knows."

Their hired car pulled up to the hospital entrance. Hunter kept a firm arm around her as they settled into the comfortable leather seat. Even though the world seemed to be in a shambles around him, an unexpected contentment settled deep in his soul when Juliana pillowed her head against his shoulder.

He hoped her visit with her father would bring her peace. Maybe, who knew, the visit from his daughter would give Goodhew the will to survive.

Hunter instructed the driver to take them to the nearest take-out restaurant where they ordered grilled chicken sandwiches and fries. Juliana only managed to eat half her sandwich and a few of the fries in the short drive to the field where the chopper would be landing.

In spite of how drained he knew she was, a smile transformed her face as she moved to Cort. "There's my pumpkin. Oh, I've missed you sunshine! Were you a good boy?" She shot an anxious glance at the two bodyguards who'd been protecting him. "He didn't cry, did he?" she shouted over the whirling of the chopper blades.

"Not more than a whimper, ma'am," the self-assured black man with a jaw like an ice breaker told her with a grin.

"When did you last feed him?"

"At six, just as we were told. He drank the whole bottle and burped half of it on my lap."

"Sorry, Del. With all your nieces and nephews I thought you'd be wise to that trick," Hunter shouted, making sure Juliana was buckled into her seat.

"No sweat, boss. Ty and me can handle that kind of action."

Hunter felt Del's scrutiny as Juliana fussed over the baby, tucking a blanket more securely around him. Her love for the baby was evident in the tone of her voice and her tender smile.

As the chopper lifted off the ground, Hunter wondered what he'd found in this amazing woman.

FROM THE SKY AT NIGHT, the St. Lawrence River was an unfurled bolt of fabric with pinpoints of light scattered across it like diamonds on an evening gown. Juliana thought it seemed wonderfully remote. And beautiful.

"There are more lights in the summer," Hunter told her, leaning over Cort's car seat between them to point out her window. Juliana was conscious of the scent and heat of Hunter's body, beckoning her to lean into his arm, absorb his strength. "We're getting into the off season. Most of the summer homes are closed up by the Canadian Thanksgiving in October. The river doesn't freeze up until December usually. See the darker shadows in the river? Those are islands. This area is called Thousand Islands, although there's actually one thousand eight hundred and sixty-four islands. Two-thirds of the islands are in Canada. In the daylight you can see white stone markers in the water that delineate the international boundary.''

One thousand eight hundred and sixty-four islands sounded like an ideal hiding spot from a killer, Juliana thought, glancing at the rough-hewn bodyguards on the bench facing them. ''Where's your island?'' she asked Hunter.

''Out in the middle of the channel past Million Dollar Row. My grandfather—he built the house for my grandmother—was never one for crowds, which is good because we're off the charter boat tour route. We're nearly there. See the towers?''

She gaped. In the distance a castle sat like an illuminated jewel, its stone towers jutting up from a dark ring of trees.

She'd grown up in grandeur. The Collingwood estate was unparalleled. But Hunter lived in a castle. A real castle.

It was only one of several magnificent buildings on the island. Juliana noticed a tennis court, docks, an extensive garden and landing pads for two helicopters.

The chopper touched down on an empty pad. Hunter climbed out first, carrying Cort in his car seat. Then he offered a hand to Juliana to help her descend.

A shiver whispered up her arm as he brought her hand to his lips and pressed a warm kiss on the back of it. His voice rumbled with gruff emotion over the slowing whine of the chopper blades. ''Welcome home, Cinderella.''

Chapter Ten

The spectacular cabinetry and warmth of the foyer took Juliana's breath away. A massive staircase wrapped up the intricately molded paneled walls for four or five stories to a stained-glass dome.

A face appeared just for an instant over a railing on the second floor. "Hunter, you're home!"

Seconds later a slender brunette in tan corduroys and a leaf-motif sweater tread lightly down the carpeted staircase. She slowed as her gaze landed on Juliana and the baby. "Oh!"

Though she was emotionally and physically exhausted, Juliana felt a smile forming on her lips as she returned the woman's interested gaze. Was this Hunter's sister?

She'd always wanted a sister.

Tucking her sleek bobbed hair behind her ears, the woman continued down the last few steps at a more sedate pace. "You've brought guests. What a surprise." She held out her hand as she reached the mosaic-tiled main floor.

Curiosity sparkled in blue eyes that were a shade lighter than Hunter's. "Welcome to FairIsle. How do you do? I'm Brook Sinclair, Hunter's *much* younger sister."

Hunter's shielding hand settled at the small of Juliana's

back. "Brook, I'd like you to meet my wife, Juliana. And this is my son, Cortland."

"Your son? Your wife?" Brook's smile slipped from her face, then reappeared as her eyes darted to her brother's face. "Oh, my God, you're not joking, are you? Congratulations!"

Her cool fingers warmly clasped Juliana's hand. "My brother has a lot of explaining to do, keeping a secret like this from me. Not even a word of warning so I could prepare a special welcome." She beamed at Juliana. "But any wife of Hunter's is a dear friend of mine."

Juliana decided then and there that she would like Brook very much. "I'm pleased to meet you. I've heard so much about you and your boys. I'm looking forward to meeting them, too."

Brook gave her brother a congratulatory peck on the cheek, causing him to turn an interesting shade of crimson. Juliana had never thought Hunter could look embarrassed.

"The boys have been in bed for hours," his sister prattled excitedly. "The beginning of school is always exhausting. But they'll be thrilled to wake up and find their favorite uncle is home—with a new cousin. May I hold my new nephew? He looks like an angel, blond like you, Juliana. How old is he? How did you come up with the name? Is it a family name?"

Cort immediately seized a lock of Brook's hair and gave her a beauteous smile. "Urgh!"

Brook pelted them with questions as Hunter directed the butler to bring their bags upstairs and asked for coffee to be brought into the drawing room. Juliana did her best to answer her new sister-in-law's questions as Brook carried Cort into a comfortable book-lined room with huge picture windows. The carved woodwork and the plaster ceilings were magnificent, but Juliana immediately fell in love with the time-worn furniture, the checker table near the fireplace, the shells and pebbles lining the windowsill and the walkie-talkie jammed between the cushions of the antique sofa. This room had been used and loved and lived in for decades. Cort would be happy growing up here.

She glanced up at Hunter, catching him watching her intently as if trying to gauge her reaction. This was another glimpse of her husband she hadn't anticipated. This was his home, the place where he was most comfortable. Was he wondering how she would fit in here?

Juliana was wondering, too. Feeling Brook's watchful eyes on them, she sat beside him on the sofa and laid her hand on his hard, muscled thigh.

Hunter covered her hand with his, his thumb massaging her palm.

Juliana caught her lower lip between her teeth as she felt the stirring effects of his caress create an ache deep inside her. How on earth could just this slight touch make her breasts feel heavy and sore?

She shifted her thigh against the hard length of him, not sure if she wanted him to stop this erotic torture. Telling herself that this was an act he was putting on for his sister's benefit failed miserably at dampening her response.

Brook kissed one of Cort's tiny hands. "I want to know everything. How you met. How old this little guy is. And when you got married. I don't remember receiving an invitation."

"We got married yesterday as a matter of fact," Hunter explained, giving her an anecdotal account of the first-meet story they had concocted.

Juliana attempted to add in the appropriate details, but the seductive play of Hunter's thumb on her palm, circling, stroking, kneading her fingers, was far too hypnotic. Her body clenched in tandem with the rhythm he set.

Her breasts ached for the same caresses.

She was ready to jump out of her skin by the time Lars, the butler, who looked as if he could win a gold medal in an Olympic triathlon, brought in a tray and laid it on the coffee table.

To Juliana's dismay, Hunter's ministrations abruptly ceased as Brook served the coffee like an experienced hostess and mother, expertly juggling the baby, cups and dessert plates.

Juliana drank the coffee, which was strong and delicious, and ate a slice of the lemon-blueberry pound cake, her mind struggling to grasp a few of the facts that Brook was telling her about the history of the house.

With one hundred and two rooms, she and Hunter would surely have their own suites. Their own space. They'd be able to maintain the relationship they'd agreed upon.

Even as she repeated this to herself like a mantra, Hunter set down his coffee cup. "Thank you for your warm reception, Brook. If you'll excuse us, I'd hoped to romance my wife on our first night home."

Juliana felt her body zing with heat and her knees start to quiver. "Promises, promises," she said lightly, setting down her own cup.

Hunter shot her a wolfish gaze that made her throat constrict. Dear heaven, if she didn't know better, if she didn't know *him,* she'd think he meant every heated word.

Brook looked amused. "I can take a hint." She reluctantly handed the baby to Hunter, then gave Juliana a sisterly hug. "Go easy on him. What he knows about marriage would fit onto the head of a pin. But he'll stick with you through thick and thin, which is more than I can say for my three husbands."

Hunter scowled at his sister. "Thanks, Brook. Don't you have a hotel chain to run?"

"As a matter of fact I do. No thanks to you." With a cocky salute to her brother, Brook sauntered out of the drawing room.

Feeling suddenly self-conscious, Juliana tilted her head to one side and eyed her husband appraisingly. One of Cort's tiny hands explored the contours of Hunter's chin, while the other patted the column of his strong neck. "She didn't tell me anything I didn't already know."

He raised an arrogant brow. "How reassuring." Juliana couldn't tell if he was annoyed or amused, he hid his emotions so well. But her mouth went dry as a wry smile touched his lips and a marked huskiness entered his voice. "It's been a long day. Let's get our son to bed."

Our son. Warmth shimmered over her skin. Standing in the living room with Cort battened protectively in Hunter's arms, Juliana saw all she wanted in her future displayed before her. This strong noble man and this adorable little baby.

With a small sigh of gratitude, she let Hunter guide her toward the stairs, goose bumps raising on her arms when his hand grazed the small of her back. She could only imagine how many nights they would climb the stairs together, only to part and go to separate rooms and separate beds. She wouldn't think about that now. At least they'd all be safe.

"I'm afraid my mother's rooms haven't been used in a long time. They'll need a good cleaning before you can move in. I've asked the staff to set up a crib for Cort in my sitting room. We'll make do for tonight in my room and sort the rest out in the morning. Brook might think it odd if I gave you a guest room."

The edge in his tone rubbed the glow off her mood. It was obvious he was trying to establish distance between them. Setting the boundaries. "Of course. I'm so tired, I don't care where I sleep."

Liar.

Her heart was already racing, her fingers and toes already curling at the prospect of sharing a bed with him. She hadn't forgotten what he looked like with his shirt off. She doubted any woman could.

On the north wing of the second floor, Hunter opened a pair of dark paneled doors to a room that was rich and masculine. William Morris area rugs scattered over the oak floors added color and interest to the paneled walls and the massive wood pieces. He'd probably hate it if she told him how much she saw of his personality in the fish and the acorns carved into the bedposts and the telescope placed in the bow window of the sitting room formed by one of the towers.

He fished his cell phone out of his pocket and handed it to her. "I'll get Cort settled for the night. You call the hospital and check on your father. Then have a bath. Your clothes are in your dressing room through that connecting door."

Juliana couldn't argue with him, not when the baby seemed perfectly trusting of Hunter's care. She tousled Cort's corn-silk hair and kissed his warm silky cheek, every nerve in her being attuned to the bulk and the strength of the man holding her precious charge. "Good night, pumpkin. Don't forget to give him his antibiotics."

Cort didn't look the least bit upset or anxious as Hunter carried him into his dressing room. The little traitor.

No, he wasn't a traitor.

He recognized a pair of arms he could trust.

She kicked off her shoes, listening for a moment to the deep rumble of Hunter's voice and Cort's giggles as the diaper tape was ripped open.

With a small sigh, Juliana punched in the hospital's number. Unfortunately, the nurse informed her, there was still no change in her father's condition.

She moved around the room, adding Cort's favorite blanket to the crib and lowering the Roman blinds over the windows in the sitting room so he wouldn't wake at the crack of dawn.

Her dressing room was cavernous and stripped bare of any form of decoration, the paneled woodwork painted a dreary shade of goldenrod that she didn't care for. Her clothes—all neatly hung or folded and placed on the shelves—took up only a small portion of the available space. She saw her purse on a shelf. A quick check revealed her wallet, her ID and her gun were present and accounted for.

She pulled the new midnight-blue nightgown and the matching robe she'd bought Saturday from their hangers and entered the bathroom. Someone had gone to the trouble of preparing the room for her. The mirrors sparkled. Pillar candles on iron stands ringed the old-fashioned claw-foot tub and a basket of toiletries was set out for her use.

Juliana filled the tub with steaming hot water, adding a generous dollop of bath oil and a sprinkling of the dried herbs and flowers from a crystal jar. Then she lit the candles, dropped her clothes to the white tile floor and sank into a warm scented heaven that made her body limp at the luxury. The only thing that could make it better was sharing it with Hunter.

An ache she'd never experienced for any other man settled between her thighs. Someday she'd like to see his beautiful chest—and the rest of him—sluiced with water.

Still, she'd settle for the joy of waking up beside him and a glimpse of watching him sleep.

Twenty minutes later, her muscles blessedly free of tension and her toes wrinkled into prunes, she entered Hunter's bedroom. The lights were dimmed and he was gently laying Cort in the crib. A fierce longing gripped Juliana as she stared at them from across the room.

Hunter looked up and Juliana's breath evaporated from her lungs at the sudden flare of hunger in his eyes.

Her nipples beaded with primitive awareness. Her satin nightgown and robe felt too thin. Too revealing. The thought that Hunter found her attractive, desired her, was both alarming and thrilling.

But in the blink of an eye, the hunger she'd seen was gone and his face grew tight. Masklike. He didn't glance at her as he drew the moss-green velvet draperies along the wooden rod that offered the sitting room privacy from the sleeping area.

Juliana's heart slammed like a fist against the vulnerable wall of her feelings. She didn't need a translator to interpret his behavior.

It was as plain as the granite set to his jaw that he didn't want to desire her. The stripped walls of her dressing room were evidence that Hunter didn't want any woman to make a lasting mark on his life.

She turned her back on him and fumbled with the thin satin ties of her robe. She wanted to climb into bed, close her eyes and put an end to this horrible day before she made a fool of herself. All the wishful thinking in the world wouldn't turn their marriage into the passionate relationship Ross and Lexi had shared.

ANY THOUGHTS HUNTER'D had that he could make it through this night unscathed fled when he looked across the room and saw Juliana standing near his bed in a midnight-blue nightgown that made her skin glow like cultured pearls. Her hair tumbled down around her shoulders like spun gold.

He'd never broken a contract in his life. An honorable man would turn away, leave the room.

He'd buried his best friend today. He wanted solace with the one person who would weep with him.

Juliana's robe slipped off her shoulders. The skimpy satin nightgown she wore beneath it was little more than two tiny straps of satin over her shoulders and a meager amount of fabric that dipped low down her back and barely covered the lush curve of her bottom.

God, she was so beautiful. So graceful. He'd never been so fascinated, so spellbound by a woman's back—the line of her neck, the angles of her shoulder blades, the hollow of her spine and the twin dimples just above her buttocks. He wanted to chart those dips and angles with his fingers and his lips and claim them as his own.

She climbed into his bed, on his side, no less. Without giving him a second glance, she pulled the covers up over her shoulder and lay silently.

In the hush that fell over the room, Hunter heard the sound of his heart pounding and cold reason gradually returning. They had an agreement with each other. No matter how much the idea of peeling off that nightgown and making love to her appealed to him, he respected her too much to risk their arrangement.

With a conflicted heart, he tucked the covers more securely around her and bent to kiss her head. Her hair smelled like a summer garden. Not apple blossoms.

Another unexpected change to add to his growing confusion over what to make of his wife.

"Good night, Cinderella. Sleep well."

She didn't answer. Her breathing was slow and even. She'd fallen asleep.

Thank God for small favors. Hunter made his escape.

Juliana was dreaming....

She knew she was being a bad girl, disobeying Papa's rules. But Papa had so many rules—"must nots" she and Michael called them.

No one would know if they each sneaked a ride down the smooth polished banister in the big house. Just for a treat. Oh, it was such fun—similar to going backward on a swing, only higher. And when you reached the bottom you were propelled through the air like an acrobat for just the tiniest bit. Juliana would land with her knees bent and her arms out, wanting to do it all over again.

Michael was already scampering up the knobby spindles to the banister with eager hands. "Me first, Juli. Me first!"

"Wait! Let me help you." Before she could steady him, he was zipping down the railing like a wet bar of soap on porcelain.

Her smile of delight froze in terror as he slipped off his perch and fell. Surprise widened in his dark eyes as his head struck the nose of a stair with a sickening thud. She cried out Michael's name, her hands rising to cover her ears to block the horrible thunking sounds her brother made as he tumbled helter-skelter down the stairs to the marble floor below.

From out of nowhere Juliana heard her Papa's condemning voice muffled by an ear-piercing roar. Then the pop and hiss of flames. Her father wouldn't speak to her.

Her pleas and apologies fell on deaf ears.

Papa had turned his back to her, was leaving her. Walking into the fire. Anger and frustration surged through her, made her reckless. She grabbed the tail of his jacket to stop him from leaving, to force him to acknowledge her. "If you die, I'll never forgive you! Do you hear me? I'm your daughter. Your only daughter. I need a father!''

Gradually Juliana became aware of strong arms securing her to a bare oak-hard chest. Of warm hands stroking her back, comforting her, not condemning her.

"Shh! It's okay, sweetheart. You're having a bad dream.''

She felt the tender brush of a kiss on her forehead. A kiss that acted as a balm, leaving her feeling cherished. Wanted.

"Hunter? Thank God!'' Her fingers dug into the hard muscle of his shoulders. Her lips pressed against his chest as if seeking assurance from the taste and texture of his skin that he was there in the flesh and this was not part of her dream.

His fingers splayed over her back, cupping her bottom and pulling her into the notch of his thighs.

Juliana gasped as the steely evidence of his maleness fit intimately against her belly. Desire and the need to be close to this man, to have no barriers between them, swelled inexorably in her, drawing her to his heat and his hardness and toward whatever the future may bring.

Hunter said her name on a ragged cry, his lips grazing her temple, her cheeks. The rasp of his beard and the warmth of his breath on her skin was a sweet torture. Juliana responded, running her hands over the ridges of muscle and bone, gripping his hips and pulling him closer still. His mouth claimed hers fiercely, his kiss so hot and demanding it left no room for doubts.

All she knew was that he was kissing her as she wanted to be kissed, holding her as she wanted to be held. Not as a servant or his wife in name only. But as a true wife. His lover.

He pushed a strap off her shoulder and Juliana felt the

scrape of stubble on her tender skin as he broke their kiss and sampled the sensitive skin beneath her jaw, then the curve of her shoulder and, finally, her breast.

She bucked against him as a fire bolt of pleasure shot through her. Sweet heaven, nothing had ever felt so incredibly wonderful in her life as he suckled her breast, his tongue laving her nipple, coaxing it into a tight nub.

Generously he laved attention on her other breast, kneading her soft flesh, nipping and suckling until her legs were moving restlessly and her hips were lifting off the Egyptian cotton sheets.

"Soon, my Cinderella, soon," he whispered, his lips tilting into a smile against the fullness of her breast.

She threaded trembling fingers through his hair and silently urged him to continue the sweet torture. Slowly, deliberately, he changed the pace, nibbling her neck, her ears, kissing the corners of her mouth, touching the tip of his tongue to hers, then deepening the kiss as his hands descended down her ribs to her belly and slid her legs apart.

Juliana nearly cried out when his hand molded over her damp panties, then moved slowly back and forth creating a friction that mounted in her like a secret aching to be told. He captured her mouth in another deep kiss that took her to another realm as his fingers slid inside her panties and created a new ultrasensitive friction that had her keening in the back of her throat.

She'd made love before, but not like this.

Instead of hiding her feelings and wanting to please, this time she yearned to open herself to Hunter, to soar wherever he took her. Forever.

HUNTER DESPERATELY tried to hold on. The frenzy that had gripped him when he'd tried to comfort Juliana was building to a shattering point. He couldn't remember ever desiring a woman this badly and was almost grateful for the darkness that prevented her from seeing the depth of his need.

She was so hot and tight all he could think about was the satiny texture of her skin and burying himself into that creamy sweetness. Blessedly, he felt the beginning quiver of her climax caress his finger. Her name shuddered through him to the tip of his tongue.

She was so sweet. So hot. He almost lost it right there like an inexperienced frat boy.

He remembered his manners. Sinclairs always remembered their manners. "Are you ready for me, Cinderella?" he demanded hoarsely, his thumb expertly finding the tiny pulsating pleasure point in her hot silky folds.

Her back arched off the bed, rocking with tremors. "Yes. Oh, yes!"

He raked her panties off her with one tug. Then shucked his boxers and moved between her parted legs.

Slowly, slowly, grasping the last vestiges of his control, he slid into her.

And found heaven.

Sweat popped on his brow. The muscles corded in his neck as he braced his arms on the bed as if sheltering and protecting the vulnerability of this act between them. The fluttering contractions of her orgasm brought him perilously close to the edge of release. His forearms and triceps shuddered as he withdrew, then plunged into her again. Deeper, this time.

Her body tightened around him, welcoming him. Offering him a harbor from old hurts and fears.

"Oh, Hunter, I need you so much."

Her words unleashed a part of him he'd kept protected and hidden for so long. Her fingers feverishly feathered over her chest and abdomen as her legs locked solidly around his hips.

He needed no further encouragement.

He thrust into her, mindless of rhythm or anything else but the unstoppable need to be joined with this amazing woman. To surrender his senses to total awareness of her. Her scent. Her feel. Her taste. And the cries of her passion. All that mattered was sustaining this union at whatever cost—emotional, physical, spiritual.

With one last thrust his release came, wondrous and sacred as an ethereal mist rising from the river on a winter's morning. Hunter collapsed beside her, pulling her against him.

Wrapping his arms tightly around her waist, he kissed the back of her shoulder and drifted into the most contented sleep he'd ever known.

WHAT HAD HE DONE?

Hunter took a sip of black coffee and grimaced as he watched the sun's first rays streak out from a ball of pink fire and light the sky. The river and the dozens of darkened islands in his field of vision slumbered on, ignorant of the crisis of conscience he'd woken up to.

Last night had been… Well, he still hadn't decided on the right words to describe exactly had happened between them. Memories of the taste and feel of Juliana in his arms twisted his gut into knots…right down to the realization that he'd had unprotected sex with her.

He set his coffee cup down on his desk too hard, the hot liquid splashing over the rim. What had he been thinking?

He obviously hadn't been thinking, damn it.

He'd foolishly, irresponsibly broken his contract with her. Crossed every boundary of honor and decency in their marriage that shouldn't have been crossed. Now she could very well be pregnant with his child.

His child.

A brother or sister for Cort.

He ran his fingers through his hair, petrified by the possibility of being the parent of yet another child. And taunted by images of how this child was conceived. For a fantasy-filled moment he pictured himself still in bed with Juliana this morning. Imagined her sleek satiny flanks snuggled against his thighs and the softness of her breasts filling his palms. Imagined making love to her again, more slowly this time without any barriers of darkness to hide behind.

Imagined her stomach rounded with his baby.

Panic scattered through him like a flock of birds startled into flight.

He shook his head, steeling his heart.

It was one thing to enter into a marriage of convenience to ensure his godson was well cared for, but quite another to commit himself to a relationship that was governed by emotion and lust. He was already susceptible to Juliana—last night had clearly demonstrated that. He didn't want love to enter into the equation. To ruin their clear-cut arrangement.

Love had only made his father and his sister miserable. Gave them impossible expectations. He respected Juliana. Admired her. He needed her to steer him through raising Cort.

He'd apologize for what happened last night. Assure her it would never happen again. He'd sleep on the floor if need be.

And if she was pregnant he'd deal with it—if and when the time came.

He took another fortifying sip of coffee and reached for a fax that had come in overnight, determined to tear his mind away from what had happened between him and Juliana and concentrate on the Collingwood investigation. There was still no word yet from Investigator Bradshaw about Robert Lance, the man who'd purchased the pager used to detonate the bomb. The fact that eight hours had passed since they'd gone to pick him up for questioning suggested they'd had trouble locating him. Was Robert Lance involved in the bombing?

Hunter scanned the fax. It was from an operative assigned to do a thorough background check on the Collingwood's missing cook, Nonnie Wilson.

He nearly choked on his coffee as he read through the report. Had Goodhew known any of this when he'd hired the cook? She threw parties where she cooked in the nude for her guests. She'd been arrested twice for trespassing on private property—allegedly picking wild mushrooms and herbs. Her bedroom was decorated like the sleeping quarters of an officer in the *Star Trek: Voyager* series. And her sister claimed she liked to visit New Age retreats when her aura was dull and needed recharging. She also entertained the Collingwood staff by reading their tarot cards.

Hunter punched in the operative's cell phone number. It was an ungodly hour, but they had a murderer to catch. "Edwards, I just read your fax. Get on the Internet and see if there are any Star Trek conventions taking place this week. While you're at it, get a list of New Age retreats within a day's drive of New York City. Then get on the phone. I've got a feeling Nonnie has a dull aura."

He looked at the list of possible leads he'd scratched onto a legal pad after he'd crept out of bed this morning. There were far too many suspects and no concrete evidence. The information about the senior management and board of directors that his operatives had been filtering hadn't indicated anything sinister. But the theft of Juliana's purse yesterday indicated the killer still considered her a threat. Who knew what the killer had planned to do with Juliana's cell phone?

There was some comfort in knowing Juliana and Cort were safe on the island, but he wouldn't rest easy until the killer was apprehended. There was also the real possibility that Annette could be a target. From what Juliana had told him about her conversation with Annette yesterday, the woman was a loose cannon. He'd get working on the arrangements today to have her brought to the island ASAP.

He studied the next item on his leads list and called the operative assigned to doing a background check on David Younge, the controller. Juliana had told him that Younge's wife, Sarah, had waylaid her in the ladies' room at the estate just before Juliana discovered her purse was missing.

Sarah had brought up the subject of her husband's recent private meetings with Ross. Hunter wasn't accepting Sarah's explanation at face value. He wanted verification that Ross had been advising David to take family leave and sort out his troubles with his teenage son. Ross might well have been informing David not to count on being promoted to senior vice president and chief financial officer on Kendrick Dwyer's retirement or that his work was suffering and he'd soon be out of a job if he didn't shape up.

He'd just completed the call when his sister opened the door to his study, a frown hovering over her blue eyes. "I thought I'd find you in here," she said.

"What has you up at the crack of dawn?" he asked mildly, noting her rumpled hair and chenille bathrobe and slippers.

She closed the door and jammed her slender hands into the pockets of her robe. "You have to ask? You, my confirmed bachelor brother, waltz in here with a wife and a five-month-old baby without giving me any notice. What's going on?"

He averted his gaze. "I wanted to surprise you."

"Liar." She sat down in the chair opposite his desk. "Are you sure the baby is yours?"

Hunter's gaze leaped sharply back to his sister's "don't try to pull one over on me" expression, the one she used with mediocre success on her ex-husbands and her hellion sons. It didn't work any better on him. "I think you know me better than that."

"I thought I did, but then I never anticipated you behaving this impetuously, either." She cracked a self-deprecating smile. "That's usually my department. Are you in love with her?"

Her question hovered in the air.

Was he?

Hunter shifted the papers on his desk to hide his irritation. He knew Brook would sit there doing her sisterly duty until he gave her an answer or his nephews brought the house crashing down around their ears. "Brook, let me assure you that my decision to marry was neither impetuous nor hasty."

Now she looked offended. "You mean, unlike my marriages?"

His lips tightened. "I didn't say that."

"Then what are you saying?"

"I'm saying, my nosy sister, that Juliana is the most courageous woman I've ever met. And far more than I deserve. Now make yourself scarce, I have work to do."

Brook sighed and rose to her feet. "You know, it took me three marriages and two years of therapy to realize I had a problem saying, 'I love you.' I hope you don't suffer from the same affliction."

Hunter crumpled a report on his desk after she'd gone. He appreciated Brook's concern, but she didn't know what she was talking about.

JULIANA SHOULDN'T HAVE been surprised to wake up and find herself alone in Hunter's bed. Still, it hurt.

She touched the pillow beside her that bore the indentation of his head, feeling uncertain and more than a little scared. If she hadn't already admitted her feelings for Hunter to herself, her body now radiated them.

She *loved* him. Loved his steely strength and his uncompromising determination to protect Cort at all costs. Loved the little displays of thoughtfulness that he tried so hard to hide. She'd always be grateful to him for forcing her to visit her father.

And she'd never forget the way he'd made love to her last night. As a wedding planner, she'd naively thought lovemaking was all about creating a romantic mood, creating just the right setting with flowers and soft music and candles. What she'd shared with Hunter had been so emotional and passionate she was still flushed and trembling from the wonder of it. No wonder newlyweds made love two, three times a day!

She laid her head on Hunter's pillow. Last night had given her hope that he might return her feelings. She'd seen the desire in his eyes.

But you never knew with men. Men desired and took what they wanted to fill their hungers—especially rich men. Ross had been like that with his female conquests until he'd met Lexi. And Hunter had made it plain that there wouldn't be a physical side to their marriage. A shadow crossed over her heart. Would he blame her for what happened last night? Think she was trying to seduce him for his money? Would he send her packing?

Anguish fought with anger inside her.

She was *not* leaving Cort.

As though sensing he was the subject of her thoughts, Cort gave a startled little cry. He sounded confused that he'd woken up in strange surroundings.

"I'm coming, baby," she said, reluctantly leaving the warmth of the bed. She straightened her nightgown, her face burning with erotic images of Hunter's lovemaking and tied her robe around her. Then hurried to the sitting room.

"Good morning, pumpkin."

Cort immediately brightened and lifted his arms to her, his cheeks warm and pink from sleep.

Juliana scooped him up and nuzzled his cheek, his sweet baby scent working its calming magic on her. One by one, she raised the roman blinds in the tower sitting room, letting in the light of day.

"Oh, my," she breathed, gazing out at the view. She'd landed in paradise. The river spread out around FairIsle as far as her eye could see—a moving, shimmering carpet patterned with islands in varying shapes and sizes. Some populated with grand mansions or modest summer cottages, others scarcely more than a handful of evergreens rooted to massive outcroppings of granite.

Looking down, she could see a fountain splashing in the center of the formal rose garden. And flower beds lining a path to an ivy-covered building that might be a greenhouse. She'd always wanted a garden to tend.

She kissed Cort's temple, wondering if Lexi had felt this overwhelmed when Ross had brought her to the Collingwood estate for the first time. Even though she'd lived around luxury all her life, Juliana had always been aware that it didn't belong to her. Lexi hadn't grown up in luxury, but she'd walked into Ross's world as if she were entitled to it. If she'd been overwhelmed, she hadn't let it show.

Juliana decided she wouldn't, either.

She'd change the baby and give him his morning bottle, then have a quick shower and find Hunter. She couldn't put off facing him. They needed to talk about last night.

Chapter Eleven

The house was even lovelier in the daylight than it had been last night. The vibrant reds, blues and greens of the stained-glass dome over the foyer cast streamers of colored light onto the mosaic-tiled floor. Cort tried to capture the beams of light in his hands as they descended to the main floor.

The house was curiously quiet. She doubted the family had breakfast in the formal dining room. Surely there was a breakfast or morning room. If Hunter hadn't eaten yet, she'd take a tray to him, wherever he was.

She headed for the kitchen, always the best source of information in the workings of a fine home like this. She'd only been introduced to Lars, the Olympiad athlete butler last night.

She pushed a paneled swinging door and found herself in a spacious kitchen with an immense black granite-topped island in its center. The woodwork and custom cabinets were painted a lemony yellow. Terra-cotta pots planted with herbs stood in front of French doors that looked out over a terrace. The cook was monitoring several pots and pans on the commercial range.

At least half a dozen people, the staff, she presumed, were seated at an antique farmhouse table enjoying coffee and cinnamon rolls and gossiping about Hunter's sudden marriage.

A sudden hush fell over the kitchen as Lars scraped back his chair and rose, laying his napkin on the table. "Mrs. Sinclair."

Telling herself to behave as Lexi would, Juliana approached the table, smiling. "Good morning, Lars. Please, call me Juliana. I'm so happy to meet all of you."

Lars made introductions. She greeted the maids, the head gardener, the maintenance engineer, the boatman, the cook and the friendly red-cheeked nanny named Prudy.

"Have I missed meeting Brook's sons?" Juliana asked.

"Mackensie is off to school already," Prudy replied, tweaking Cort's toes with a mischievous smile. "And Parrish has play group on Tuesday and Thursday mornings. Brook dropped them both off on her way in to work. The chopper takes her to the head office of the Clairmont Hotels in Syracuse. Shall I prepare a bottle for this young man?"

"Please do." She looked to Lars. "Has my husband already eaten this morning?"

"Not yet."

Juliana enlisted the staff's cooperation in stealing a few minutes alone with her husband. The cook prepared a tray loaded with freshly sliced fruit, cinnamon rolls, a carafe of coffee and glasses of orange juice. Prudy had volunteered to give Cort his morning dose of antibiotics and was feeding him a bottle and fawning over his sweet disposition and his fine long lashes. Lars informed her that Brook used the first floor study as her home office and that Hunter conducted his affairs from an office on the third floor.

The butler led the way upstairs, carrying the tray. Juliana's heart knocked in tandem with her knees and her palms grew moist. She hoped she wasn't making a mistake. But she couldn't very well change her mind in front of

Lars. It might be spread all over the kitchen within a few minutes.

Lars punched a code into a keypad before a closed door on the third floor, but Juliana stopped him from knocking. She wanted an unshielded glimpse of Hunter's face. "I'll take it from here, thank you."

His expression clearly suggested he didn't like the idea of her entering Hunter's domain unannounced.

"It's quite all right. I'm well aware of the sensitive nature of his work. We don't have any secrets from one another."

That seemed to satisfy him. "Very well. I'll be available to give you a tour of the house at your convenience. There are several sets of furniture in the guest bedrooms that you could choose from to appoint your suite until you've had time to redecorate it according to your tastes. Enjoy your breakfast."

Juliana waited until he had reached the second floor landing before she quietly opened the heavy, steel-reinforced door. Taking her cue from Brook's attire last night, she'd dressed casually this morning in slacks and a blouse.

Hunter's back was to her. His dark head bent in concentration. Her stomach clenched. Desire welled in her to encourage him with a stroke of her hand or a squeeze to his muscled shoulder. He was working on the computer, the sleeves of his navy sweater shoved up to just below his elbows. Unlike the rest of the house, the furniture here was sleek and modern, in keeping with the bank of televisions and other high-tech equipment that Juliana didn't recognize.

She set the tray down on a coffee table in front of a black leather sofa.

Hunter swiveled around in his office chair. "Is Juliana

awake—'' His voice broke off abruptly when he noticed her. ''Oh, hi.''

Hi? For a brief instant, Juliana rejoiced in the narrowing of his azure eyes on her like the lens of a camera sharpening into focus and his obvious discomposure. Hunter, with his formal education, was not the kind of man who said hi.

Confidence glowed in her like a lit candle as she remembered the way he'd pulled her into the shelter of his arms after they'd made love. Maybe after last night, he was one step closer to trusting her. ''As you can see, I'm fully awake. I brought you breakfast.''

''I didn't hear you knock.''

She bristled at the subtle reprimand in his tone and the rapid alignment of his features into a cold impenetrable wall. Her confidence waffled and was in immediate danger of being snuffed out. He was pushing her away again. Distancing himself.

Well, she wasn't going to make it easy for him. She lifted a crystal tumbler of orange juice from the tray and held it out to him, so that he'd have to come to her to get it. ''I didn't knock,'' she said with mettle in her tone, ''because I'm your wife. I thought we should discuss what happened last night.'' She held up a hand to stop him from interrupting. ''Don't worry, I'm not going to get hysterical or blackmail you because we shared more than your last name for a few minutes.'' Her body simmered with the remembered warmth of his touches. ''I've had sex before. Several times, in fact.''

Somehow, Hunter wasn't the least bit comforted by the knowledge that Juliana had been intimate with other men, or her willingness to dismiss the issue so lightly. He'd been with other women. But none of those experiences had equaled what he'd felt when he'd held her in his arms.

His mouth unhinged, then snapped shut like a steel trap.

He was damned if he said anything. Damned if he didn't. He'd never forgive himself for giving in to the emotion of the moment. For letting himself be vulnerable to her.

Even now he was experiencing difficulty resisting how perfectly at ease—and very, very sexy—she looked standing in front of the black leather sofa in tailored plaid slacks and a copper-hued silk blouse. Only four primly placed buttons stood between him and the remembered delights of her cleavage. Her hair was pulled back into a sleek ponytail and her face was devoid of makeup with the exception of a trace of gloss on her lips. She'd braved the lion in his den, entering unannounced. He had to give her credit for that.

Reluctantly he rose from his desk and took the proffered glass of juice from her hand.

It was a serious error in judgment. She'd washed her hair again this morning. The scent of apple blossoms was back.

He paced back to his desk, contemplating dangerous thoughts of easing her onto the sofa and releasing those buttons one by one in the full light of day. "Be that as it may," he said rigidly, "I owe you an apology for breaking the terms of our agreement."

Her determined little chin lifted gracefully. She even smiled. *Smiled.* Though he detected a shadow behind it.

"You have nothing to apologize for. I had a nightmare, you comforted me and one thing led to another. This last week has been difficult for both of us."

He told himself he was a stronger man, more disciplined than his father. He wouldn't put himself at the mercy of emotions that couldn't be controlled. "It was a breach of trust. I assure you it won't happen again. I'm sure you agree that it would be best if we didn't overstep certain boundaries in future?"

Her mahogany eyes swirled like shifting pools, making it impossible for him to decipher her thoughts. Was she relieved? Disappointed?

He hated the weakness in him that made him care.

"Please don't give it another thought. Roll?" She passed him a plate that held one of the cook's legendary cinnamon rolls. "I'll see to it that my suite is prepared today." She nabbed a wedge of cantaloupe and a cinnamon roll from the tray with a linen napkin and took a bite of the roll as she headed to the door. "I know you're busy, so I'll let you get back to work."

He had the uncomfortable feeling she'd just dusted her fingers of him. "Wait. How's your father this morning?"

He could see her squaring her shoulders, taking a fortifying breath. "Still in a coma. Your operative kindly held the phone to my father's ear so I could at least speak to him for a few minutes." Her eyes shone with moisture. "Please find out who did this to him."

The door closed firmly behind her rigid spine. Not quite a slam but certainly with more force than necessary.

Hunter ate breakfast alone, debating whether he'd effectively made his point.

JULIANA COULDN'T STOP her legs from shaking. She hid her disappointment about Hunter's rejection behind a determined smile and devoted herself to the tasks of preparing her suite and becoming acquainted with her new home and the staff.

Hunter couldn't have been more clear. After all he'd done to protect her and Cort, the least she could do was respect his need for privacy and distance. As Prudy gave her a tour of the nursery Juliana realized that most of her life had been spent trying to earn back her father's love and approval, curbing her own thoughts in deference to his, doing what was expected of her, burying the hurt. She'd realized sadly, while at his bedside, that no matter how many times she tried to please him, it would never be enough. Her father simply wasn't willing to forgive her.

By the same token, she could show Hunter in countless ways that she loved him and that he could trust her with his heart, but if he remained unwilling to commit himself to an intimate relationship their marriage would remain as it was—an amicable arrangement in name only. She would simply have to accept that and enjoy her life within those parameters.

"The nursery is lovely, Prudy," Juliana said, eyeing with pleasure the ducklings and bunnies that had been hand-painted on the pale-blue walls. Cort swung back and forth in the baby swing, his blue eyes bright as he pointed at a robin and big fluffy clouds painted on the ceiling. "This will be fine for Cort's naps, but I'm not sure I'm ready to have the baby sleep so far from me at night."

"Brook felt the same way when she was visiting and the boys were babies. She'd have the extra crib Cort slept in last night moved into her dressing room."

"I'll do the same."

Prudy excused herself to pick up Parrish at preschool and bring him home for lunch. Lars gave Juliana and Cort a tour of the house and the guest rooms. Juliana suspected that in addition to being the butler, he served as a body-guard. While he was courteous and deferential, his eyes carried questions. He was suspicious. She and Hunter would have to convince everyone they were in love, starting with Lars.

When Lars opened the door to a guest room on the third floor opposite the wing containing Hunter's offices, she exclaimed in delight at the white-painted furnishings with their quaint crystal knobs and the comfortable sofa and side chairs in a blue-and-white French print. "I love this. It'll brighten up that dull goldenrod until it can be repainted." She pointed out several other accessories she thought would furnish the suite temporarily, laughing when Cort nearly bent over backward reaching for a Chinese vase on a table.

Juliana got a better grip on his squirming body. "I think you'd better include the vase, Lars."

The stony-faced butler's lips twitched. "We'll start moving in the furniture after lunch. It will be good to see that room in use. It's been empty far too long." His incisive gaze seemed to take her measure.

She smiled at him over the top of Cort's head, warming to his concern for Hunter. "I couldn't agree with you more. Now, how do I find a decorator in this neck of the woods? That paint has got to go as soon as possible. By the end of next week I want a room that's warm and romantic and knocks Hunter's socks off, not a festering ground for bad memories."

Lars grinned, showing large white teeth. "Leave it to me."

"WHERE ARE YOU?" the killer demanded.

"In Alexandria Bay, New York. That's *bay* as in *river*. This Brook Sinclair lives on an island somewhere in the St. Lawrence. We're talkin' a big river. I just bought a map. You know how many friggin' islands there are out here?"

"No, and I don't care to know. I just want to know how long it's going to take you to confirm whether or not Juliana and the baby are staying with this Brook Sinclair."

"I'm going to charter a boat and scout out the territory by day. Find a way to sneak onto the island after nightfall."

"Excellent. Don't disappoint me. It's such a tragedy that so many babies die in their sleep. Sudden Infant Death

Syndrome they call it. They just stop breathing—like they've suffocated.''

"Have I disappointed you yet?"

"The tracking device wouldn't fit in the damn phone."

"And somehow that's my fault? That was a top-of-the-line product—the smallest available on the market."

The killer sighed in exasperation. "I'm sorry, you're right. It was a minor setback and you've already proven your worth by finding Brook Sinclair so expediently."

"That's more like it. It's an in-and-out job. No sweat. No one will even know I've been in the house."

The killer pressed the end button on the cell phone and verified that no one was nearby who could have overheard the conversation. Soon, very soon, there would be no more sucking up. The baby would be dead and finally there would be some justice in the world.

Chapter Twelve

Hunter knew he should make an appearance downstairs for lunch. His nephew Parrish would be home from play school and he hadn't seen the rascal in over a week. But it would mean encountering Juliana in front of an audience.

Keeping up the image of a newly wedded couple in front of his family and his staff wasn't making it any easier to keep their relationship strictly platonic in private. It was all too easy to lower the barriers he wanted to keep firmly in place when she looked at him as if he were some kind of hero.

Still, he couldn't hide out here behind the bunkers of paper that had been spitting out of his fax machines the last few hours; the majority were associated with this case, but a few updated him on other ongoing cases. Hunter had been diligently attacking the self-replenishing pile, setting aside information that warranted further action from him and delegating other tasks to his operatives.

At some point, he'd seriously have to consider taking on a partner. Maybe Del.

Del had come up the secret passageway to the safe room hidden behind a bookcase in Hunter's office while making his morning rounds and they'd drafted a plan to whisk Annette out of the Collingwood estate. If someone at the estate was involved in the bombing, she could be in danger.

It was a risk to bring her to the island, but he needed her cooperation if they were going to succeed in keeping Cort's identity hidden from the world. Plus, she needed confirmation that her nephew was alive.

Hunter had just finished making arrangements so that Gord Nevins could spend a few hours at Juliana's father's bedside this evening, when his cell phone rang.

"Bad news, we've reached a dead end with Robert Lance," Investigator Bradshaw barked in Hunter's ear. "We finally picked him up this morning at his place of employment. He had nothing to do with the pager that detonated the explosion. He lost his wallet on the subway a few months ago. We've verified his story with his credit card companies and it all checks out. He reported all his cards lost on the same date."

Hunter pinched the bridge of his nose. Unlike Riana's abduction, in this case they had a preponderance of information and suspects. A solid lead *would* turn up, he told himself. They had to keep plugging away until that happened. "So, whoever bought the pager used Lance's stolen ID?"

"You got it."

"Anything turn up with the florists?"

"Not yet. If the guy's clever, he went to three different florists and paid cash for each purchase."

"What about latent fingerprints on Juliana's purse?"

"We're way ahead of you. We lifted Juliana's prints and Stacey Kerr's prints. And two others which are unidentified. Definitely not Sable Holden's. We took the liberty of comparing the prints she left on her coffee cup during her interview with the prints found on the purse."

Hunter frowned. "Think it's significant that Stacey was

the one who just happened to find the purse? She was Lexi's personal secretary. Maybe Lexi confided in her about Cort or Stacey stumbled across the information. Juliana saw Stacey at the funeral in a private conversation with Kendrick Dwyer. Later, at the reception, Stacey asked Juliana if she had pictures of the baby with her.''

Bradshaw played devil's advocate. ''Maybe Dwyer's sleeping with the secretary. He wouldn't be the first man his age to want a beautiful Southern trophy on his arm.''

Hunter agreed that Bradshaw had a point. He told the investigator about Juliana's conversation with Sarah Younge in the ladies' room and voiced his doubts that Ross had been encouraging the controller to take family leave.

''I'm keeping close tabs on David Younge,'' Bradshaw assured him. ''We're looking into his personal finances. Maybe he's got a gambling problem. Ross gave Juliana a corporate check to fund her care of the baby. Younge could have been suspicious about the check and traced it, just like we did, to a bank in Cleveland.''

''I've got operatives tailing the senior executives. Sooner or later someone's going to get sloppy.''

The trooper sighed. No doubt he'd been living on coffee and deli food the last week. ''From your lips to God's ears. I've got brass breathing down my neck and TV cameras up my ass. Any promising tips coming in from the hot line?''

''Nothing that twigs. An FBI expert is going through them first, looking for connections. Did your men dig up anything suspicious on Annette? I'm planning to unite her with her nephew tomorrow, provided her background check is clean.''

''She looks clean as a whistle.'' He heard Bradshaw rifle through a file. ''Not even a parking ticket. We talked to friends of the family and former neighbors. Her parents were middle-class overachievers. The mother put Lexi in beauty contests from the time she was three. Annette was more into books and brought home all kinds of school awards. She had her own used-book stand she'd drag around the neighborhood in a wagon. Not surprising she works as a copy editor and fact checker for a women's magazine. Her boss says she does a good job. Said Annette was very close to her sister and wouldn't tolerate people who asked her nosy questions about her sister's personal life.''

"What about boyfriends who might have figured out that she could inherit a fortune if all Ross's heirs were dead? Juliana mentioned someone named Darren spoke to Annette at the funeral. She wasn't pleased to see him.''

"That must be Darren Black. He's a mathematician at Cornell. Annette was engaged to him a few years ago, but that seems long over. Her phone records show no current contact with him or any other boyfriend in her life. Since someone at the estate may be in on the bombing, she'd probably be safer with you than on the estate.''

Hunter drummed his fingers on his desktop. "That's my take.'' He sketched out his plan for escorting Annette to the island. After he'd hung up, he checked his watch and secured his office, then hurried downstairs.

He couldn't put off lunch any longer.

"UNCLE HUNTER! Wanna play baseball?''

Three-year-old Parrish's chair fell sideways and struck the floor with a crash as he bolted out of it and launched himself like a red-haired missile at his uncle's knees.

Cort, startled by the noise and the shouting, screwed up his face and started to cry, smearing baby cereal and pureed peas into his eyes.

Juliana quickly reached for a facecloth to wipe him off. "It's all right, sweetheart."

"Parrish, I'm sure your uncle appreciates the enthusiasm of your welcome, but we don't jump off chairs as if we're kangaroos," Prudy gently scolded. "Now pick up the chair and say you're sorry to your aunt Juliana for making the baby cry."

Parrish poked his head out from between Hunter's knees, his ears red and his freckled little face set stubbornly. "No."

Juliana suppressed a laugh as Hunter pushed Parrish out from between his legs. He frowned down at him, "You heard, Prudy. Pick up the chair and apologize."

Parrish eyed Juliana distrustfully. He didn't budge. Juliana saw more than a little of Hunter in him. "I think he's objecting to the explanation that I'm his aunt."

Hunter knelt down beside his nephew. "I know this is sudden, Parrish, but this very pretty lady is my wife. And the cute little green guy is my son. He's your cousin. They're going to live with us."

"Not in my room."

"No, not in your room. They'll have their own rooms. Now the thing you have to remember about babies is that they aren't as strong as little boys like you and they can get hurt easily. You have to be very gentle with him until he's big like you and then you guys can do boy stuff together like play baseball."

Parrish's brown eyes popped. "Baseball?" he repeated hopefully, hopping around Hunter's feet.

"Pick up the chair and apologize and we can play baseball when Mackensie comes home."

Parrish managed to right the chair with a little assistance from Hunter, then put his hands behind his back and turned to face Juliana looking angelically contrite. "Sorry, baby,"

"Par-rish," Hunter rumbled in a warning tone.

"I'm sorry I scared the baby, aunt lady."

"Apology accepted." Juliana met Hunter's neutral gaze, her heart splintering into a dozen pieces beneath her smile as he delivered a chaste kiss to her temple. Maybe he wasn't capable of being a genuine husband to her in every sense of the word. But no doubt about it, he'd be a genuine father to Cort.

She could live with that.

WHEN HUNTER KNOCKED at the door adjoining their suites, Juliana yanked the door opened before he could do it again, a finger laid to her lips. "Ssh! Don't knock. Cort just fell asleep. He was exhausted from watching Parrish and Mackensie at dinner. I never realized raising boys takes so much energy."

Hunter frowned down at her, as if he wanted to say something, but then his gaze took in the rest of the room that had once been his mother's.

She clasped his hand and pulled him into the room, sensing his reluctance to cross the threshold. That old wall was coming up. Well, she was going to ignore it. "What do you think? I found the furniture in a guest room on the third floor. I'm afraid I kept Lars and the handyman lugging heavy furniture all afternoon." She beamed at the results. The white furniture and the upholstered pieces had brightened the room as she had hoped. She'd even cut a bouquet of misty pink roses from the garden to fill the Chinese vase.

Hunter hadn't set foot in this room in twenty-four years. Hadn't so much as opened the door since that horrible night when his father had raided his mother's room and thrown her things out into the garden below. Even now, a sense of apprehension pinched his shoulders. Like a distant echo he could hear the smashing of glass and his mother's hysterical pleas for forgiveness. He closed his eyes tightly before an image of his mother hanging by a silk scarf from a pipe in the greenhouse could form fully in his mind. To this day he'd never told anyone that he'd found her first.

He drew a ragged breath and opened his eyes, forced himself to absorb the changes Juliana had wrought to the room. The furniture, the vase of flowers, the wool throw on the sofa, the candles and the pile of books on her bedside table infused the room with her warmth.

There was nothing here to remind him of his mother. The room held Juliana's stamp now.

He felt a loosening in his chest as if he'd finally let go of a breath he'd been holding and gazed down with gratitude into Juliana's expressive eyes. Strands of her silver-blond hair had slipped loose of her French braid and framed her face. Like a rose, he thought, she bloomed more beautifully with each passing day. Became harder and harder to resist.

He tucked a strand of hair behind her ear. "It suits you. This was Brook's furniture once."

"Do you think she'll mind that I've scavenged it?"

"Not at all. She'll be flattered."

"I was disappointed she didn't return for dinner. At least Mackensie was there. Your nephews are quite a handful."

"Worried?"

She laughed, a sound Hunter had rarely associated with this room.

"No, delighted. Thank you for bringing me and Cort into your home." He stiffened as she raised on tiptoes and kissed him lightly on the mouth, her lips warm and enticing and capable of chasing away old demons. "I'm honored."

Then she stepped back and stared up at him, as if defying him to reprimand her. Hunter found that he couldn't. Not when she'd told him she had a soft spot for his hellion nephews.

"I thought you'd want to know that Gord's visit to the hospital went off without a hitch. We've got another one scheduled for tomorrow evening. And we've booked him into a hotel near the hospital for the weekend."

Hope danced in her eyes, casting an irresistible spell on his heart. Making him more determined than ever to keep from hurting her. She'd gone through enough already.

"I'm so glad. Gord's a caring man. It will mean a lot to my father to hear a friend's voice."

Hunter nodded. "I also came to tell you that I'm leaving shortly for New York to pick up Annette and bring her back here for a few days. She'll stay in the Windermere guest house. We should be back by morning. But before I go, there are a few things you should be made aware of, for your safety."

"Of course."

"Follow me." He led her out of the room and up the stairs to his office. "Lars will provide for your personal security, and Del and Ty will remain here to ensure the island is secure. They're staying in the Chelsea guest house. You can reach them by picking up any phone and pushing the Chelsea button." He punched in a code to unlock the door to his office. "Your emergency code to enter my office is 'wife.'"

Hunter grinned when she rolled her eyes.

"I'm so glad you're finally accepting that notion. But why are we here?"

He approached the wall of bookshelves fitted between the bank of TVs and showed her a button concealed beneath the lip of a lower shelf. Juliana pressed the button and the center bookcase silently swung open. In the wall behind, a panel simultaneously slid over to reveal a hidden room.

Her eyes widened in surprise.

"This is a safe room. I had it built into the house in the event someone might come after me and pose a threat to my family or the staff. Only Lars, Brook and Del know it's here. It's stocked with enough food and water to last several days. And, of course, weapons." He pushed another code into a keypad on the wall and a door on the far wall of the safe room slid open. "This is an emergency exit. Use the same code as my office. But don't leave this room unless you feel you must. The exit will let you out behind a row of shrubs on the west side of the house. There are some strategically planted hedges to provide cover all the way to the woods and the boathouse."

"I hope you're not suggesting I jump in a boat and head out onto the river. I know as much about boats as I know about camping, Hunter. I'm not even a very strong swimmer."

He smiled, remembering her idea of camping. He'd make a point of teaching her some basic boating skills. "Live with me long enough and you'll discover I always have a backup plan."

"Tell me something I don't already know," she said, looking less than amused. "What's the backup plan?"

"Head through the woods to the western tip of the island. There's a rocky point. You'll see a sundial and a bench. The sundial faces north. Walk fifty-three paces southwest from the sundial and you'll spot a chip in the rock face that looks like an arrowhead. Just to the right you'll find a slit in the rock face. Slide your fingers in that slit and pull. It's actually a door. The cave is stocked for emergencies. Hide out there until I come for you."

A worried frown crossed her face. "Now I'm wishing

I'd accepted Lars's offer of a tour of the island today—I only went as far as the garden. I'm not even sure which cottage is which.''

He touched the corner of her mouth with his thumb and felt her jump at his touch. ''Relax. I told you this so you'd know what to do—just in case. Windermere has the star-shaped window in its tower. Chelsea has the twin scalloped-shaped windows. If you're out wandering by yourself or with the boys, stay away from the shore. The current is strong. Can you remember all that?''

''Wife, fifty-three paces southwest, look for the arrowhead. Got it.'' Her mahogany eyes searched his face, concern evident in their shadowy depths. ''Hurry back, okay?''

He squeezed her shoulders. ''I'm supposed to be on my honeymoon. I'll be back.''

He regretted the words almost instantly.

The warmth evaporated from her expression and she stepped away from him abruptly. ''Just remember you said that. Not me.''

SHE COULDN'T SLEEP. Memories of last night played along her nerves, making the idea of sleep impossible. The house, without Hunter's reassuring presence, seemed full of strange sounds in the dark. Just after eleven she heard a helicopter land, likely Brook returning from her long day at the head office of Clairmont Hotels. Juliana was tempted to go downstairs to greet her and offer to make a cup of tea for them both, but didn't want to intrude. Brook was probably tired.

Juliana wasn't sure when she drifted off, but a small noise woke her just after 3:00 a.m. She lay in bed listening, trying to determine the source of the sound. Had Hunter already returned with Annette? She hadn't heard the helicopter.

The muffled squeak of a door hinge reached her ears. She heard a definite footfall that sounded as if it were coming from the direction of Hunter's suite. Had he gone into her dressing room via the corridor that connected their suites to check on Cort?

Juliana climbed out of bed, anxious to reassure herself that he was home safely and Annette was comfortably installed in the guest house. "Hunter?" she called softly, padding toward her dressing room where Cort slept.

There was no response.

Thinking he hadn't heard, she called again softly.

She heard a faint audible click like a lock being set.

It was then she realized that the connecting door that led to her dressing room was closed. How odd, she'd left it open before she'd gone to bed so she could hear Cort.

Had Hunter closed it? She turned the knob.

It was locked from the other side.

Her heart started to pound. She rapped her knuckles lightly on the door. "Hunter, open the door please!"

There was still no answer.

An ill feeling stuck between her shoulder blades. She slapped her palm against the door, the fear of waking Cort the least of her concerns. "Hunter, you hear me? Open this door!"

The racket she made roused Cort. At least his plaintive wail was reassuring. But she wasn't going to feel better until she had her baby safely in her arms. And to think her gun was in her purse high on the shelf in her dressing room!

Fear chasing her heels, she ran out of her room and into the hall. Down at the end of the corridor a shadow seemed to move, but her mother's instinct to go to Cort was stronger than the desire to investigate the shadow. The door to Hunter's suite stood open. His bed was undisturbed. He wasn't back yet.

The door to the connecting corridor was also open. Juliana rushed into the corridor, turning on lights. To her relief, Cort was in his crib in the dressing room on his hands and knees, his bum jutting up into the air, cranky sobs shaking his tiny body.

"I'm here, pumpkin. Mommy's here now," she said, shushing him as she lifted him into her arms. She tucked his favorite blanket around him and marched into Hunter's room. Snatching the phone from its cradle, she punched the button to summon Lars.

"Lars, I need help," she said, trying to sound calm. "Someone entered Hunter's room a few minutes ago—and it wasn't Hunter."

Wrapped in Hunter's bathrobe to take the chill off, Juliana was pacing back and forth in Hunter's room, trying to put Cort back to sleep when Lars arrived. He'd pulled on jeans and a T-shirt that revealed muscles layered one atop the other like scoops of hard-packed ice cream. She felt moderately better. He wasn't Hunter, but he'd do in a pinch.

"What happened?"

She calmly explained.

Lars examined the door. "It was probably Parrish."

"Parrish?"

"He has monster nightmares and he probably came to get Hunter to chase them out a window. Happens at least three times a month. This door has never been unlocked and he knows it stays locked and that he's not allowed in there. The boys don't respect many rules, but they do know that Hunter's office, that room and the greenhouse are off limits. Parrish probably saw the door was open and locked it, then got scared when he heard your voice. I'll go check on him."

Juliana breathed a sigh of relief as she massaged Cort's

back. ''Thank heavens that's all it was. Please tell Parrish I'm sorry I scared him.''

She'd crawled into Hunter's bed with Cort snuggled beside her and was dozing off when a discreet tap sounded at the door. ''Come in,'' she called softly.

Lars stuck his head into the room. ''Thought you'd want to know that Parrish did have a nightmare.''

''Thank you, Lars.''

''Sleep well, madam.''

''I will once my husband gets home.'' Juliana kissed Cort's downy head and smiled into the darkness, taking comfort from being in Hunter's room, among his things, in his bed.

She'd go back to her own bed once he returned.

HUNTER'S PLAN TO RETRIEVE Annette was put on hold by a phone call from his operative who'd located the Collingwoods' cook, Nonnie Wilson, at a New Age retreat in a small Quebec village about one hundred kilometers east of Ottawa.

''There's more,'' Edwards told him. ''The sous-chef told me Nonnie has a thriving catering business on the side. Does the odd special job for some of the Collingwoods' friends and associates. The Collingwoods didn't seem to mind as long as it didn't affect her responsibilities to them.''

''Did the sous-chef mention any names?''

''Several. Simon Findlay, David Younge and Sable Holden.''

Hunter didn't need to think twice about making a detour to Canada. He called Investigator Bradshaw and told him he'd personally escort the cook back to New York.

Then he called the operative assigned to Simon Findlay. ''What's Findlay been up to lately?'' he demanded.

"Right now, he's having dinner with his fiancée and another woman at Tavern on the Green. The fiancée's a looker, if you know what I mean. I gotta say, for a man who buried his boss yesterday, Findlay looks very happy. He just ordered a bottle of champagne."

"Who's the other woman?"

"I don't know. But I'm on it, boss."

"Let me know as soon as you find out."

Hunter dropped the cell phone back into his pocket and massaged his temples. So many leads. So many possibilities.

He just had to stay focused.

He'd deal with Nonnie Wilson first.

Full-figured, with an unruly mop of corkscrew curls, Ms. Wilson was not thrilled about having her Ayurvedic massage cut short. She stormed into the Indian-style lodge wearing a thick white bathrobe and leopard-print slippers. "This had better be important," she told him.

Hunter led her to a pair of chairs in a quiet corner and introduced himself as The Guardian.

"I've heard of you," Nonnie said impatiently. "Don't tell me Mr. Collingwood changed his mind about giving me this week off and sent you to find me. Doesn't anyone understand that I need this time to balance myself spiritually, emotionally and mentally? Hands are the servant of the brain."

"Have you watched the news lately, Ms. Wilson?"

She looked at him as if he didn't have a brain. "No. What's the point of going on a retreat to escape the outside world if you bring it with you?"

"I'm sorry to be the bearer of bad news, but Mr. and Mrs. Collingwood died tragically last Friday evening. The funeral was Wednesday."

Nonnie let out a high-pitched squeak that raised the skin

on the back of his neck and brought the clerk at the desk running to inquire if everything was all right. Hunter dispatched the clerk to fetch Nonnie a glass of water.

"The police have been searching for you. They'd like to ask you some questions."

Her face turned pasty. "Me? Why?"

"The Collingwoods were murdered in an explosion. Your unexplained disappearance suggests you may have been involved."

"That's ridiculous. Why would I kill them? Do you have any idea how much money they pay me?"

Probably far more than she was humanly worth, Hunter guessed, judging from her lack of emotion over her employers' deaths. "When did you speak to the Collingwoods last?"

"Thursday morning. Mrs. Collingwood came into the kitchen with a beautiful smile on her face and told me that she and Mr. Collingwood were going on an unexpected trip and I could enjoy a much deserved holiday."

"Did Mrs. Collingwood mention their destination?"

"No."

Her pencil-thin brows drew together with mounting alarm. "Did you say the funeral was Wednesday? That can't be. Was there a reception? Who prepared the food? Why was *I* not contacted?"

"Did you leave a number with someone?"

"Yes. With Goodhew."

"He was injured in the explosion and is still in the hospital in a coma."

Nonnie took this news as if it were another inconvenience to her personally. "I suppose this means I'm unemployed."

"I'm sure a chef of your renown will have offers to choose from. Perhaps Mr. Findlay or Mr. Younge—or even

Ms. Holden—will snap you up? I understand you've catered private functions for them?''

''Only Mr. Findlay's engagement party and a birthday party for Mrs. Younge. She loves my vegetarian torta, and I'm the only chef she trusts implicitly with her special dietary needs.''

''What about Ms. Holden?''

''That woman? *Please!* She had a red aura around her that was too draining. I met with her once to discuss the possibility of a small dinner party— six guests—but I couldn't work under those conditions.''

He didn't trust a word out of Nonnie's mouth. Maybe Investigator Bradshaw would get more out of her. He told her to pack her things. He was taking her back to New York tonight.

''But I'm supposed to have my Shirodara treatment! It has to be left on overnight.''

''I apologize for the inconvenience. But I'm sure you don't want to keep the police or the network entertainment shows waiting. There's been a lot of speculation about your disappearance.''

That perked up her attitude. He gave her a ten-minute head start, then went to the desk to settle her bill. He studied the computer printout of her room charges. Just as he'd hoped, Nonnie had made a brief long-distance phone call the minute she'd returned to her room.

He punched the number into his cell phone.

''Younge residence,'' a tense female voice said.

He hung up thoughtfully. Was Nonnie the mole in the Collingwood staff?

HUNTER WASN'T BACK by morning.

Cort woke her just before seven with a ditty of vowel sounds, his blue eyes joyous as a sunny day. Juliana shared a morning cuddle with him, peppering him with kisses. Oh, she loved him! She couldn't even remotely consider taking care of him as being a sacrifice on her part. He was such a good baby!

She promised herself and she promised Lexi that Cort would have a happy life. Lexi had embraced life, lived it with courage in the face of losing her first child, and Juliana would do no less in her memory. Even if it meant accepting that Hunter would never love her the way she loved him.

Reaching for the phone, she called the hospital and checked on her father. There was still no change in his condition. But she wasn't giving up hope. She asked Hunter's operative to hold the phone to her father's ear and talked to him for a few minutes, telling him that Gord was coming for another visit tonight and would stay nearby over the weekend.

She prayed that even though he was unconscious her father would be reassured by her voice and that it would make a difference in his recovery.

She debated calling Hunter on his cell phone, then decided he would call if he was going to be delayed much longer.

She brushed her teeth and combed her hair. Still wearing Hunter's bathrobe and her slippers, she followed the scent of coffee downstairs.

The household was awake and lively. As she reached the foyer she could hear Mackensie and Parrish making engine noises in the morning room and the clink of dishes in the kitchen.

As she entered the morning room, Brook glanced up from the table where she was reviewing Mackensie's homework. "Good morning." Her expression instantly turned contrite. "Oh, dear. You look as if you could use a cup of coffee. I'm sorry about last night. I was so tired I didn't hear Parrish get up and neither did Prudy.''

"No harm done, really.'' Juliana smiled at Parrish, who'd dropped the slice of honeydew melon he was using as an airplane and was studiously ignoring her. "I didn't know it was you in Hunter's room.''

Parrish looked at his mother, his brow furrowed. "Did the monster scare the aunt lady, too?''

"Yes, that's why I'm wearing your uncle's bathrobe.'' Brook tapped her son on the tip of his freckled nose. "Her name's Juliana.''

"There's no such thing as monsters,'' Mackensie said with the bored arrogant tone of an eight-year-old who knows everything. With his dark good looks and competitive streak, Juliana had no doubt Mackensie would be running the family business one day and making money hand over fist.

Smothering a grin, Juliana slid Cort into his highchair and put a couple of toys on the tray to amuse him. Lars brought in Cort's antibiotics and a bottle, but the baby was too engrossed in Mackensie's and Parrish's antics with their banana-chocolate-chip pancakes to drink it. Juliana decided to start with coffee and work up to an appetite.

Brook handed Mackensie his homework. "It looks great. Finish your breakfast. The chopper leaves in fifteen minutes and you still need to brush your teeth. Prudy will take you in today. I'm taking the morning off to spend with Juliana.''

Juliana met Brook's gaze over the rim of her coffee cup.

"If I'm not imposing,'' Brook added.

"Not at all, I'd love it.'' She had a feeling Hunter was going to be the topic of conversation, which suited her just fine.

Brook finished her coffee. "Let me get Mackensie off to

school. When you're ready, I'll give you a tour of the island.''

After Brook had hustled Mackensie upstairs to brush his teeth, Juliana tried again to give Cort his bottle.

Parrish sat in his chair eating his pancakes, a watchfulness in his brown eyes that reminded her of Hunter. Like his uncle, Parrish didn't trust easily.

Suddenly he hopped off his chair and tugged on the sleeve of her robe. ''Aunt lady, did you make the monster go out the window?''

''What? Yes, sweetheart, I did,'' she assured him, remembering what Lars had told her about Parrish's monsters.

Parrish nodded his head. ''Good. He was a big one. I think he wanted the baby.''

IN THE BASEMENT, the killer's accomplice had found a hiding spot.

He'd ended up in the basement through a door beneath the main staircase and had wandered through the warren of stone tunnels until he'd found an unlocked storage room. Light from a small dirt-streaked window made it possible to make a pallet on the hard-packed gravel behind an old trunk using some drop cloths he'd found folded on a shelf.

He stared up at the brick ceiling.

He'd missed his chance last night. Juliana had almost caught him. But now he knew where the baby slept.

There'd be other chances. He just had to be patient.

Chapter Thirteen

Brook insisted they leave Cort and Parrish in the servants' capable hands for the duration of the tour. "I can't utter a coherent sentence when I'm watching Parrish. He's so curious. Last month he picked up a black rat snake and brought it to show me." She put her hand over her heart. "Thank God they aren't poisonous! I let Lars take care of the snake."

Juliana laughed as Brook shuddered. With every passing moment she liked her sister-in-law more.

They went out the main entrance and down the grand granite staircase Juliana remembered from her arrival. It was a beautiful late September morning. Sunshine spilled around them taking the chill out of the wind from the river, and a herring gull circled overhead. "I wanted to show you the front of the house in the daylight. It faces the main river channel. When my grandparents and my parents entertained, guests would arrive in their yachts at the dock and pass through the stone arch and stroll through the gardens up to the main entrance. There were lanterns in the trees and a string quartet. My mother loved garden parties."

Juliana could imagine it all. "It must have been lovely."

Brook's eyebrows arched. "It was an illusion and like all illusions it finally shattered."

A chill passed over Juliana's spine at her words. Was her marriage to Hunter only an illusion?

Brook hooked her arm through Juliana's, taking her on a stone-walled path around the east wing of the house, past a terrace that was perfect for outdoor entertaining to the formal rose garden and symmetrically arranged flower gardens at the rear of the house. They stopped to admire the wood nymph fountain that was the centerpiece of the rose garden. "Did Hunter tell you about our mother?"

"Some. He mentioned her infidelities and that she committed suicide."

"I'm surprised he told you that much. He keeps all that locked up along with the greenhouse and mother's room."

Juliana's gaze was drawn to the greenhouse at the rear of the garden. Tucked behind two mature trees with vibrant purple foliage, the stone foundation and glass walls of the greenhouse were nearly obscured by vines. "Why does he keep the greenhouse locked?"

"That's where my mother entertained her lovers. It was her favorite place. No one ever questioned the time she spent there—except our butler. He'd convinced himself he was doing my father a favor by revealing mother's indiscretions."

Juliana felt nauseated. The family butler had blackmailed Hunter's father! Little wonder Hunter had questioned her father's generous inheritance from Ross. He'd learned from bitter experience that even the most trusted servant might be capable of betrayal. Did Hunter think she would betray him? Was that why he kept holding her at arm's length?

Brook tucked her short dark hair behind her ears, her voice resigned. "It's also where she chose to die."

"Oh, Brook, I'm so sorry. Hunter didn't tell me that." She squeezed her sister-in-law's arm in sympathy. "My mother died when I was twelve. I don't think missing them is something you ever get over.''

"Yes, well, it was a long time ago. We were children." They retraced their steps to the fountain and took another path between a row of boxwood hedges and flower beds. "At least Hunter's opened the door to mother's room by marrying you."

Juliana found herself blushing. "Yes, it's been opened and will be redecorated very soon."

"Sooner than you think. Lars asked my advice about a decorator and I took the liberty of calling an old friend. She'll be here early this afternoon with paint and fabric samples. It's on me. Consider it a wedding present."

Juliana stopped on the stone path. She and Brook hardly knew each other, but she hugged her tightly. After the last year of isolation in Cleveland, it felt wonderful to have a friend her age. Emotion choked her voice. "Thank you. I don't know what to say."

With a laugh, Brook wiped a tear off her own cheek. "You're going to be good for my brother. Just don't let him push you away."

Don't let him push you away!

Truer words were never spoken, cutting through the miasma of doubts that had been circling in Juliana's mind since she'd made the heartbreaking discovery that Hunter was fighting his desire for her with every ounce of determination in him. Her heart pounded unsteadily against her ribs.

He'd made love to her with such fierce unrestrained emotion that she couldn't let herself consider for an instant that it hadn't been genuine.

He needed her. His kisses and his touches gave him away. But he was so afraid of being betrayed, so afraid of completely trusting her and loving her——of being made a fool of as his father had been—that he would deny that need existed.

And she'd allowed him to keep her at arm's length without a word of protest, just as she'd enabled her father's efforts to push her away after Michael's death. The fear that Hunter would banish her from Cort's life and that she would once again fail her father's expectations of her had pushed her into agreeing to Hunter's terms of their marriage.

Well, no more.

Finding the courage to express her anger to her father had been freeing, had released nineteen years worth of confusion and pain. Even if her father hadn't heard her, she'd put into words the outrage of a six-year-old who didn't understand why her father wouldn't hold her anymore when he read her a story. Or kiss her good-night.

She'd reached rock bottom in that regard. If her father recovered, and she prayed that he would, she was not going to spend one more moment chasing his affection. Nor was she going to spend the rest of her life being denied the physical comforts of her marriage.

Hunter deserved to be loved. To have the old hurts of his past healed.

Even at the risk of being banished from Cort's life, she had to tell him clearly, unequivocally, that she planned to spend their marriage showing him in thousands of different ways that she loved him and flaying his attempts to dismiss her. It was the only way she'd ever find out if their marriage had a chance of becoming real.

A gust of wind rippled through the trees and stirred a clump of hollyhocks, the flowers ruffling like ladies' party dresses at a ball. Lexi had waltzed into Ross's heart and his home never doubting she was his equal. Juliana thought it was high time she asked her own prince to dance.

She hooked her arm back through Brook's. "I love your brother and I have no intention of ever letting him go. Now, show me the guest cottages. Hunter is bringing a guest back with him today. He seems to be a bit behind schedule, though."

They took a wide stone path that wound into a woods dense with pine and birch. "Yes, he warned me there would be extra security for a while, but of course, I don't know why. I'm taking the boys to New York for the weekend to see their fathers. All the live-in staff but Lars are off for the weekend. They leave at three and return Monday morning at seven."

As they rounded a bend in the path a charming stone cottage with a slate roof came into view. Twin decorative stained-glass windows shaped as scallops bordered the carved oak door. A pot of pink geraniums stood on the front steps.

"This one's the Chelsea," Brook said. "Windermere is farther down this path. The cottages are fully stocked and self-sufficient and the guests look after themselves. Hunter doesn't even allow staff in to clean until after the guests have departed, but I understand the reasons for his caution. He's protecting his clients as well as his identity.

"Many of the Clairmont's guests are repeat customers who seek out our hotels because of the extraordinary level of security we can provide. A guest at the Clairmont doesn't worry about the paparazzi or the crust of their breakfast toast being auctioned off on the Internet."

"Then you won't think I'm being paranoid if I ask you to show me where the cave is? Hunter gave me directions but I'd feel better if I knew exactly where it is."

"You're not being paranoid. You're being smart. Hunter's occupation isn't without risk. But then, life is one risk after another. The trick to surviving is being knowledgeable and prepared. I'll show you Windermere, then we'll head over to Rocky Point. It's on the other side of the island.''

''Good, and on the way, you can tell me about your ex-husbands. All three of them.''

Brook rolled her eyes. ''That's a short story. Mackensie's father was the quintessential handsome, older man. I married him to escape my overbearing father only to discover that Howard didn't respect my needs any more than my father did. The second husband loved me for my money—which Hunter wouldn't let him have. And the third one, Parrish's father, well, let's just say I threw away the best thing that ever happened to me. With the help of a good therapist, I'm trying to move on with my life.''

''So, you're still in love with him?''

''Yes.'' One word and it was said with the confidence of a determined woman. Brook flushed becomingly. ''But you don't know Rand. There's little chance he'll ever forgive me for hurting him. Still, he did invite me to stay and have dinner with him on Friday when I drop off Parrish. That's a first.''

''Only dinner?''

''Yes, only dinner! But it may give us a chance to talk.'' A wistful smile touched her face. ''I'm hoping he's ready to listen.''

Juliana nodded knowingly. ''Pack some lingerie just in case. A woman has to be prepared to take risks.''

AFTER DELIVERING NONNIE into the hands of the state police and conferring with Investigator Bradshaw about the Younges' possible involvement in the murder, Hunter raced to the Collingwood estate with a security team and a state trooper.

Gord Nevins and Stacey Kerr appeared shaken by his

predawn arrival. The papery texture of their skin and the dark shadows beneath their eyes showed the strain they were living under.

"Is Goodhew…?" The household manager's question trailed off incomplete.

Hunter quickly reassured them that Goodhew was holding his own, but something had arisen in the investigation and the police felt it prudent Annette be moved to an undisclosed location.

Stacey glanced uncertainly at the state trooper and smoothed a hand over her hair. "Shall I wake her?"

"Not just yet. There were a couple of other matters we thought you could help us with. I understand that David and Sarah Younge sent a gift basket to Goodhew."

"Yes," Gord acknowledged. "We put it in his quarters, since we didn't know where to send it. I thought I might bring one of the books on tape with me for the weekend visit."

"Trooper Jones would like to examine the basket. We'd also like to know if you have a record of who delivered it?"

"I believe so. If Trooper Jones will follow me, please."

Hunter turned to Ms. Kerr as the trooper and the household manager left the room. "We'd also like a list of the floral deliveries made to the house and the funeral. Did you keep a record of which deliveries came from which shop?"

"Certainly. Cards occasionally get switched and this way we can double-check if there's any doubt before a thank-you card is sent out. The list is in my office. It'll take a few minutes for the photocopier to warm up."

"Make two copies while you're at it."

Hunter followed her through the house to the secretary's office where a mountain of sympathy cards piled high on a table, waited to be filed into boxes lined up on two library tables.

"What's this all about?" she asked as she switched on the photocopy machine.

"That's confidential, I'm afraid."

She flushed. "But the police are getting closer to finding out who did this?"

"Who do you think did it, Ms. Kerr? You knew the Collingwoods. Lexi probably spoke more openly to you than anyone else in the household."

She blinked at him, her eyes suddenly guarded. "I don't know. I can't imagine anyone wanting to hurt them—Lexi especially. She was such a gracious lady."

"Not even Kendrick Dwyer? I understand Ross was pushing him to retire."

"Is that fact or speculation?"

Hunter folded his arms across his chest. "You tell me. You're the one sleeping with him."

She pressed her lips together and tapped a manicured fingernail on top of her desk. "How did you know?"

"Educated guess."

"It was very brief. He's sicker than he's letting on. And no matter what you might think of me, I have no desire to be a rich widow."

"What were you arguing about at the funeral?"

"He wanted to make sure I didn't tell the police about our involvement. He thought it would jeopardize the company's stability if it came out. He's going to try to keep his illness from becoming public as long as possible, then he's going to throw his support behind the person he felt Ross would have handpicked to succeed him."

"And who would that be?"

Stacey selected a folder from her desk and moved to the photocopier. "David Younge."

HUNTER SENT THE TROOPER back to Investigator Bradshaw with a copy of the floral delivery list and the gift basket, hoping that David or Sarah Younge's fingerprints could be lifted off the contents and compared to the unidentified prints found on Juliana's purse. Or, that the Younges had made a stupid mistake and ordered the flowers which had concealed the bomb from the same florist who'd prepared their sympathy arrangement for the Collingwoods' funeral.

This could be the lead he'd been hoping for, though he still felt as if a piece of the puzzle was just beyond his grasp.

Annette's gratification at being taken to see Cort was obvious. As soon as they'd stepped outside the house, Hunter had pulled her aside and informed her they were going to see Cort.

"It's about time! Where is he? Who has him?"

"All your questions will be answered once we safely arrive at our destination," he assured her. "For now, all you have to do is sit tight and act as if you're going away for a few days."

Annette hugged him. "I can do that."

They stopped to refuel the chopper and to eat breakfast. Annette, her thoughts obviously far away, pushed her scrambled eggs around on her plate. Her eyes held a disturbing emptiness that made him want to reassure her that she would always have a place in Cort's life. But now wasn't the time.

As they returned to the chopper, Hunter took the seat on the bench beside her and patted her hand. "It won't be long now."

Her brief smile was taut with nerves. "It feels like I've been waiting forever."

"WHY CAN'T I COME UP to the house now to see him?" Annette demanded when Hunter showed her to Windermere cottage and told her he'd be returning shortly with her nephew.

"Security reasons. With footage of the funeral all over the media, I don't want to take the chance that one of the servants might recognize you. I know you're anxious. Bear with me."

Hunter felt his heart give pause as he came around the edge of the house and saw Juliana and Brook seated on the terrace, their heads close together, enjoying the late-morning sunshine and a cup of tea. Cort rocked in a baby swing, a colored block grasped in each tiny hand, while Parrish swiped at plastic golf balls on the lawn with a toy club. He heard Juliana laugh and a smile began deep inside him and pushed itself to the surface.

Juliana lifted her silver-blond head, the sun bathing her profile with a gilt halo. Hunter felt himself stumble into a void of confusion and desire when she turned her head and saw him, her face softening into a welcoming smile.

He ceased being able to function, his chest tightening with denial as she leaped to her feet and came to greet him. She was wearing jeans this morning and a cream cable-knit sweater.

"There you are, my prince!"

Surprise and wariness at her teasing tone spilled through him as she stroked his cheek then slipped her hand behind his neck and nudged his head down for a kiss. The determined glint in her eyes warned him something was different about her a split second before she kissed him. His hands tightened reflexively around her waist, pulling her lovely jeans-clad body against him as her tongue parted his lips in the sweetest of invasions.

He instantly forgot about Brook and Parrish as his right hand slid up her spine and twined in her loose hair. Slanting his mouth over hers, he countered her sweet invasion with one of his own, taking control of the kiss.

He'd been thinking about kissing her like this ever since he'd made love to her. Once ignited, desire long denied held him hostage until something hit him in the leg and brought him back to the edge of reason. He reluctantly tore his mouth from Juliana's and looked down at one of Parrish's golf balls.

Parrish was eyeing him intently, his hands on his bony hips. "Sorry. I said 'fore' like I was supposed to, didn't I, Mommy?"

"You certainly did," Brook said with a chuckle, "but I don't think Hunter heard you. I think we need to excuse ourselves and leave these two newlyweds alone."

"Aw, do I have to 'xcuse myself? I wanna play golf with Uncle Hunter."

Hunter gave Juliana one last hard kiss on her mouth as if to remind himself where they left off and hunched down beside his nephew. "We'll have to play another time. I've been working all night and I've got more work to do."

Brook took her son's hand. "Come on, kiddo. We need to pack your bag for your visit to Daddy's tonight."

Hunter ruffled his nephew's hair. "Have fun at your dad's. I'll see you Sunday night."

Juliana pushed back the feeling of shyness as Brook and Parrish walked away. She and Hunter had made love, there was no reason to be shy with him. Resting her head against his chest, she slipped her fingers inside his jacket to warm them. "I was getting worried. You were gone so long. Is everything okay? Is Annette with you?"

He laughed, the sound rumbling against her ear. "That's a lot of questions." His arm looped around her, his fingers lightly stroking her hair. She sighed contentedly. She hadn't exactly told him she loved him and wanted to renegotiate the terms of their agreement, but this was a promising start.

"I've got a lot to tell you, but there's someone in Windermere who's waiting anxiously to see Cort. Let's pick him up as if we're going for a stroll. We can talk on the way over."

Juliana extracted herself from the warmth of his embrace, her heart paining her as she took a closer look at him. Even with a day's worth of stubble shadowing his jaw and weary lines bracketing his eyes and mouth, he was the sexiest man she'd ever seen.

Her pulse skipped in anticipation of spending a lifetime comforting him. Sharing his bed. Showing him in numerous ways that she loved him. She caressed his shoulder as he scooped Cort up out of the swing. "Are you making headway in the investigation?"

He swung around with Cort in his arms, his eyes steely with determination. "Yes, finally. We located Nonnie Wilson last night at a New Age retreat in Quebec. I know you don't want to hear this, but she may be the mole in the Collingwood household."

Juliana listened with growing skepticism to his account of his conversation with the Collingwoods' cook. "Admittedly Nonnie's eccentric and narcissistic, but she's not exactly Mata Hari. So what if Simon Findlay, the Younges and Sable Holden approached her about catering a private function? That's not so unusual. She's an exceptional chef."

Hunter's left brow lifted to a cynical angle. "So why did she call the Younges right after I interviewed her?"

"Probably because she wants to work for them. Or she feels some sort of loyalty toward them and warned them you were asking questions about them. You know, just because your family butler betrayed your family doesn't mean that someone on the Collingwoods' staff betrayed Ross and Lexi.''

Every angle in Hunter's face hardened. ''Who told you that?''

''Your sister.''

His stride lengthened. ''She talks too much.''

''She thought I should know.'' Juliana touched his arm. Felt the tight bunch of muscles reacting to her touch. ''I'm glad she told me. It explained a few things.''

He stopped abruptly and swiveled toward her. ''What things?''

Cort's eyes grew round as if he sensed the tension between them. ''Ba-da?''

Juliana held her ground and calmly faced him. ''Like why you wanted a marriage free of emotional and physical entanglements. And why you don't trust me.''

''You think I don't trust you?''

''You can hardly say the word without flinching. I saw it in your face in your bedroom Wednesday night. And in your office the next morning.''

''I don't think this is the right time for this conversation,'' he ground out.

''There'll never be a right time for this conversation, Hunter. My father never let me talk about Michael because it was too painful for him. He never touched me, never hugged me after my brother died. I have been through too much with my father to suffer that kind of treatment from my husband. This may not have started out as a real marriage, but I promised to love and honor you and I'm giving you notice that I intend to keep that promise.''

''You're what?''

''You heard me. I love you! And not because of the zeroes in your bank account or that very handsome face of yours. I love you because you have everything and you know that none of that matters as much as protecting and caring for the people you love. So get used to the idea of me loving you.''

It was neither ladylike, nor romantic and it wasn't quite how she'd planned to share her feelings, but the words had flown out of her mouth and Juliana couldn't take them back. Wouldn't take them back. Heart pounding, she turned and stomped down the path toward Windermere.

THUNDERSTRUCK, HUNTER STARED after her as Cort started to cry.

Had Juliana just told him she loved him?

Funny, he didn't remember anything about Cinderella shouting at her Prince Charming.

But then, Hunter admitted to himself, he hadn't been the least bit charming. He was not even calm. His knees, in fact, were unsteady. She'd poured her heart out to him and he'd stood there like a Neanderthal trying to make sense of a foreign language, wanting to rage that he'd never asked her to love him.

He didn't want her to love him.

And furthermore, he absolutely did not want to be standing here watching her walk away from him with this sick feeling of dread in his stomach.

Should he go after her? His heels dug into the path.

And tell her—what?

That he needed her. Oh, God, he needed her! Making love to her the other night had been his salvation and his downfall.

She loved him.

Hunter let the enormity of that thought sink in beneath the din of the baby's cries as Cort butted his head into his shoulder, seeking comfort. Hunter rubbed his little back. ''It's all right. Don't cry. Mommy's just a little upset.''

The thought that he was hurting Juliana sliced his heart into ribbons. She was so beautiful. So good. She'd given up so much for Cort. How could he deny her the affection she so rightly deserved—the affection he craved to give her?

He strode down the path after her, rounded a bend and found her seated on a bench, her back to him, looking out at the river.

He stopped behind her and touched her cheek, feeling the damp path of her tears on his palm. Helpless to know how to prevent those tears. "Juliana, I don't pretend to know anything about love. The whole institution of marriage terrifies the hell out of me. But as God is my witness, kissing you is no pretense. And staying out of your bed is the hardest thing I've ever had to do. I don't want to hurt you."

She clasped his hand and pulled it to her lips, sealing her words with a kiss. "I know."

She did? Was he that transparent?

Hunter tugged on her hand, urging her off the bench. The hope and the love welling in her eyes as she faced him humbled him. He wasn't worthy of her. But for Juliana, for Cort, he would try. He erased the tears from her cheek with his thumb, then leaned down and kissed her damp lips. Peace settled in his stomach. "Annette's waiting. Join me for a shower later?"

Her smile was more radiant than a sunrise as she took Cort from his arms. "If you'll be naked, I'll be there."

"YOU'RE WHAT?"

"I'm Cort's legal guardian," Hunter explained gently as Juliana placed the baby in Annette's waiting arms. "Ross and I were friends for years."

"Umpf!" Annette said, momentarily distracted by the

squirming bundle of little boy. "He's so big. And beautiful! He's blond like Ross. I imagined he'd be darker like Lexi."

Juliana stood back and looked from aunt to nephew. "I think he has your nose."

"I have my father's nose."

Frowning up at this new stranger, Cort tentatively explored his aunt's face with his tiny fingers.

Juliana beamed. "See, he's warming up to you. He's a little cranky. It's almost time for his nap."

Cort gave a sharp high-pitched squeal, making Annette laugh. "I can't imagine why anyone would want to hurt this little guy. Has he been staying here since…?" Her sentence trailed off as if she couldn't bring herself to mention the bombing.

Hunter exchanged a glance with Juliana. "Actually Juliana and I were married last Tuesday. I've brought them here as my wife and son. Given the circumstances of your sister and her husband's deaths, I thought it necessary to protect their son's identity until he's old enough to receive his inheritance."

"You married *her* just like that?"

Hunter ignored her rudeness. "Juliana's been caring for Cort since birth. He's better off with two parents than one."

Annette appeared to think that over for a moment. "And how do I fit into this cozy little family scenario? He's my nephew."

Hunter sat down on the ottoman in front of her. "How about as a close friend of my wife who visits frequently on weekends and holidays?"

"Really?"

Juliana squeezed Annette's shoulder. "Of course. You're Cort's family. He needs you. And you need him. You can stay as long as you like, so get settled and make yourself comfortable. You've got lots of privacy here and we're going to do everything we can to make this difficult time easier for you. After the servants leave at three, you're welcome to come up to the house and spend more time with the baby—and join us for dinner.''

''That sounds wonderful. Thank you.'' Her green gaze flicked to Hunter. ''Do the police have any suspects?''

''They have some promising leads, but nothing conclusive,'' he admitted. ''They reached a dead end with the pager and haven't located the florist that had prepared the flower order. And we haven't ruled out a connection between Riana's kidnapping and the bombing. I'm not giving up on finding Riana.''

Annette captured Cort's tiny wrist with her fingers, her expression pensive. ''I still think Sable Holden's behind this. Only a jealous woman would kill with flowers.''

HUNTER STEPPED INTO the shower, his heart pounding and anxiety making his muscles feel leaden. They'd returned to the house and had lunch with Brook and Parrish. Then Juliana had whisked Cort upstairs for his afternoon nap. She'd join him in a minute.

He was iron-hard with wanting her and naked in more ways than one.

He worked soap over his body. Being this vulnerable didn't fit comfortably on his skin. The door to the bathroom opened.

''Hunter?'' Juliana's voice was soft and melodious.

He had to swallow hard to make his throat work. ''In here.''

The curtain around the old-fashioned bathtub slid open and Juliana stood within arm's reach, naked, her glorious hair spilling over her shoulders. Her eyes admiring and wanting.

Hunter offered her his hand, a tremor shuddering through

him as she delicately placed her slim hand in his and stepped over the wall of the bathtub.

The spray from the shower sent beads of water trickling over the milky globes of her breast. "You are so beautiful, I'm afraid to touch you. Afraid you'll disappear if I do."

She smiled up at him, a siren's smile. "Then I'll touch you first. Prove to you I'm real."

Her fingers cupped him, stroked him. Hunter groaned his pleasure. "You're very bold, Cinderella."

She pressed a kiss to his collarbone. His skin lit on fire. "I know what I want. I want you." She kissed his chest, increasing the intensity of the heat searing him with very clever flicks of her tongue.

Her mouth moved lower still to his abdomen, tracing circles of fire around his navel, inciting his hips to rock with tingles of heat. And then she went down on her knees between his thighs and ran her tongue lightly over the tip of him and Hunter couldn't restrain himself from touching her any longer. His fingers wove like ribbons into her hair as she took him deeply into her mouth.

His control exploded, emotions ripping through him like bolts of lightning. It was too much and not enough. And the only way he knew to tell her what she was doing to him was to lift her from him and kiss her, his tongue plunging into her mouth as his hands found home on her water-slick breasts. He sat her on the rim of the tub, hot water pelting his back as he eased her legs apart. She opened to him with the shy beauty of a rare orchid, each part so delicate and perfectly formed.

He stroked her breasts reverently, rolling the swollen tips between his fingers. Then sucked each tip until Juliana made that lovely keening noise in the back of her throat.

His hunger to know this incredible woman was unstoppable. He kissed the soft skin of her belly and the insides of her petal-soft thighs and very, very gently tasted her sweetest offering. Not for a moment did he ever want her to doubt his desire to touch her. Pleasure her. With his tongue and his fingers he brought her to a sharp gripping climax, then rose and lifted her to his hips. Her legs locked around his.

Water surrounded them in a fine mist. His gaze firmly holding hers, he lowered her wet silken body onto him, inch by inch.

"I love you," she said clearly. Irrevocably.

Warmth invaded his heart, piercing his doubts, filling him until he thought he would burst. Was this overwhelming feeling love? Would it last a lifetime like the love Ross had for Lexi? He gazed at Juliana's eyes, molten with gold and red flecks, her desire-swollen mouth, yearning to give her back even a little of what she'd given him—trust, faith, love.

He swallowed hard and prepared to open himself completely for the first time in his life.

"Cinderella…"

His cell phone rang.

Chapter Fourteen

Juliana shuddered as Hunter climbed out of the tub. Her nerves clamored in protest from the sudden severing of her body from his.

His voice sounded strained as he answered the phone. "Bradshaw. What's going on?"

Juliana turned off the shower and reached for a towel. Whatever the BCI investigator wanted, it was obviously important. Hunter's muscled body had gone perfectly still, then in a fluid motion he grabbed his clean clothes and a towel.

"I'll be there in an hour and fifteen minutes tops," he said curtly and hung up.

"What was that all about?" she demanded, wrapping the towel around her.

"Bradshaw just finished interviewing the principal at the private school the Younges' oldest son attends. David Jr. was suspended for playing a prank on a science teacher. He left a package on his desk containing what appeared to be sticks of dynamite and a note that said, 'Bang.' The boy came forward and confessed. His parents donated a huge sum of money to the school and the principal let him off with a two-week suspension."

Juliana's face drained of color. "Do you think David Jr. orchestrated the bombing?"

"I don't know. According to Bradshaw, the boy's seventeen. He's not a child."

"But how would he have known about Cort?"

"Maybe he overheard his parents talking about it. Sarah has five children, she might have guessed Lexi was pregnant before Lexi knew herself. And David did have access to the Collingwood Corporation's bank accounts. Bradshaw traced the check Ross gave you to a bank in Cleveland. Younge may have, too."

Hunter jammed his legs into his briefs and his slacks. Then pulled on a shirt. "Bradshaw's waiting for me. He's bringing the Younges in for questioning. I'll call you when I have news."

He was almost out the door when he stopped suddenly and turned back to look at her, a grin tugging at his mouth and heat smoking his eyes. "I'm sorry about the interruption. I promise we'll finish what we started when I return."

It wasn't exactly a declaration of his feelings, but it would do for now. She dropped her towel to the floor and smiled sweetly. "Just so you don't forget where you left off."

SINCE THE CALL that had awakened him earlier—informing him that Annette was on the island and altering his instructions—he had been busy conducting reconnaissance. Learning the layout of the island, taking note of the two tough-ass guards who discreetly patrolled the grounds and conducting a head count.

From his vantage point in the upstairs room of the old greenhouse, he watched Hunter Sinclair depart in a helicopter. Then a boat arrived at the dock. A woman and a man carrying heavy leather cases walked up to the house.

He worried they were staying the night, but Juliana and the baby escorted them down to their boat two hours later.

Just before three, Brook Sinclair, her youngest son and seven other people plus the pilot crowded into the second helicopter.

He made a careful count on the dusty windowpane. That left Juliana, the butler, the two bodyguards and the baby.

A petite figure moved into the garden below, casting nervous looks over her shoulder. Another woman.

Annette.

She and Juliana and the baby would be alone in the house with the butler.

Now those were the kind of odds he liked. But first, he'd eliminate the guards.

Helping himself to a heavy rabbit figurine from a bed in the greenhouse he slipped through the woods. Finding a branch of a tree that jutted out over the path, he climbed the tree and waited.

It wasn't long before the guard passed.

The figurine hit him in the head dead center.

With a low grunt, the guard dropped to his knees, then fell face forward to the ground.

Smiling, he jumped out of the tree to the path below and rolled the guard over to check his pulse. There wasn't one.

Too bad, he was a good-looking kid—except for that nasty indentation in his head.

"I'm telling you, I didn't make any bomb. And I didn't hire anyone. My parents were friends with the Collingwoods. Why won't you believe me?"

Through the one-way observation window Hunter eyed the scrawny teen with the peach fuzz dangling from his knobby chin. He had a feeling Investigator Bradshaw was barking up the wrong tree. He saw an indulged kid who'd pushed a joke with a teacher too far, not a cold-blooded killer.

His cell phone rang and Hunter snapped it open.

"It's Edwards. Remember the woman who joined Findlay and his fiancée last night? I've spent the morning tailing her. Turns out she's the fiancée's kid sister. She works as a clerk in a law firm."

"Which firm?"

"McGuire, Bainbridge and Willoughby."

Hunter swore. Tom McGuire was Ross's lawyer. He was one of the few people who knew of Cort's existence. Hunter rapped sharply on the window to attract Bradshaw's attention.

The investigator came out of the interview room a few seconds later.

"What's up?"

Hunter told him. He snagged the list of florists that Stacey Kerr had given him from his jacket pocket. "Have you had anyone check out Findlay's florist yet?"

"Someone is working their way through the list."

"Let's beat them to it."

THE FLORIST ON THE upper west side was a diminutive powerhouse of a woman in a green smock. She climbed onto a raised platform behind the counter and asked if she could help them.

Hunter gave the woman an encouraging smile as Investigator Bradshaw showed her his badge. "We'd like to ask you about a couple of flower orders."

She slipped on the pair of reading glasses that dangled from a silver chain around her neck and examined the state trooper's ID. "It's a crime to buy flowers now? Geesh!"

Hunter let Bradshaw run the show.

"Do you remember a Simon Findlay ordering a funereal

arrangement to be delivered to St. Patrick's on Wednesday?''

''Sure, I remember. I might be old, but I don't have dementia. That was for the Collingwood funeral. Sad, a young couple like that. It wasn't Mr. Findlay who ordered the flowers. It was his fiancée. Pretty girl, but not too bright upstairs. She came in here asking for a sincere and expensive arrangement—the larger the better. Imagine that? Size matters, even in flowers. I told her I could do her something 'very sincere' for $425.00 plus delivery. She left smiling.'' The woman held her liver-spotted wrists out to the BCI investigator. ''For that you're going to arrest me?''

Hunter struggled to hide a grin.

Investigator Bradshaw cleared his throat. ''No, but we would like to know whether Findlay or his fiancée ordered any flowers the week before. It would have been three large arrangements.''

''Doesn't ring any bells.'' She thumbed through a stack of yellow invoices stuck on a metal pick.

Hunter leaned on the counter. ''It was probably a pick-up order for Thursday morning. One of the arrangements was in a white wicker basket. It might have been under the name of Goodhew.''

''Sorry, fellas. Nothin' under Findlay or Goodhew. The only thing I got is a pick-up order for three arrangements on Wednesday night. One was in a basket but that was a special order for a wedding anniversary. The customer came in the beginning of the month and placed the order.''

''What's the name?'' Bradshaw asked.

''Robert Lance.''

Hunter exchanged a now-we're-getting-somewhere glance with the investigator. The pager used to detonate the bomb had been purchased with Robert Lance's stolen ID.

''You got an address or a phone number?''

"No. He paid cash when he ordered it. Said he didn't want to leave a number because he didn't want to take the chance of someone calling from the shop and ruining the surprise."

"Can you describe him?" Investigator Bradshaw asked.

"Geesh! I saw the man twice. He was an ordinary Joe. Nothing special. Bit of a receding hairline."

"Hair color?"

"Dark, I think."

"Eye color?"

"I'm an old lady. Who notices these things?"

Hunter frowned. "What about the order itself? What was so special about it?"

"Now *that* I remember. He had a picture from their wedding and wanted me to reproduce the arrangement with the basket as closely as possible. Then he asked me to do two other similar arrangements in large vases."

"Do you still have the picture?" Bradshaw asked.

"It's in the back. You want to see it?"

"Definitely. We'll come with you."

They followed the florist through a beaded curtain into the cluttered back room. A bulletin board mounted on the wall near a large worktable had a jumble of orders and photographs pinned to it. The florist indicated a photo with a gnarled finger.

Hunter leaned closer to examine it. The photograph had been cut down with scissors to the size of the basket. It was impossible to tell where it had been taken, though there was a hint of a blue gauzy background visible. But he knew Juliana would know whether that specific arrangement had been used in Ross and Lexi's wedding.

Investigator Bradshaw used a pencil to lift up the photo and look on the back. "There's no writing or identifying marks, Ma'am," he said, straightening. "You and the picture are going to have to come with us. We need to take your fingerprints.''

THE SUN WAS SINKING into the horizon when Hunter called. Juliana and Annette were appreciating the spectacular show of the sunset with a glass of wine when Lars came into the drawing room with the portable phone and announced Juliana had a call.

She set down her glass of wine on the coffee table and took the butler's cell phone from him. ''Excuse me, Annette.''

Hunter's voice warmed her ear and sent shivers over her skin. ''Sorry to disturb you.''

''I'm not sorry.'' She glanced at Annette who'd leaned over to talk to the baby. Cort lay on his back beneath an activity set, batting his hands and feet at the colorful toys dangling just within his reach.

''There's been a new development I thought you could help with.'' He described the basket arrangement the florist had made. ''Does it sound like something from Ross and Lexi's wedding?''

''Your description leaves something to be desired,'' she said tactfully. She got up and walked out into the hall.

''Here, talk to the florist yourself.''

''Who am I talking to?'' She heard a woman ask Hunter.

''My wife. Describe the flowers.''

''Geesh,'' the florist said into the phone. ''Is your husband always this bossy?''

Juliana smothered a chuckle. ''I'm afraid so.''

''Well, at least he's a handsome devil. Listen, honey, here's what I did. First, I started with an old-fashioned Victorian wicker basket. Then I added…''

Juliana's heart stilled at the florist's description.

It matched the basket of flowers Ross had specially requested for the room at the estate where Lexi had dressed for their wedding. Annette had been right. That was something a jealous, angry woman would do. A woman who'd lost her family's company and wanted Ross to suffer personally, as well. Juliana just prayed that Sable Holden hadn't been sick enough to kill Riana. "Please put my husband back on the phone."

"Is everything all right?" Annette asked when Juliana returned to the living room a few minutes later.

"Oh, yes. But Hunter's going to be delayed."

"TY, YOU IN HERE?"

Del checked the cottage, wondering if Ty was heating himself up a TV dinner or was in the latrine. Del hadn't seen him in over an hour and his cell phone appeared to be out of service. Ty had probably accidentally turned it off.

Del didn't like it.

He'd trace the perimeter of the island one more time in case he'd somehow missed Ty, then check up at the house. Maybe Ty had bummed dinner off Lars.

Dusk was falling, enveloping the woods in shadows as he patrolled the back side of the island. A slight sound warned him a split second before something struck him from out of nowhere. Excruciating pain ricocheted through his left shoulder, making him stumble. Instinctively, he reached for his gun with his right hand to defend himself. But before he could draw his weapon, he was tackled. Del rolled with his assailant, going for his jugular with his right hand. His left arm was completely useless.

His assailant was strong. Skilled. Del saw the glint of the blade, managed to kick it from the man's hand. A booted foot hit him in the ribs, cracking bones. Del grabbed the foot and twisted, pulling the bastard to the ground. Trying to break his ankle.

Too late, Del saw the blade flash again. But this time he was helpless to stop it.

AT HALF PAST SEVEN, Cort rubbed his tired eyes and let it be known that he'd had enough for one day.

Juliana rocked him in her arms. "I'm sorry, Annette. It's his bedtime. Would you like to help me bathe him and get him settled? We could talk or watch a movie afterward."

Annette uncurled herself from her niche in the sofa and stifled a yawn. "Actually I wouldn't mind a long bath and a good night's sleep myself. I haven't slept much in the last week. And now that I've seen the baby, I think I'll be able to."

Juliana gave her a one-armed hug. "Good night, then. If you feel up to company in the morning, call me. Cort's usually up before seven."

"All right, I will."

She and Cort walked with Annette to the door.

A haunting sadness filled Lexi's sister's eyes as she touched the baby's head. "Do you think Lexi regretted marrying Ross? She thought it would bring her happiness, but mostly it brought her pain."

"I can't speak for her. But I do know that the love they had for each other lives on in their children."

"I'll hold on to that thought." With a wave, Annette descended the granite steps and disappeared into the night.

Juliana went upstairs to bathe Cort, dwelling on what Annette had said. Had that been Sable's plan—to make Ross and Lexi regret their marriage?

ONCE THE STATE POLICE fingerprint expert had taken the florist's fingerprints and removed several latent fingerprints from the photograph, he promised to contact them as soon as he had any results. In the meantime, Hunter and Investigator Bradshaw headed to Long Island with the photograph in an evidence bag. Hunter wanted to look through the photo album of Ross and Lexi's wedding.

Stacey Kerr brought them the album and left them to work in private in Ross's study. The photos the photographer had taken of the bride getting dressed were near the beginning of the album.

Investigator Bradshaw tapped a photo of Lexi and her mother beside a wicker basket of flowers. "There's the basket. This is the same photo." He laid the cut-out basket on top of the photo.

It was a perfect fit.

"Look at the truth it tells," Bradshaw said softly.

Hunter swore as he studied the photo of Lexi and her mother. Mrs. York wore an expression of pride and joy as she adjusted her radiant daughter's tiara. Lexi looked like a princess. The love between mother and daughter was like a glass shell, enclosing them, excluding others. Annette was not included in the picture. Hunter had a stomach-clenching feeling there was some symbolism in her absence.

He thought of Juliana and her conviction that her father loved her brother best. Was that how Annette had felt about her sister? That Lexi was the favored child? Hunter checked the other pictures in the album. He found one of Annette and Lexi. But Annette's smile was forced as if she wished she were anywhere else but at her sister's wedding.

Hunter vaguely remembered Juliana repeating a comment Annette had made the day of the funeral about postponing her wedding to Darren Black because of Lexi's pregnancy. It hadn't registered then, but it registered now.

Sable Holden hadn't killed Ross and Lexi out of revenge.

Annette had. And she'd been misdirecting the investigation by casting suspicion on everyone but herself.

Hunter reached for his cell phone, fear dwelling in his heart. Annette was on FairIsle. He had to warn Lars and Juliana.

"WHAT'S KEEPING LARS with your bottle?" Juliana asked Cort, smoothing his furrowed brow with her fingers. "I know you're tired, my grumpy pumpkin. Here, I'll put you down in your crib with your blankie and be back in a few minutes with your bottle."

Cort started to fuss the moment she laid him down. "It's all right," she murmured to soothe his cries. "I'll be right back. Lars probably got tied up with something."

Juliana went out into the hallway and leaned over the banister, looking for the butler. "Lars?"

There was no answer from downstairs. The house was silent. Had he gone outside for a minute? Or taken a phone call?

She hurried down to the kitchen. Cort was so tired. If she didn't get his bottle right away, he'd probably fall asleep then wake up in a few hours hungry as a bear.

Lars wasn't in the kitchen. The overhead lights had been turned off, but the under-cabinet lights glowed softly on the granite countertops. Juliana grabbed a bottle from the refrigerator and popped it in the microwave to warm.

As she stepped back from the microwave, she slipped on a sticky substance on the floor. They must have spilled some red wine earlier. She crossed to the sink to grab a dish cloth, leaving a tacky trail. She swiped at the sole of her shoe, startled to see the stain was a vibrant red. Like blood.

Had Lars broken a wineglass and cut himself?

Juliana switched on the overhead lights. The blood was

more visible now on the black-and-white tiled floor. Alarm creeping through her, she followed the trail to the door of the butler's pantry and pushed the door open.

A scream rose in her throat.

Lars lay on the floor unconscious and bleeding. He'd been stabbed several times.

"OH, GOD. LARS?"

Juliana felt in his pockets for his cell phone, panic spiraling through her. This wasn't happening. It couldn't be happening. Lars needed a hospital. Now.

His cell phone wasn't there. Nor was his gun.

But the butler was still alive; she could hear him breathing. She grabbed an apron hanging from a knob and bunched it over the wounds in his abdomen, laying Lars's hands over the cloth. She had to alert Del and Ty there was a dangerous intruder on the island.

The microwave pinged. Juliana nearly jumped out of her skin in fright. She needed to do something. Cort was upstairs alone. She had to find a phone. Get help.

A bead of perspiration rolled down her spine as she grabbed a marble rolling pin off the pastry board. Taking a steadying breath, she stepped back into the kitchen and made a wild dash for the portable phone sitting in its base at the message center.

She hit the talk button, then hit the button for the Chelsea cottage. Oh, damn. There was no dial tone!

A receiver must be off the hook in the house somewhere.

Juliana felt panic seizing her. What should she do? Go find the other security guards?

No! She had to get upstairs to Cort. Her baby could be in danger. Her gun, the replacement cell phone Hunter had given her and the safe room were up there, too. She could call for help for Lars from the safe room.

Not knowing whether Lars's attacker was still in the house, she moved cautiously through the house, avoiding the servant's staircase off the kitchen and the main staircase. She'd take the back staircase at the far end of the house that brought her near the nursery and Brook's suite.

Her heart beat with a deafening roar in her ears as she crept up the stairs. Please God, keep Cort safe.

She entered Hunter's room first, locking the door behind her and nearly succumbing to tears at the strong sense of his presence in the room. Give me strength, Hunter. Give me strength, she prayed.

She could hear Cort snuffling in his crib and her heart leaped. Almost there.

She eased the door open, entering the corridor that connected her suite to Hunter's. The door to her room was ajar—the way she'd left it. Her heart pounding wildly, Juliana crossed the corridor and locked her door. Then she peered into her dressing room, looking for places someone could hide. Satisfied that no one was hiding in wait, she grabbed her purse from the shelf and pulled out her gun.

Feeling safer, she lifted Cort from his crib and swaddled his blanket snugly around him. To her relief, he burrowed his head into the curve of her neck and sighed.

There was no sign of her cell phone. Where had she left it? In her room?

Somewhere in the house Juliana heard a door slam. The kitchen door, she thought. Oh, God!

She had to get Cort upstairs to Hunter's office. Now.

Gun raised, she unlocked the door to Hunter's room and crossed the hallway to the main staircase. It was the most direct route to Hunter's office.

One flight up to safety, and a chance to save Lars.

Hugging the wall of the staircase, she moved up the

stairs, praying Cort wouldn't make a noise and give away their location.

Five more steps. There! Her fingers shook as she punched in the code to Hunter's office: *Wife*. What a wonderful word! Thank God for a husband with backup plans. She pushed the heavy door open. Not a moment too soon.

Shots splintered the railing behind her and dug into the paneling to the left of the door. She darted into Hunter's office, closing the door behind her. Then headed straight for the bookshelf and the hidden button.

She could hear more shots being fired out in the hallway. She had no idea how long the door to his office might hold back an intruder. She wasn't taking any chances. Maybe there was a cell phone in the safe room.

She hit the button, and the bookcase and the panel behind it granted her access to the safe room. Relief poured through her as the entrance sealed automatically, securing them inside.

Juliana laid Cort on the carpet and searched the locker. There was no cell phone. But she found more guns.

She took one for backup, blessing Hunter for his cautious nature. Oh God, she wished he were here now! She was so scared.

She emptied the locker so she could use it as a crib for Cort. She couldn't take him with her. It was much too dangerous. He'd be safer here in Hunter's secret room. Her heart in her throat, she gave Cort a goodbye kiss and laid him in the locker. "I love you, baby. I'm counting on you to bring your sunshine into Hunter's life."

Choking back tears, she hit the keypad for the emergency exit. She couldn't leave Annette and Lars to certain death. She had to find a phone that worked.

AVOIDING THE PATH, Juliana moved along the shore of the island toward Windermere, terrified that one false step in the dark would send her falling into the river. The night was cold, the stars distant and blurred. But she couldn't think of failure. She had to think about saving Annette and Lars.

Somehow Sable had found out where The Guardian lived.

Juliana tripped over a rock and fell, scraping her hands on some stones. She didn't have time to feel any pain. Not when Lars could be dying. May already be dead. She glimpsed Windermere through the trees. Saw lights on. Saw a shadow move in front of the window and glimpsed the gold sweater Annette had worn to the house earlier.

Thank God she was unharmed.

Juliana crept up to the door of the cottage and entered without knocking.

Annette whirled around, dropping a cushion she had clutched to her stomach. "Juliana! What's wrong? What are you doing here?" she asked in alarm.

Juliana locked the door. "Quick! Try the phone. We need to call the state police. Lars has been stabbed. He's dying."

Annette reached for the phone and lifted the receiver. Juliana cried out with relief at the sound of the dial tone. She snatched the phone from the smaller woman's hand. Setting her gun on the sofa table, she dialed for help.

"This is Juliana Sinclair," she told the emergency dispatcher. "I'm on FairIsle. There's an intruder in the house. He stabbed the butler and hid his body in the pantry. I'm in the guest cottage with Annette York. There are two security guards on the island, but I can't reach them. We need help now!"

The dispatcher told her to remain calm, the police were

on the way. Juliana disconnected the call and pressed the button to reach Chelsea cottage.

The phone rang and rang.

"Damn!" She hung up in frustration. "Come on, we're getting out of here. We're sitting ducks." She turned and reached for the gun. It wasn't there.

Annette had it. Her face was white and her hand was trembling. "I'm not leaving until you tell me where Cort is."

"He's safe, Annette. I hid him."

"Tell me where."

Juliana thought about drawing the gun she'd tucked in the back waistband of her jeans. But she didn't want to risk either of them getting hurt. Annette was scared. She might pull the trigger. "Put down the gun. We don't have time for this. The killer could be headed for your cottage right now. I know a secret cave where we can hide. Hunter showed it to me."

Annette motioned with the gun. "Let's go, then. Out the back door."

Chapter Fifteen

Hunter was frantic.

He and Investigator Bradshaw had been trying the phone lines to FairIsle in vain as they flew back to the island in Hunter's helicopter. The main phone line to the house was busy. The cell phones belonging to the security team were not currently in service. There was no answer in Chelsea cottage. And Juliana's cell phone rang incessantly.

Investigator Bradshaw had called the state police to the island. Would they be too late?

Guilt and despair racked him at the thought of Juliana being ripped from his life. He saw her beautiful face as she'd dropped the towel from her body so he wouldn't forget where he'd left off.

As if he could.

Selfishly, foolishly, because he'd been too cowardly to make himself vulnerable to her, he hadn't told her he loved her.

He was an idiot. Not saying the words didn't negate the feelings. Didn't mean they weren't there, buried in him. Making him ache.

She could be hurt. She could be dying.

The most courageous woman in the world had told him she loved him today. Twice. And he'd failed her.

"How much longer?" he shouted at the pilot, searching the dark landscape below for familiar landmarks.

"Forty-two minutes."

Investigator Bradshaw touched his arm. "The troopers will be there any minute."

Hunter nodded grimly, tortured by the fear they would be too late. Just as he'd been too late to save his mother.

JULIANA KNEW SOMETHING was horribly wrong when she heard Annette's voice. "I've got her. We're on the path heading toward the garden. Meet us at the fountain."

She stopped and whirled around. Annette had a cell phone in her hand. The last thing Annette had said before she'd left the house this evening took on a new and horrifying significance in Juliana's mind. Had Annette wanted to make Lexi regret her marriage to Ross? To what lengths had she gone to bring pain and unhappiness to her sister's life? "You did this? How could you kill your sister?"

"How could I?" Annette gave a short bitter laugh. "Do you know what it was like being Lexi's younger sister? Lexi, who won beauty competitions. Who only had to walk into a room and people adored her. I was invisible! Nothing I did ever mattered. I got straight A's in high school. Was valedictorian of my class. When I got a scholarship my mother told me it was just as well because they couldn't possibly afford to put us both through college.

"I was engaged first. Did you know that? My one shining moment that eclipsed Lexi. Darren was a mathematician. An academic. He was going to be brilliant—and he loved *me*. For twenty-four whole days I had Mother's attention. She called me almost every day to talk about the wedding. And we even met for lunch. Lunch! That was something she normally only had time to do with Lexi. We were planning *my* wedding. My future, my happiness. And it was going to be beautiful.''

Juliana tried to edge away from Annette and the gun in the dark. She could dart into the woods behind a tree and be in a position to defend herself.

''Is Darren helping you? Did he make the bomb?''

''No! You're so stupid. You underestimate me—just like Lexi. She told me they were going to see Cort and gave me the address. I made the bomb with castor beans—simple research on the Internet. Darren had nothing to do with it. I simply couldn't marry him, not after Lexi came home with the baron of Wall Street and announced she was pregnant and they were getting married.

''Pregnant.'' Annette spat out the word. ''If I'd come home pregnant my parents would have disowned me. But not their beautiful, perfect Lexi who'd never so much as had a pimple her entire life. She'd nabbed a goddamn billionaire! Mother told me that we'd have to postpone my wedding because she couldn't possibly be expected to plan two weddings at once. Lexi's wedding had to come first because of the baby.''

Annette pointed the gun straight at Juliana's heart. ''Of course, I understood. Lexi always came first. She was their princess and her marriage to Ross was my parents' crowning achievement. Now, keep your hands up and keep moving!''

Juliana's heart folded in two as she resumed walking. ''Did you take Riana?''

''No, I only wish I had! For the first time, Lexi's life wasn't so perfect. She had to wallow in misery like the rest of us. Except Lexi's misery killed my parents. The doctor told me mother's heart attack was probably stress-induced because of Riana's abduction. And father, the police said he hadn't been paying attention while driving due to grief over Mother's death. Lexi took everything from me! Now I'm taking everything from her.''

"By killing Cort?'' They were nearing the fountain. Juliana could hear the splashing of water. "How can you kill him? He's never done a thing to you. I know what it feels like to be the least favored child. I had a brother whom my father still has on a pedestal even though he's been dead for twenty years. But Cort is just a baby. You're his only living relative. He'll grow up knowing you, loving you, maybe more than anyone has loved you in your life.''

"But he's *her* baby. Besides, I'm not going to kill him just yet, thanks to you. If Hunter was willing to marry you to give Cort a mother, he'll be willing to marry me. He's very handsome don't you think? More handsome than Ross—and he has the sexy alter-ego thing going.''

Annette's voice curled with disdain. "You were just Cort's nanny. I'm his godmother. And if Cort happens to die in a tragic accident a few years from now, no one will be the wiser. I can't inherit the Collingwood estate until Riana's been missing at least seven years and been declared legally dead. Marrying The Guardian will suit me just fine. The Collingwood estate was nice, but this is a *castle* and I'll be the undisputed queen. Mother and Daddy would be so proud.''

Cold fury raced through Juliana's blood. She wasn't about to let this woman harm Cort or claim Hunter's bed.

A male voice drifted across the garden. "Where are you?''

"Here,'' Annette called.

Juliana's heart pounded in terror as the lights in the shrubbery revealed the approaching figure of a man clothed all in black. He had a gun in his right hand.

"Kill her.''

Juliana dived behind the boxwood hedge, reaching for

the gun hidden at her waist as shots fired in the night. Rolling onto her knees, she took a wild shot at them and followed the hedge west toward the woods as Hunter had told her.

"Where'd she go?" Annette screamed.

"Over there. I've got her."

Juliana heard two shots and a grunt of surprise.

"You bitch. You shot me? What'd you do that for?"

Annette's voice was cold and unemotional. "Yeah, life is a bitch, isn't it?"

Another shot rang through the night. Followed by a chilling, horrifying silence.

Juliana kept her head low and made a straight cut across the path into the woods on the other side toward the shoreline. The police were coming. If she could beat Annette to the cave, she could survive. At least Cort was safe.

Four strides off the path, she tripped over a log and fell headlong to the ground. The gun flew from her grasp.

She patted the ground, looking for the gun. Where had it gone? Her hands found something. Cold fingers, attached to a body. She shrieked, nausea burning in her throat.

Oh, God, it was Ty! She could make out the white streak of skin at his neck. She thought he was dead.

She heard crashing in the underbrush somewhere behind her. Annette was coming.

Juliana rose, running blindly through the woods in the dark. Trying not to sob. Shots fired around her, instilling her with more terror. Annette was too close. Juliana wasn't going to make it to the cave.

The trees parted ahead of her. Juliana saw the rapid movement of the river and two police boats approaching the island, emergency lights flashing and floodlights blazing. A bullet whizzed past her head.

Juliana didn't think twice. Hunter and Cort needed her. She dived into the river and swam for her life.

HUNTER FOUGHT TO CONTAIN the panic roaring through him as the chopper neared FairIsle. Juliana was missing. The troopers had already landed on the island and found Annette bleeding from a stab wound in her left arm, screaming hysterically that an intruder had attacked them and Juliana had shot him. But she didn't know where Juliana, the baby or the intruder was. The troopers had searched the house and the island. They'd found Lars barely alive in the butler's panty. Hunter had given them instructions to the safe room where they'd found Cort safe and sound, sleeping. But there was no sign of Juliana.

The troopers were searching the other buildings on the island and the woods. Hunter counted off the last few minutes until the helicopter would reach the island, praying the troopers would find Juliana in the cave.

"Sorry, sir," a trooper told Hunter over the cell phone. "We just checked the cave. She's not there. But we found both guards in the woods."

Fear gripped Hunter's heart. "Are they alive?"

"One of them is. He's in pretty bad shape. African-American male in his thirties. He's been stabbed, too, like the butler. Looks like he crawled a considerable distance to try to get help."

Del. Oh, no!

"I don't think the other guard knew what hit him, sir," the trooper continued.

Hunter worked his jaw silently, grieving for Ty, praying he wouldn't be burying Lars and Del and Juliana, too. Where was she? Why hadn't they found her yet?

"We'll keep searching the woods near the cottages.

That's where she was when she talked to the emergency dispatcher.''

''Wait a minute!'' Hunter said suddenly, his head shooting up. If Juliana had gone as far as the cottages to call for help, she'd have tried to make it to the safety of the cave from there. Unless she couldn't make it. Annette might have caught her off guard in which case Juliana would have fought back, perhaps have done something brave and unexpected to save herself.

Dread burned in his soul. He knew exactly what she'd done.

''Get a boat out on the river. I think she's in the water, and she's not a good swimmer.'' He turned and tapped the pilot on the shoulder. ''Bring us down low and approach the island from the east. The current will pull her that way.''

The pilot nodded and brought the chopper down.

Hunter and Investigator Bradshaw scanned the dark flowing water for signs of life.

ONE, TWO, THREE, BREATHE.

With a froglike motion of her arms and legs, Juliana popped her head out of the water and fought back fear. The current was rapidly pulling her farther and farther into the main river channel. Though she'd tried to draw attention to herself, the engines of the police boats had drowned out her cries for help.

But she wasn't giving up. Something glowed white in the water a hundred or so yards ahead of her. One of the markers that delineated the international border, she thought. At any rate, it would be something to hang on to until daylight. Tomorrow was Saturday. There would be plenty of boats passing that could come to her rescue. She was *not* leaving Cort and Hunter to Annette's mercy.

She and Hunter had unfinished business. Words and feelings still left unexplored between them. She didn't want to miss out on any of it—especially the joy of hearing him admit he loved her.

Juliana moved her arms through the water and lifted her head out to take another breath. A strange whipping noise reached her ears. What was that? Then, blessedly, she saw it. A halo of light descending from the sky, sweeping over the river. She lifted her arms, waving them over her head, and tread water. "Over here! Over here, please!"

The beam caught her in its glare a second before she caught a mouthful of river water that had her gagging and sinking into the water's powerful embrace.

No! She flailed her arms like she was spreading peanut butter and kicked her legs like they were egg beaters, pulling herself to the surface again.

"Help!"

To her great joy, a figure dropped out of the helicopter and into the water. Seconds later, he surfaced and swam toward her.

"Juliana!"

Even beneath the roar of the helicopter she recognized that voice and swam toward the man she loved. Hunter had come. He'd saved her!

Relief and joy broke through Hunter when he covered the last few yards and stretched a hand through the water, grabbing Juliana's arm. "I've got you," he said, pulling her into an embrace. "This is one hell of a way to pick up where we left off."

She pressed her cold lips to his, her fingers clutching his shoulders. "I love you. Annette was going to marry you and hurt Cort. She wanted to destroy everything Lexi had."

He didn't know what the hell she meant about Annette planning to marry him but it didn't matter. She was safe.

They had a lifetime together to sort out Annette's twisted schemes. He held his cherished wife close in his arms. "I love you, too, sweetheart. So much it scares me."

For the first time since he'd found his mother's lifeless body, Hunter found real peace.

EIGHT SOMBER DAYS LATER, Hunter took Juliana's hand as she was preparing to leave for the hospital to visit her father and asked her to come out into the garden with him.

It was early October and the deciduous trees were showing their yellow and scarlet colors against the backdrop of the dense pine woods. In the last eight days they'd buried Ty and rejoiced at both Del's and Lars's recovery. And they were steadily weathering the media storm.

Surprisingly, Annette hadn't breathed a word about Cort's true parentage or Hunter's identify as The Guardian. Hunter suspected that Annette probably thought drawing attention to Lexi's son and his legal guardian would be like putting Lexi in the spotlight again.

And Annette wanted all the attention for herself. She was already mounting her defense in the media. The prosecutor was asking for the death penalty and Annette was granting interview after interview, proclaiming her innocence and insisting that her sister's and brother-in-law's killer was still at large.

She claimed that the intruder on the island had attacked her as well, and that Juliana had shot and killed him. It was Juliana's gun. And it was her word against the word of the butler's daughter.

But Annette's story gathered more momentum when the intruder's body was identified and the police discovered he had connections to the Mafia. Annette insisted that the intruder had been hired by one of the higher ups in the Collingwood Corporation and she was being framed. Hunter knew that even if his identity leaked out, he'd continue on as The Guardian. He'd protect Cort. And protect Juliana.

Grateful that Annette was securely behind bars, Juliana had devoted as much time as she could to being at her father's bedside and helping Hunter cope with the invasion of his beloved island and the loss of one of his men.

"Close your eyes," Hunter said when they reached the fountain.

"Why?"

"Because I asked you very nicely to close them."

Juliana obediently closed her eyes. Felt the warmth of the sun and a light southwesterly breeze touch her face as Hunter guided her with his hands. She guessed where they were going before she heard the key turn in the lock.

The squeak of rusted hinges brought tears to her eyes.

She felt the texture of cobbled stones beneath her feet and smelled the decay of vegetation.

"Open them."

Juliana opened her eyes. As she'd suspected, they were in the greenhouse. The glass ceiling soared a good twenty feet in the air above them. Stone-edged beds curved along paths that radiated out from a small central courtyard. In the center of the courtyard, stood a cloth-covered pedestal.

Hunter cleared his throat. "This was my mother's favorite place.

She curled her fingers around his, absorbing his strength and love. "I'm sure it was very beautiful."

"You asked me once to tell you a secret to prove that I trusted you."

She shook her head. "You don't have to prove anything to me. You've shown me in so many ways that you trust me. That you have faith in me." She drew a shaky breath. "If you hadn't shown me the safe room or told me about the cave, Cort and I might not have survived. And neither would Lars and Del.''

Regret echoed in his voice. ''I should have been here with you. Protecting you.''

''You were there when I needed you most,'' Juliana insisted. ''Besides, you were doing what you were supposed to be doing. You found out that Annette was the killer and you got the police out here in time.''

She leaned her head against his shoulder. ''I don't want you to stop being The Guardian. It's who you are. I love that about you. And I'm still hoping that you'll find Riana. Annette insisted she had nothing to do with her abduction. I'm not sure I believe her.''

Hunter touched her hair, his gaze solemn. ''I promise you, we'll keep looking. Bring her home with us here, with Cort. Now, back to my reason for bringing you here. Do you see that pipe there?'' He pointed with his finger, his jaw tight. ''That's where I found my mother the day she died. I never told anyone until now. The gardener discovered her later.''

Juliana took his dear face in her hands, her heart breaking at the painful memories in his eyes. ''Oh, Hunter, I'm so sorry. That's an awful burden for a child to deal with.''

''I've locked up that memory like my father locked up this greenhouse, thinking if I ignored it, it would go away. I realize now that all it did was prevent me from being able to see the possibilities of the present and the future.''

He leaned down and kissed her. ''I love you, Cinderella. You're my present and my future. Will you accept this greenhouse as my wedding gift and bring it back to life like you've brought me back to life?''

Juliana's throat swelled with emotions and a tear rolled down her cheek. ''Oh, yes!''

Hunter kissed her reverently, deeply. ''I was hoping

you'd say yes. But just in case you didn't, I had a backup plan.''

''Oh?''

He stepped away and pulled the cloth off the pedestal revealing a beautiful dainty sculpture of an old-fashioned ladies' slipper. The slipper was encrusted with sequins of glass that twinkled in the morning sunshine like diamonds.

Juliana laughed. ''It's a shoe!''

''No, it's not. It's Cinderella's slipper. It's to remind you that I'm your perfect fit.''

Juliana tugged the tails of his shirt out of his slacks. ''Care to show me what you mean by a perfect fit?''

Hunter laughed huskily. ''Give me a second to lock the door. There are children running around.''

As if by magic, Mackensie appeared at the open door to the greenhouse, out of breath from running. ''Mommy says to come quick. The hospital's on the phone. Aunt Juliana's father is out of the coma.''

She reached for Hunter's hand. Hand in hand, they ran toward the house. Brook met them on the back terrace, trying to hold back tears as she held the phone out to Juliana.

Juliana gripped the phone with a shaking hand. ''Papa? It's me. I'm so glad you're back.''

Her father's voice was slurred but recognizable. ''Me, too, little girl. Love you so much. Are you coming to see me?''

Juliana beamed up at Hunter and squeezed his strong fingers. ''I'm on my way, Papa. And I'm bringing company.''

Epilogue

Four weeks later

The cursor blinked on the computer screen as Riana's kidnapper reread the short letter:

> Riana Collingwood is alive. She is a bright, pretty child with her father's eyes and her mother's smile. Prepare a five-million-dollar cash ransom and await further instruction.

The kidnapper printed the letter. Then printed an envelope with the address of the Find Riana Foundation.

Wearing gloves, the kidnapper opened the envelope and slid Riana's hospital ID into it. As a finishing touch, two fine dark hairs plucked from the child's head were taped to the bottom of the letter.

That ought to get The Guardian's attention.

* * * * *

*Don't miss the next story
in Joyce Sullivan's thrilling
Collingwood Heirs miniseries.*

*OPERATION BASSINET
Harlequin Intrigue #726,*

*available September 2003,
only from Harlequin Books!*

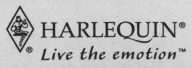

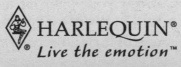

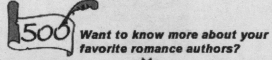

HARLEQUIN®
INTRIGUE®

presents another outstanding installment
in our bestselling series

COLORADO
CONFIDENTIAL

**By day these agents are cowboys; by night they are
specialized government operatives. Men bound by love,
loyalty and the law—they've vowed to keep their
missions and identities confidential...**

August 2003
ROCKY MOUNTAIN MAVERICK
BY GAYLE WILSON

September 2003
SPECIAL AGENT NANNY
BY LINDA O. JOHNSTON

In **October**, look for an exciting short-story collection
featuring *USA TODAY* bestselling author
JASMINE CRESSWELL

November 2003
COVERT COWBOY
BY HARPER ALLEN

December 2003
A WARRIOR'S MISSION
BY RITA HERRON

PLUS
FIND OUT HOW IT ALL BEGAN
with three tie-in books from *Harlequin Historicals*,
starting January 2004

Available at your favorite retail outlet.

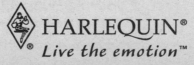

HARLEQUIN®
® *Live the emotion*™

Visit us at www.eHarlequin.com

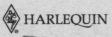

#725 SPECIAL AGENT NANNY by Linda O. Johnston
Colorado Confidential

After someone set fire to the records office at Gilpin Hospital, Colorado Confidential agent and arson investigator Shawn Jameson agreed to work undercover as a nanny to find the culprit. But when he met key suspect Dr. Kelley Stanton and started caring for her three-year-old daughter, he knew she couldn't be the one to blame. Could he protect her from the real arsonist, and win her heart?

#726 OPERATION BASSINET by Joyce Sullivan
The Collingwood Heirs

Detective Mitch Halloran had some bad news to break to stay-at-home mom Stef Shelton—the child she'd been raising wasn't really hers! The two embarked on a mission to find the kidnapper and get her baby back. But as they delved deeper into the mystery, they couldn't deny the growing passion between them....

#727 CONFISCATED CONCEPTION by Delores Fossen

Accountant Rachel Dillard thought she was safe in protective custody. Safe from her boss, whom she was going to testify against, and safe from her mixed emotions for soon-to-be ex-husband, Jared Dillard. But when Jared told her that one of their frozen embryos had been secretly implanted in a surrogate mother, she knew they had to team up to find their child. But would working together tear them apart for good? Or bring them closer than ever....

#728 COWBOY P.I. by Jean Barrett

The last thing private investigator Roark Hawke wanted to do was protect Samantha Howard. The headstrong beauty didn't even want his help—or the ranch she was about to inherit. Then an intentional rockslide nearly killed them, and Samantha was forced to put her life in Roark's capable hands. Could he discover who was trying to kill the woman he'd fallen for—before it was too late?

Visit us at www.eHarlequin.com

HICNM0803